Taking the Lead

"I could be dangerous," he murmured, his voice lowering to a near whisper as his eyes flirted with her shamelessly. "A stalker. An axe murderer. Once you left here with me, you would be in my clutches."

"Or you could be in mine," she whispered back, just as playfully.

"I would count myself lucky."

Harmony stilled the laughter rising in her throat at the outrageous comment. Laughter wasn't something she was used to, yet this man seemed to inspire it within moments of meeting him.

Ducking her head, Harmony fought to hide the smile trembling on her lips as she lifted her glass once again and took a fortifying sip of her drink.

"Second thoughts?" he asked.

Harmony lifted her head, swallowing tightly as she considered fighting the attraction. Perhaps for a second.

"I never have second thoughts," she finally assured him. "You?"

"Never." Male confidence surged through his expression. "Would you like to dance?"

"I would love to." She finished her drink before gathering her courage and laying her hands in his.

Berkley Sensation titles by Lora Leigh

HARMONY'S WAY
MEGAN'S MARK

HARMONY'S WAY

LORA LEIGH

BERKLEY SENSATION, NEW YORK

THE BERKLEY PUBLISHING GROUP
Published by the Penguin Group
Penguin Group (USA) Inc.
375 Hudson Street, New York, New York 10014, USA
Penguin Group (Canada), 90 Eglinton Avenue East, Suite 700, Toronto, Ontario M4P 2Y3, Canada
(a division of Pearson Penguin Canada Inc.)
Penguin Books Ltd., 80 Strand, London WC2R 0RL, England
Penguin Group Ireland, 25 St. Stephen's Green, Dublin 2, Ireland (a division of Penguin Books Ltd.)
Penguin Group (Australia), 250 Camberwell Road, Camberwell, Victoria 3124, Australia
(a division of Pearson Australia Group Pty. Ltd.)
Penguin Books India Pvt. Ltd., 11 Community Centre, Panchsheel Park, New Delhi—110 017, India
Penguin Group (NZ), Cnr. Airborne and Rosedale Roads, Albany, Auckland 1310, New Zealand
(a division of Pearson New Zealand Ltd.)
Penguin Books (South Africa) (Pty.) Ltd., 24 Sturdee Avenue, Rosebank, Johannesburg 2196, South Africa

Penguin Books Ltd., Registered Offices: 80 Strand, London WC2R 0RL, England

This is a work of fiction. Names, characters, places, and incidents either are the product of the author's imagination or are used fictitiously, and any resemblance to actual persons, living or dead, business establishments, events, or locales is entirely coincidental. The publisher does not have any control over and does not assume any responsibility for author or third-party websites or their content.

HARMONY'S WAY

A Berkley Sensation Book / published by arrangement with the author

ISBN 978-0-7394-7673-4

BERKLEY SENSATION®
Berkley Sensation Books are published by The Berkley Publishing Group,
a division of Penguin Group (USA) Inc.,
375 Hudson Street, New York, New York 10014.
BERKLEY SENSATION is a registered trademark of Penguin Group (USA) Inc.
The "B" design is a trademark belonging to Penguin Group (USA) Inc.

PRINTED IN THE UNITED STATES OF AMERICA

HARMONY'S WAY

◆ P R O L O G U E ◆

BOULDER, COLORADO

Harmony Lancaster flipped on the television as she pulled the damp towel from her hair. Long, damp strands of black, brown and sunlit blond fell down her shoulders as she picked up her manicure set and propped herself on the bed to watch the news conference.

Good ole Reverend Henry Richard Alonzo, head of one of the largest and fastest growing supremacist societies in the nation, was once again holding court and spouting nonsense. If only those to whom he preached were aware of who and what he was really all about. A son and grandson to members of the highest order of the Genetics Council. A man whose family had helped to create the monsters he now railed against. If Breeds could be called monsters.

A cynical smile shaped her lips: Well, perhaps in her case.

Returning to the States hadn't been an easy decision to make, especially to this area. But the job she had come here to do required it: rescuing the kidnapped daughter of a wealthy industrialist. The little girl had been amazingly brave during the rescue. It had made the job that much easier when it came to getting her out of the shack where she was being held.

As for the kidnappers, they would never be found. Harmony had made certain of it.

"The very creation of the Breeds is an abomination to the natural order and law of mankind," Alonzo was stating rationally, though his blue eyes glowed with fanatic fervor. "Allowing them to run loose, to crossbreed and live as human is the most unconscionable mistake we can make. They were not created by our great and mighty God. They were created by man. They are the beasts that will mark us with their corruption. Is this what we truly want? To tempt our downfall into hell?"

"Give me a break," she muttered, turning her attention to the news conference as she ran a file slowly over her short nails, watching the arrogance that filled Alonzo's lined face.

How old was he now? Sixty-five, seventy? Shouldn't he be dead by now? The man was a plague, a blight on society, and if he would just mess up a little bit, then she would be happy to take him out. But until she found the blood on his hands, there wasn't a damned thing she could do.

If the Breed Ruling Cabinet wasn't very careful, then Alonzo was going to manage to eventually destroy them. He was gaining momentum and power. The once splintered supremacist groups were now slowly banding with him, creating a single entity that could, in time, turn world sentiment against the Breeds.

Race wars. They had been a part of the world for as long as humanity existed, in one form or another. They were gaining in momentum with the emergence of the Breed population. Sometimes, Harmony wondered why Callan Lyons, the leader of the Feline Breeds, had made the decision to publicize their existence. Yeah, Breeds were free. They weren't dying in labs anymore and they weren't imprisoned. Now they were hunted and reviled, and the world was slowly becoming divided once again. This time over species distinction rather than race.

Were the Breeds human? Unfortunately, as far as Harmony was concerned, they weren't. Humanity was stripped from them the first five years of their lives. And now Alonzo threatened the fragile balance the Breed Ruling Cabinet was attempting to bring to those fighting to regain their humanity.

That was, if Alonzo didn't die first. His wealth and fervor were the guiding forces behind the rapidly organized Blood Purity Society. And that sucked. Because killing him would require a lot of work, and it would really prick her conscience a bit. Of course, that wouldn't bother her overmuch if it weren't for the fact that another fanatic would just take his place. There were always other monsters out there waiting to replace the ones that fell.

"Mr. Alonzo, scientists from every nation have declared the Breeds as human," a reporter pointed out. A very nice lady and proponent of Breed rights. "At this point, isn't it a little late to consider locking them up again? They aren't animals."

"That's exactly what they are," H. R. Alonzo snapped. "They are animals, and our women are breeding with them, creating more animals. Before it's finished, the purity of our God-given genetics, the creation of our almighty God, will be tainted with them. Our children will be animals. Is this the world we want to live within?"

"We want a world without racial discrimination." The reporter smiled smoothly. "What you're suggesting is the worst possible scenario for just such discrimination. If we allow your views, what's to stop the violence against other races as well?"

Alonzo stared down from his podium at the reporter as the television cameras panned in on her. Harmony sat up, crossing her legs on the bed as she watched the reporter. She was wearing silk and pearls, a very sedate statement of power. Harmony liked that.

"Would you take your dog to your bed, my dear?" he sneered. "Or your cat?"

The reporter's brow lifted. "Neither my dog nor my cat walks on two legs, speaks in my language, or eats with a fork, Mr. Alonzo. Nor is their blood compatible to mine. Excuse me if I disagree with your vision here and say that if it walks like a human, talks like a human, and bleeds like a human, then it's my guess it's human." Her attractive features were flushed with her ire as her gray eyes narrowed on the good reverend with disapproval.

"And it's my guess you have no idea of the additional elements of that blood you speak so highly of, my dear," he sneered. "Do your research, then come talk to me about the difference between humans and animals."

The reporter opened her mouth to respond, only to be brushed aside as Alonzo called on another reporter. Harmony shook her head as he carefully maneuvered the rest of the news conference.

Alonzo was determined to bring a bill before Congress that would severely limit the rights the Breeds now enjoyed. If he continued as he was starting, there was every chance that he could do just that.

Harmony tightened her lips at the thought as she turned her gaze to her nails and the careful filing process that would heal any tears beginning in the tips. Suddenly, she narrowed her eyes, swinging her head toward the door as an odd scent caught her sensitive nose.

A Breed scent.

Harmony rolled smoothly from the bed, jerking her knife from beneath her pillow as she scrambled to the side of the door and flattened herself against the wall. If Jonas was out there, he would come in fast. The door would fly open and he would roll in before coming up with his weapon. He wouldn't expect her to slip out behind him.

She had no intention of fighting her own brother. But she wouldn't be taken, not now, not for a crime she had every right to commit. She was code-named Death for a reason. She would not be taken easily.

Tensing in readiness, she inhaled, trying to pinpoint how many were waiting outside for her. She remembered Jonas's scent; he wasn't there, but one of his men was. She would know Mercury Warrant's scent anywhere; he was so Breed that it literally rolled off him. And it was possible he was masking any other Breeds who were with him.

There was no doubt that he was after her. She could feel it. Hell, she had felt them tracking her for weeks. She was obviously getting soft; otherwise, they would have never managed to find her so easily.

God, she didn't want to do this. She didn't want to fight her own kind. But as the door slammed inward, Harmony threw aside her reluctance and fought for escape. This time Jonas wasn't playing around. He had found a way to trap her and then sent his best. And the odds sucked.

SANCTUARY
VIRGINIA, SIX HOURS LATER

Jonas watched as the small, slender form of the female Breed was literally dragged into the holding building with its single cell and interrogation room. The three Breeds hauling her into the cement building looked the worse for wear. Bruised faces, split lips and blood marred their savage features, and the most powerful of the three, Mercury Warrant, had a tourniquet tied high on his thigh, above the knife wound he had received. The sleeve of Rule's black uniform was sliced and wet with blood. Lawe would carry another scar on his face, low along his chin.

Harmony was dumped into the small metal chair beside a

scarred wooden table, the manacles at her wrists and ankles attached to a metal ring in the floor. She was secured, confined. Dressed in light gray boxer-style underwear and a matching tank top, she showed no reaction to either the chill of the air or the bruises and scrapes that covered her shoulders and arms.

Her breathing was slow and easy, her overall demeanor calm as her oddly streaked black hair covered her face and hid her expression from him. What more would he see if he could stare into those incredible eyes? Had she only strengthened her ability to hide there as well?

Harmony had grown as a killer over the years, as a fighter. Self-control, twenty years of military training and a fierce determination to live and to exact vengeance had made her a commodity eagerly sought on the killing market.

He stared at the file that rested on the monitor shelf in front of him. It bulged with evidence of suspected kills, sightings and psych reports.

She had taken her first job no more than a year after her escape from the labs ten years before; she had become more proficient and deadly over the years. She had also become better at hiding. There were any number of people after the woman called Death. Not just because of her reputation for being the best, but because of the information she had taken the day she escaped the labs, and the information she had stolen since.

His lips quirked in amusement as respect curled within him. She had outdistanced the projections the scientists had made in regards to her ability, to become the perfect assassin.

He watched as the door to the confinement cell opened and the scientist over the Breed medical facility walked into the room, carrying the plastic medical tote that held the syringes and vials for the samples she would need.

"Harmony, my name is Ely." Elyiana Morrey's voice was soft, sympathetic. "You're not in any danger here."

There was no response.

"I need a few blood samples and a saliva swab. It won't take long and I promise it won't hurt."

Jonas had a feeling Harmony really didn't give a damn. As Merc moved in closer to protect the scientist, she stopped at Harmony's side, lifting her arm to the table.

Harmony stayed relaxed, still, as Ely tied the rubber strap around her upper arm and moved to test the veins. Jonas watched the muscles in Harmony's arm flex, then tense. The action would prevent the needle from effectively finding the veins beneath the skin. The ability Breeds had learned in the labs, to control their muscles, had been developed just for this purpose. Ely's gaze was concerned as she looked up at the camera, meeting Jonas's.

"Tell her you'll sedate her if she doesn't cooperate," Jonas ordered coldly.

Ely's gaze snapped with disapproval as his order came through the comm link she wore.

"Do it, Ely. Now is not the time to argue."

Her lips thinned.

"Harmony, I've been ordered to sedate you if you don't cooperate. Please don't make me do that."

Jonas almost grinned at Ely's compassion. Harmony would slice her throat without a thought if that were what it took to escape.

But Harmony relaxed, never betraying a flinch as the needle found her vein. Two vials later Ely pulled a cotton swab from the tote.

"Open your mouth, I need a saliva swab now." Harmony stayed still.

Jonas sighed. "Merc, pull her head back and force her mouth open."

Harmony wasn't going to make this easy for anyone.

As Merc pulled her head back, his powerful hand clamping on her jaw, Jonas saw her face. He leaned forward, his eyes narrowing on the delicate bone structure, the wide tilted eyes with their sooty lashes, the glimpse of green fiery rage in her eyes.

Ely took the swab quickly, stored it, then moved back from the table as Merc released the girl.

The blood and saliva samples were imperative. For their plan to work he had to prove the suspicion his senses had picked up, and make certain Harmony hadn't yet mated. That could really foul his plans.

The only way, at this point, to neutralize Harmony was to kill her. Killing her would not give Jonas or the Breed Ruling Cabinet the answers or the information they needed. Killing her would destroy his soul, but he knew Harmony would never trust him now. She was harder, too cautious and too aware of how easily she could be betrayed.

First, he had to weaken her, he had to find a vulnerability.

If his suspicions were correct, that vulnerability was strutting around Broken Butte, New Mexico, with all the arrogance and control of a man comfortable in the domain he had created.

At that thought, Jonas's lips curled in a satisfied smile as he rose to his feet and moved for the doorway of the office and the interrogation cell beyond. Before leaving the room, he picked up the brush lying on the desk, tested the bristles against his palm and nodded shortly.

It had been many years since he had calmed her by brushing her hair. He wondered if she was still susceptible to what few good memories the labs had held. They had been few and far between, but despite the years they had spent apart, he was still her brother. Not just of the same species, but of the same mother.

The mother she had killed.

◆ CHAPTER 1 ◆

BROKEN BUTTE, NEW MEXICO
TWO WEEKS LATER

She was being watched. Harmony pulled her sporty Jeep into the parking lot of the small, rundown little bar just inside Broken Butte and considered her options.

She was scheduled to arrive at the Sheriff's Department in the morning, or else. Jonas's "or else," of course. So what the hell was she doing here when she should be going over those files tucked in her suitcase back at the hotel?

Because she was bored. Bored and restless and damned pissed at herself for allowing it to happen. The combination of emotions was depressing, and Harmony didn't do depressed well. She needed just a little fun. Just enough to maybe liven the night a bit. Nothing too heavy. A drink, maybe a good fight.

Her eyes narrowed at the entrance to the bar. With any luck, her tail would decide to make his way inside to be certain she was there. If she didn't tag him, then she was going to have to go hunting. And she just didn't have time to go hunting right now.

No, Harmony Lancaster, once known as Death, was going to have to toe the good-girl line for a six full months.

Which meant no going hunting. No unauthorized bloodshed. She grimaced at that, as she slung her tote over her shoulder and slammed the door to the Jeep closed.

Death, a good girl. Now there was an oxymoron. The very thought of it was enough to leave a sour taste in her mouth. It was one of the reasons she was making her way into this seedy little bar rather than researching her upcoming opponent: the good sheriff of Broken Butte.

Pushing her way through the old, saloon-style doors, she paused at the entrance, her gaze going over the array of cowboys staring back at her.

As she slid onto an empty bar stool, Harmony let her eyes sweep over the dancers at the far end of the room.

"What can I do for ya, honey?" She turned to the bartender's booming voice.

Tall, broad and bald, with a friendly smile, he reminded her of the bartender at her favorite biker bar in Chicago. Perhaps New Mexico wasn't as far from civilization as Jonas could possibly send her after all.

"Whiskey."

"Shot or glass?" he asked.

"Glass, no ice."

"You got it, honey." He nodded.

Picking up the drink, she turned her back to the bar and once again surveyed the room.

What the hell had convinced her that she could return to the States? No matter how important the job.

Children were her weakness. The plea had come from a former client, to help a friend locate his kidnapped daughter. A little girl no more than five, with big brown eyes and a mischievous smile. Harmony had been insane to agree. She had known Jonas was stalking her for nearly six months now. She should have never returned. Because she knew what he wanted in the end, just as she knew he more than expected her to fail at this chance he had given her to escape Breed Law.

She shook her head at the thought. Her brother had aged more than he should have in the last ten years. The bitterness and cold, hard purpose in his eyes had only grown.

Like her, his French accent had totally evaporated since his escape from the labs, and his English was fluid and flawless. They had been trained to blend in, no matter where they were sent.

As she lifted her drink to her lips and ignored the frankly sexual glances she was receiving, she caught movement at the doorway from the corner of her eye. Turning her head, Harmony watched in appreciation as the thoroughly male form strode into the bar.

Now, she very much doubted this was her tail, though she wouldn't have minded in the least being his. At least six feet, three inches of broad, muscular male moved with lazy, casual grace.

He was dressed in jeans and a dark blue denim shirt that emphasized the heavily tanned contours of his face. His features were rugged, with high cheekbones, a sensually full lower lip and eyes a deep, navy blue that gleamed with suppressed amusement as he met her gaze. He was taking stock of her as carefully as she was taking stock of him. And it was evident that, as she did, he liked what he saw.

Had she ever so fully noticed a man before? Sexuality fairly screamed off this male, from the bulge in those snug jeans to the wide, muscular width of his shoulders. Shoulder-length, thick, straight black hair flowed around the arrogant features of his face and softened them just enough to make him seem approachable.

Harmony had admitted long ago she wasn't necessarily a sexual being, despite some of her more animal-like genetics. But this man, he made the feline inside her stand up and roar.

She could feel a strange receptivity flowing through her veins, peaking in her nipples and the suddenly sensitive folds of her pussy.

"Hey, Lance, buddy. 'Bout time you made it around to see us." Behind her, the bartender called out a greeting as the cowboy moved to the bar stool beside her. "Beer?"

"Beer works good, Stan," Lance answered with a slow drawl that had a shiver working up Harmony's spine.

She loved that voice. It was as smooth and dark as her whiskey.

Turning on the bar stool, Harmony met the bartender's gaze as she slid her glass forward for a refill.

"I'll get the lady's too, Stan."

Harmony nearly missed the offer, her senses suddenly infused with the scent of midnight storms and dark desert nights. The scent of the male at her side. Strong. Pure. No, this wasn't her tail, but for just a moment she could imagine him behind her, his hands shaping her rear before sliding against her, nudging her thighs apart.

"Thank you." She breathed in deeply as she turned her head, keeping her smile light, hiding the sharp canines at the side of her mouth.

Hers were smaller than most Breeds', and rarely noticed for what they were, but flashing them wasn't something she did often.

"You're welcome." The slightly crooked smile he gave her did something to the pit of her stomach. It fluttered. Hell, she had never had anything either on or in her body flutter in her entire life.

"My name's Harmony." She stuck her hand out, tilting her head to get a better look at his face.

"Lance." He nodded, extending his hand, his large, calloused palm engulfing her fingers.

The feel of his flesh against hers startled her. She could feel her hand sensitizing, her fingers tingling. Heat, unlike anything she knew, flowed from a simple handshake, from his body to hers.

Harmony's eyes widened as his narrowed, a small frown creasing his brow as he glanced at their joined hands. Did he feel it? That exchange of heat, of awareness?

"Well, that was odd enough." His smile was still lazy, but his gaze had sharpened with sensual awareness.

"Wasn't it?" Harmony cleared her throat as she brushed the long strands of her newly colored hair back from her face. She liked the soft dark russet tone of the color. It gave an added emphasis to her pale green eyes and dark brows.

The camouflage was a nice addition. Her naturally streaked hair was a dead giveaway to her Breed genetics. The mix of black, browns and golden ambers would have been instantly noticed.

"I haven't seen you around. Are you visiting relatives?" he asked.

"Not really." She shook her head as she turned back to him. "I'm just passing through."

She wished. Yet somehow she had a feeling it would not serve her purposes to allow this man to know she would be here for long.

"That's too bad." The regret shimmered in the air between them.

"Yes, it is." Harmony inhaled deeply, certain she could become addicted to his scent if she weren't extremely careful.

"So you're just here for the night?" He picked up the chilled bottle of beer as he voiced the question, his gaze darkening, his intent to seduce clear.

"Just for the night." Harmony nodded slowly.

"Alone?"

She hesitated as she met his gaze.

"I was."

She watched as he set the beer back on the bar, his eyes never leaving hers, holding her captive with a deep blue fire.

"I could be dangerous," he murmured then, his voice lowering to a near whisper as his eyes flirted with her shamelessly. "A stalker. An axe murderer. Once you left here with me, you would be in my clutches."

"Or you could be in mine," she whispered back, just as playfully.

"I would count myself lucky."

Harmony stilled the laughter rising in her throat at the outrageous comment. Laughter wasn't something she was used to, yet this man seemed to inspire it within moments of meeting him.

Ducking her head, Harmony fought to hide the smile trembling on her lips as she lifted her glass once again and took a fortifying sip of her drink.

"Second thoughts?" he asked.

Harmony lifted her head, swallowing tightly as she considered fighting the attraction. Perhaps for a second.

"I never have second thoughts," she finally assured him. "You?"

"Never." Male confidence surged through his expression. "Would you like to dance?"

"I would love to." She finished her drink before gathering her courage and laying her hand in his.

◆   ◆   ◆

Lance took the young woman's hand, once again feeling the surge of sensation that traveled from his palm to hers. He'd had no intention of coming into the bar tonight. Tomorrow's meeting with Jonas Wyatt, the head of the Bureau of Breed

Affairs, would require all the patience he could muster. Which meant all the rest he could steal tonight.

Instead, the closer he had come to Stan's Last Rest, the bar at the edge of town, the more imperative the whispered warnings in the air around him had become. They hadn't screamed or moaned, and in them he hadn't heard secrets, as his grandfather often did. But he heard the demand. Just as he heard the feminine call resounding through his soul.

The moment he walked in the door he had known he was there for her. Their eyes touched and the whispering demand had eased.

Steering her to the dance floor, Lance drew her into his arms, feeling her hands settle against his shoulders as she kept just enough distance between them that the engorged length of his cock ached in disappointment.

He wanted to feel her flush against him. But not so much on the dance floor as in his bed. Naked, sweating, arching to his body as he led her to orgasm.

"Just passing through, huh?" he finally asked her as his fingers moved over her hips, growing closer to the small strip of bare flesh between her pants and her top. If he hadn't been mistaken, he had glimpsed a small belly ring when she rose from the bar stool.

"Just for the night." He watched her lips move, the soft pink curves damp and inviting.

"The night's disappearing fast." He ran his hand up her back, feeling the small tremor of her response.

He watched as she swallowed, a momentary confusion lighting the pale green of her eyes as her soft tongue flicked out to wet her lips. She wasn't nervous, but that edge of vulnerability in her gaze tore at him.

"Yes," she finally answered. "The night is disappearing fast. What should we do about that?" She wasn't playing coy or flirting. The words were a challenge, one that had the muscles of his abdomen tightening in anticipation.

"Did you come with friends?"

"I have no friends."

The odd response had him narrowing his eyes as he studied her from behind his lashes. For some reason, he had a feeling she didn't mean just in this area.

"Are you ready to leave then?" His fingertips pressed against her blouse, feeling the muscles of her back as that small tremor washed through them again.

"I'm ready." Resignation filled her tone and her expression.

Once again that strange, saddened little moan whispered past his ears as the air around them grew heavy with arousal. Hers and his. She was fighting the strength of her response to him, holding herself carefully back from him, refusing to relax in his embrace as her eyes swept quickly over the room.

Embarrassment? As though she wasn't quite certain that she wanted others to know her weakness, her arousal.

Lance waited until her gaze returned to his before speaking again.

"My place is just a few minutes from here. Are you ready to go?" he asked softly, knowing it was going to happen and damn if he wasn't looking forward to it.

He took her hand and led her from the dance floor as the music paused. "You could follow me, or I could drive you back here in the morning for your vehicle," he suggested as they stepped out of the bar.

"Could we take my Jeep?" She paused at the steps, staring into the darkness around them. "I'd hate to have it towed."

She was sure her new boss would just love having to get his deputy's vehicle out of impound if it was towed away. She'd prefer not to start this little working relationship off on the wrong foot. The next six months were going to be hard enough as it was.

"Sounds good to me." He nodded carefully as she pulled her keys from the inside of the tote she carried on her shoulder and handed them to him.

"The blue Jeep." She nodded to the wide-track, sporty Wrangler across the lot.

Keeping her hand in his, he led her across the parking lot. He unlocked the passenger-side door for her, letting her move between the door and the seat before he caught her hip with one hand and turned her to him.

He felt her tense, as though she still wasn't quite certain of what she was doing. It was obvious that leaving a bar with a stranger wasn't a commonplace occurrence for her.

"Are you sure?" He lowered his head until his lips were inches from the soft curves of hers, the scent of her wrapping around him, the smell of honeysuckle and a tint of clover infusing his senses.

"No second thoughts." Her breathing was rougher now, her lips parting as Lance allowed his hands to settle on her bare waist, to feel the incredibly soft flesh beneath them.

The temptation of those lips was too much to deny. He lowered his head as her hands fluttered against his chest, the feel of them sinking past the cloth of his shirt as he fought to rein in his desire.

Just a kiss, he promised himself as he touched her lips with his. He was the sheriff; he couldn't get caught necking in public. But one kiss surely wouldn't hurt.

Or so he thought. Until her lips parted on a soft little gasp, and her tongue touched his. The subtle taste of honeysuckle was stronger here, sweet and clean as it fueled his hunger.

Lance felt her hands slide up his chest, move to his neck, then bury themselves in his hair as a soft moan vibrated against his lips. He kissed her with soft greed, reminding himself each second that it could go no further. He could kiss her. Just a taste before the main course.

As his lips moved over hers, he found his hunger for her surging, overtaking his common sense and his control. His hands slid beneath her top, stroking the satiny flesh until they filled with the firm mounds of her breasts. And she was arching to him, her soft cry muffled by his suddenly devouring lips.

His tongue pushed against hers, twined with it, drew it to his lips and suckled it into his own mouth as she arched against him.

She tasted like hot, needy sex. Like a temptress made for lust, built for endurance and pleasure. And if he wasn't very, very careful he was going to end up fucking her right there in the parking lot.

"We're getting in trouble here." His hands slid from her breasts to her rear, gripping the snug curves and moving her against his thigh as his lips trailed over her jaw to her neck.

Lance nipped at the fragrant skin there as he felt the heated, cloth-covered curves of her pussy riding his thigh. She was panting for breath now, flushed, a soft dew of perspiration covering her skin.

"This isn't natural." Her voice was dazed, thick with need as he stroked his lips and tongue over her neck, heading for the valley of her breasts and the soft flesh he knew he would find there.

She was softer than any other woman he had ever touched. Sweeter. Hotter. And he was one second from ripping his jeans open, lifting her to the seat and fucking the hell out of her.

"I'm sure it is." Lance licked at the dampness between her breasts, tasting honeysuckle there as well. Damn, he was developing a fondness for honeysuckle. If only the taste wasn't so subtle. Then he could fill his senses with it, sate his need for it.

He flexed his fingers in the curves of her ass as he helped her ride him, swearing he could feel the damp heat of her pussy searing him through her pants and his jeans.

"You taste as sweet as summer," he growled. Her lips were at his forehead, pressing against him tentatively, causing him to pause in this frantic desperation to taste as much of her as possible, returning to him a measure of control.

Her lips touched him with feeling. He could feel it in the soft breeze that wrapped around them, the whisper of confusion and lost dreams in the air at his ear.

As though she had never willingly touched before.

CHAPTER 2

"Shhhh." Lance's soft croon whispered over Harmony's distraught senses as his head lifted from the curve of her breasts.

He lowered her shirt, the distracting touch of his hands on her breasts easing the arousal threatening to overwhelm her.

She stared up at him, dazed, as his hands pressed her hair back from her heated cheeks, before he placed a tender kiss on her lips.

"In you go," he whispered.

Moving his hands to her hips he lifted her to the seat before picking up her purse from the pavement to hand it in to her.

She had lost her only protection as he held her? Her tote held her knife and the small gun she carried when she couldn't wear her weapons. She never let it off her arm unless absolutely necessary. And she had never, ever dropped it.

She flinched as the driver's side door opened and he got in. She could smell him, an intoxicating blend of the night and the seasons merging into his scent.

"Ready?" His voice was dark, the rasp of a sexually aroused primal male ready to claim a female.

She lifted her head, inhaling deeply as her gaze met his.

"I'm ready," she whispered.

She was past ready. Her body was screaming for him now. Her senses were dazed, her mind in upheaval. She couldn't think of anything past his touch, gorging herself on him, sating the hunger raging in her flesh.

She had gone from a lifetime of never caring either way if she lay beneath a man, to being suddenly desperate to feel him covering her.

Lance started the vehicle and pulled out of the parking lot as Harmony kept her peripheral vision trained on the small mirror at the side of her door. She could see no evidence that they were being followed, but her nape prickled in awareness.

Unfortunately her survival instinct was squelched the moment Lance's hand moved from the gearshift to lift hers from her lap.

"Your hands are soft." His voice was a bit unsteady, his lust rising as he laid her hand on the gearshift, covering it with his own as he drove.

"Thank you." She had learned how to flirt within a year of her escape from the labs. She knew the word games, the social repartee that kept men at a distance. But none of it came to mind now.

All she knew was the pulse of her heartbeat in the stiffness of her nipples, in the engorged bud of her clitoris and her hungry vagina. She was so wet she could feel her own juices dampening the silk of her thong and the rasp of the swollen folds of her pussy against the ultrasoft denim she wore.

His thumb caressed over hers, the faintly calloused flesh exciting sensitive nerve endings as Harmony fought to catch her breath.

"Is this your first time to Broken Butte?" His voice was quiet in the confines of the vehicle.

Harmony shifted in her seat, swallowing tightly as she frowned at the oddly sweet taste filling her mouth. She wanted his taste. The rich earthy essence of the wind and the land against her tongue.

"Yes." She breathed in deeply, closing her eyes briefly in an effort to maintain her control.

She had never been on such an edge. She didn't feel wholly herself, and that was damned scary. She had never been out of control. She processed information quickly and her decisions were ones she knew had merit.

This hunger had no merit, it made no sense. The completely illogical clawing need was throwing her mind and her body into havoc.

She had never given her status as a female much consideration, until now. Now she could feel the weakening arousal, the pulse of melting flesh between her thighs, a hunger to submit, to be possessed.

"Have you been here long?" His thumb drew circles at the side of her hand, caressing and massaging as she turned slowly to him.

She just needed one more taste. Her breathing was heavy, labored as he flicked on the turn signal and turned off the main road onto a graveled drive. It stretched ahead of them, never ending, and the wracking desire filling her senses was finding no relief.

"I haven't been here long," she whispered in reply, her gaze centering on his lips. "Kiss me again, Lance."

His grimace was tight, pained.

"If I kiss you again, I'm not going to make it to the house before I have you beneath me."

"I don't care." She really didn't care. All that mattered was that kiss, his touch.

His hand tightened on hers briefly before he lifted her fingers and laid them back in her lap.

"We're almost at the house." His voice was as strained and tense as she felt. "Just another minute or two, sweetheart."

He shifted in his seat, obviously hoping to relieve the pressure of his jeans on his erection. She could smell his hunger wrapping around her.

Harmony closed her eyes, fighting to hold back, to wait, just a few more minutes. Her dazed senses were demanding, this strange, unknown arousal so imperative every inch of her flesh ached for his touch.

And she was on fire. She felt as though she were in the midst of a fever, flushed, so sensitive that the air inside the Jeep seemed too heavy to breathe.

"God, the look on your face." His voice was strained as the Jeep accelerated. "You're killing me here."

She opened her eyes, laying her head back on the headrest as she watched him through drowsy eyes.

"What do I look like?"

"Hungry," he whispered. "So aroused and hungry that you make me ache to see you sated."

Could she be sated?

"I want you now," she said softly. "And that terrifies me. A bit," she acknowledged with a wry smile.

Life had to mean something to you for you to fear the consequences of your actions. Her own life had never mattered much beyond fulfilling her responsibilities to others. Until now.

Living meant pleasure now. It meant his touch, his kiss, an adventure in sensation she had never imagined she would find.

"There's the house." He nodded ahead as the headlights picked up the faint outline of a single-story ranch. The sprawling design looked lazy and comfortable, the porch light bathing the front of the house in a gentle inviting glow.

Lance pulled the Jeep to a stop beside the cement walkway that led to the porch. Pulling the keys free of the ignition, he turned to his guest and watched her silently.

Her pale green eyes stared back at him from drowsily lowered lids as the flush on her cheeks and the swollen curves of her lips attested to her arousal.

He was in agony himself. His cock was like a wedge of iron in his pants, hot and throbbing in need to bury itself inside her. His tongue ached to taste her. The taste of her just might well be addictive. He was tormented with the memory of it—the subtle sweetness, the hint of heat.

"Are you ready?"

She nodded back, her expression somber as he opened his door to step out of the vehicle. But he paused. Just one taste. They were close enough to the house. He could surely keep his control long enough to taste her one more time.

He let her move ahead of him to the sidewalk, his gaze dropping to the bunch and sway of her buttocks, his hands itching to grip them, to clench and hold tight as he pounded inside her.

He grimaced at the rising lust tormenting his balls. They were as tight as his cock, tortured, aching for release. He'd thought he wanted her before that kiss, but after his lips touched hers, the hunger had only increased. Was rapidly increasing even now.

"Here we go." He let his hand rest on her hip as he opened the screen door and dug his keys from his pocket. He grunted at the pinch of the material against his erection, but managed to pull the key ring free.

He unlocked the door and stepped in, scanning the interior quickly, his senses picking up every nuance of the house as he surveyed the room.

"You have a beautiful home." She stepped into the entryway, her voice soft. The soft light overhead created a gentle halo around the silken mass of dark russet hair that fell sleekly about her face.

"Hungry?"

She shook her head no and he felt his muscles tighten further. If possible, his cock got harder.

"Drink?"

"No, thank you." Her arms hung at her sides as though relaxed, but he could feel the tension filling her.

Holding out his hand in invitation, he watched as she reached out for him without hesitation. Her slender fingers curled into his, warm. Accepting. Willing.

He couldn't help but smile down at her, loving that little light of perplexed curiosity that filled her gaze each time he did so. As though no one had ever smiled at her before.

"Bedroom?" he asked then.

She tilted her head, staring back at him as she inhaled slowly, deeply. He watched the flush deepen in her cheeks, saw the concern that darkened in her eyes.

Her tongue peeked out, swiping over her lips in the first true sign of nerves he had seen from her.

"The bedroom." Her voice was husky, vibrating with desire.

As he entered the bedroom, the automatic lights eased on, a low, dim lighting that shadowed the room and kept the intimate atmosphere he enjoyed.

He closed the door behind them, turning to her and giving her no time to voice whatever she was going to say. He wanted no objections, couldn't bear to hear her hesitation. He wanted her soft and sweet against him again, her tongue licking over his like a little cat's, the taste of her, that wild honeysuckle and clover taste overwhelming his senses as it had earlier.

His lips settled against hers as he fought to hold back his lust. His hands pulled her to him, fitting her slender curves into his taller body, his arms crossing over her back as he sipped from her lips, deep, drugging kisses that only served to further inflame the need.

She was slender beneath his hands, smaller, more delicate than she appeared. But he could feel the strength in her.

Sharp little nails pricked through his shirt as her fingers clenched against him. A tight groan escaped him as her thighs moved against his, the firm planes of her abdomen cushioning the raging length of his cock. Slanting his lips over hers, he worked his tongue into her mouth, seeking the soft slide of hers and the elixir of passion that seemed to fill her mouth.

Damn, she tasted good. Her tongue twined with his, spilling sweet honey into his senses, the taste burning through his mind like an aphrodisiac.

"Come here." His hands cupped her ass. Fully curved, firm—his fingers clenched into them as he lifted her to him, groaning as her legs curved around his hips, the soft pad of her pussy cushioning his erection.

"You're like fire." He nipped at her lips as he moved her to the bed, laying her beneath him. "So sweet and hot I could lose my mind in you."

He *was* losing his mind in her. His fingers moved to her shirt, fumbling, as he drew it over her head, revealing the lace of her bra, her heaving breasts, before he tossed it aside.

No woman had ever affected him like this, had ever made him burn, made every cell in his body ache and throb for her touch, her taste. She was so damned feminine, so soft and warm, yet firm and resilient, that he had to clench his teeth from howling with his need for her.

And she watched him, her hands falling to her sides, the sea green of her eyes blazing with passion and confusion.

He removed her shoes, the functional white socks. Her feet were slender, delicate, the high arch and painted little toenails so sweet he grimaced at the sight.

There was nothing like a woman—softly scented, lightly colored, with all their makeup tricks and confident resourcefulness that turned a man inside out. They were weak, yet the strongest force on the face of the earth. And this woman would quickly become his world. He felt it. Knew it with every fiber of his being.

She wore only the bare minimum of makeup, enough to enhance rather than cover up, but it was the scarlet shade of those little toenails that pushed him over the edge. She pampered those feet. Babied them. They were as soft as silk, perfectly trimmed and pedicured, and they shimmered with beauty.

He lifted one, watching her as he placed the arch against his whisker-roughened cheek, feeling the silken touch as her toes curled and surprise lit her eyes.

He turned his head, lowering it, then nipped at the curve of her big toe before licking over it with utmost gentleness.

Her eyes flared, shock and something akin to fear filling them.

"You have pretty feet." He massaged it for a moment before releasing her.

She swallowed, opened her lips to speak, then bit the lower curve as his fingers moved to her jeans. The snap and zipper released quickly. Her hips lifted as he eased the fabric over them, sliding them down her thighs, his fingers touching sweet satin flesh as the material cleared her legs.

She reached for him then, her hands shaking, a small, almost imperceptible moan on her lips.

"Not yet." He pushed her hands back to the bed. "Wait, baby. Let me touch you. If you get those hot little hands on me first, I'm going to lose control and fuck you until neither one of us has the strength to worry about foreplay. Just lie there. Just for a bit."

"I need to touch you." The words sounded torn from her, though she did as he asked, her fingers curling into fists as they lay at her head.

"And I need you to touch me," he admitted, fighting to clear the haze of lust from his mind. "Just not yet."

He moved back, his eyes going over the sight of her. The fragile lace of her bra that did nothing to hide her tight nipples. Her flat, tanned abdomen and the delicate white silk of her thong, the material damp enough to outline the soft curves of her pussy.

He breathed out. A rough exhalation at the knowledge that beneath the fragile silk lay bare flesh. Her sweet juices had dampened the fabric just enough to see that no feminine curls marred the luscious curves.

"Do you shave?" He jerked his boots off, unable to look away from the damp silk.

"No. Wax." She sounded uncomfortable.

He looked up, flashing her a grin of approval as the last boot dropped to the floor. He jerked his shirt over his head, not bothering with buttons, then tore at his belt before jerking the snaps of his jeans apart. His dick was killing him. He was harder, hotter than he could ever remember being in his life.

"I'm going to eat that pretty pussy," he whispered as he shed jeans and underwear in one economical move. "I'm going to spread your legs and gorge myself on you. I bet that honeysuckle taste is there too. I like honeysuckle, Harmony. I like it real well."

He wrapped his fingers around his erection, his eyes returning to hers, a tight smile curving his lips at the erotic flush covering her face, her neck. Her lips were parted, shiny from the dampness of her tongue. Her eyes were wide, her pupils dilated and filled with shocked hunger.

He should be shocked himself. He had never been this damned hot, this hard for a woman in his life. He reached over to the nightstand, jerking a condom from the drawer and quickly tearing apart the wrapper. If he didn't do it now, he wouldn't have enough mind to do it later.

He extended his hand to her then, the latex circle gripped lightly between his fingers.

He couldn't make himself say the words. If he spoke, he was going to scare the hell out of her and himself with the animalistic growl in his throat.

She looked at the condom.

"I'm protected. And I'm clean," she said.

His cock jerked at the soft sound of her voice, the knowledge that he could sink into her, bare, feel her touching him, wrapping around him.

He shook his head. "No one can be sure, baby. Come on. Touch me now."

Amusement flickered in her gaze, some hidden knowledge he hoped he could remember to delve into further. Then she was rising, sitting before him, her face level with the straining length of his cock.

She took the condom from his fingers, but as his hand dropped to her shoulder, that wasn't what she covered the head of his erection with. Her tongue, blistering with heat, like rough velvet, swiped over the bulging crest.

"Harmony . . ." His hand moved to her hair. "Baby. This might not be a good idea." His self-control was strained to the limit.

"Hmm." She hummed around the sensitive flesh as her lips opened, her mouth sinking over him, drawing a strangled groan from his throat as his fingers tightened in her hair.

Her tongue was a lash of pleasure so erotic, so hungry, he was straining to hold back, to keep from losing control and his semen between those snug, pouty lips.

But he couldn't keep from moving against her, from watching his hard flesh slide from her lips before pushing back, sinking inside her until he knew he could go no farther. And still she stared up at him, her eyes wild with lust, her body shuddering from it. Tremors shook her fingers as they moved over the shaft of his cock, the other hand cupping his tight balls, her fingers combing through the hair that grew there.

And all he could do was watch. Watch and thrust inside her mouth, slow and easy, his teeth clenched tight as he fought to hold back the release sizzling at the base of his spine.

"Enough." He pulled back, his fingers holding tight to her head as she fought to follow him, her lips shiny, swollen from his possession of them.

"I want more," she whispered as he uncurled her fingers from the pulsing flesh. "Let me touch you, Lance. Just this once."

"Soon. Not yet, baby."

He pushed her back to the bed, followed her, and when his lips covered hers, the sweet taste of her filling his senses again, he forgot about control.

His fingers tunneled into her hair, holding her head in place as he let his lips devour her. He teased her tongue, sucked at it, slow, gentle pulls that seemed to intensify the taste he craved.

He was dying for her, craving her. He was becoming addicted.

✦   ✦   ✦

Harmony fought. It was a losing battle, but still she fought to maintain enough control to be alert, to be on guard. Something wasn't right here, not quite normal. From the moment she caught sight of him tonight, she had known her fascination with him was too strong. Too intense.

But this, this lust, was insane. It clawed at her womb, dug into her pussy and sent her juices spilling from her spasming vagina. It made her clutch at him, her lips opening beneath his as he removed her bra, leaving only the thong. And that for only the length of time it took for his hands to get to her hips and tear it away.

"Fuck, you're hot." He groaned as she cried out. His fingers were sliding through the wet slit between her thighs, his thumb rubbing over her clit, circling it with devastating results as his lips moved down her neck, heading for the heaving curves of her breasts.

The pleasure was agonizing. Harmony had never known of sensations so extreme, so brutal that she couldn't focus her senses elsewhere at the same time. She had never known anything but terror that could overtake the body, the heart and the soul in one fell swoop. Until now.

Lance's hands touched her, caressed, spreading fire, creating a firestorm of bliss that burned through any other thought, any other instinct.

The need to mate became imperative. To feel his body moving over her, inside her, taking her, possessing her . . .

"Fuck me!" She barely held back the snarl as his lips and tongue moved to a painfully erect, highly sensitive nipple.

He chuckled, a dark sound of satisfaction as his finger moved from the slick contours of her pussy to grip her hip, holding her in place as she arched against him.

"Soon," he whispered. "Easy, baby. Let's see how hot it can get."

She couldn't imagine hotter. Couldn't imagine surviving it if her body became so much as a breath more sensitive.

"It can't get hotter," she gasped, no longer recognizing herself or her own body as his teeth raked over her nipple, drawing a ragged cry from her throat. If it became hotter, there was no way she could survive. No way to turn from him unaffected.

"Of course it can," he crooned, his voice husky, rough. He gave her nipple a gentle nip.

She stared down at him, seeing the sexual, sensual animal bending over her, and wanted to cry out at the injustice of it.

One night. Just one night.

Her hands were tangled in his hair, and she couldn't remember moving them from the bed. But she felt the coarse strands between her fingers, the warmth of it heating the sensitive pads.

"I need you now." She was shaking, trembling with that need, but she couldn't control the impulse to touch him. One hand fell from his hair to his face, her fingers moving over the hard planes and angles, tentatively smoothing over his lips.

He nipped her thumb, gripped it between his straight, white teeth as his tongue swiped over it with hungry heat.

"We could play later," she whispered breathlessly, on fire, feeling the thick length of his cock by her thigh as her pussy wept in need of it.

"We'll play later too." His fingers wrapped around her wrist, lowering it to his shoulder as his head dipped, his tongue trailing down the middle of her stomach in a rapid course to the tormented flesh between her thighs.

He glanced up at her with each kiss to her quivering belly, his eyes sparkling with warmth, laughter and hunger. A wild, vibrant hunger echoed and built within her until she could feel the flames overtaking her.

"Lance." The sound of her own cry shocked her—hoarse, edged with desperation as his head neared the soaked curves of her pussy. "I can't take it . . . Please . . ."

She was on the edge of a precipice that terrified her. She had never flown so high, never known such pleasure. Holding onto her control, shredded though it was, became imperative.

"Just a little bit more, baby. I just want a little taste. That's all . . . Just lay back and let it feel good. I promise to make it feel good." His wicked smile was followed by a puff of air over the violently sensitive, swollen clit.

Darkness shrouded her then. Her eyes closed, her

strength drained until she could do nothing but respond. She arched to him, a shattered cry leaving her throat as his tongue moved in to torture her, to torment her quaking cunt.

"There's a good girl." He groaned as her thighs fell open farther. "Let me show you how good it can be, baby."

Good? It surpassed good. It was torture.

His tongue was a flaming lash of pleasure, working its way slowly through the narrow slit as his fingers parted the plump lips.

"So sweet and bare." He groaned. "I love your naked pussy, Harmony. I love feeling all your silky flesh, wet and hot and straining toward me."

She strained harder. His tongue licked through each fold, tickled around her clit, slid down, rimmed the spasming opening to her vagina and then began again.

Gasping, fighting to breathe, Harmony felt her hands gripping his hair, her nails digging into his scalp as she fought to hold him in one place, to find the release hovering just out of reach.

His tongue was wicked, imperious. It sought, demanded, and drew from her a pleasure that exceeded any she had heard of, let alone known. It sent lightning crashing through her system. Tidal waves of sensation clashed through her mind, causing her to jerk, to shudder, her cries to echo around her as control was lost.

When his lips moved back to her clit, a hard male finger tested the entrance to her pussy, worked in, caressed and stroked, sending spasms racing through the very heart of her womb.

"Lance . . ." Her scream was strangled. "For God's sake. Please . . ."

Another finger joined the first. His lips covered the swollen bud of her clitoris, drawing it into his mouth, his

tongue flickering over it like flames of lust as she felt herself
fly higher. Higher.

Sensation ripped through her. Tore through her nervous
system, shredded her soul. Her orgasm slammed her, tightened her body, and sent her racing toward a heat and brilliance so extreme, so intense she lost herself within it.

Lance's hard growl filled her head as he moved to cover
her then, his thighs spreading hers farther, the blunt, thick
head of his cock separating the folds of her pussy.

"Look at me."

Look at him? She struggled to open her eyes, to make
sense of the violent tremors surging through her. What she
saw did nothing to restore her control or her equilibrium.
His eyes were so blue, a deep, impossibly brilliant blue, his
features taut, savagely so, his lips swollen as he stared down
at her and slapped a condom into her hand.

"Now." He jerked upright, the thick, pulsing stalk of his
cock angling away from his body, spearing toward her,
throbbing with the same furious, desperate hunger surging
through her cunt.

Her eyes moved slowly, reluctantly to her palm and the
condom he had placed there.

"Put. It. On."

She blinked at the guttural sound of his voice.

"You don't need—"

"Now!" His hands gripped her thighs, his eyes blazing
down at her.

She swallowed tightly, her fingers shaking, trembling as
she moved to do as he ordered as quickly as possible. She
needed him; her pussy burned, hurt. Her tongue throbbed.
Every cell in her flamed in demand.

Her fingers were shaking so bad she could barely fit the
disk over the bulging, damp head.

"I can't." It slipped, moved, slid. She couldn't make her fingers work.

"Put the damned thing on, Harmony." His body jerked, shuddered.

"Fuck it." She threw the condom, lifted her hips until the swollen head pressed against the entrance to her cunt. "Fuck me. I told you, you don't need the son of a bit—"

The invasion—it could be called nothing else, an impalement, a penetration that tore through her, stretched her and destroyed her.

Harmony heard herself screaming his name. Her legs wrapped around his plunging hips, her lips opened for his, her tongue battling his the moment they touched.

She was filled to her limit, the tearing pleasure whipping through her, overloading her senses until nothing mattered, no one mattered, the world dissolved until nothing existed but Lance. His touch. His kiss, feeling the jackhammer strokes of his cock powering inside her pussy as her tongue filled his mouth, the taste of wild honey, of spice, an aphrodisiac that heightened each sensation and sent her careening into ecstasy.

Her body jerked violently as the next orgasm ripped through her. She bucked, shuddered, fighting to scream, but only a whimper emerged as he tore his lips from hers. A strangled male cry filled the air then, followed quickly by the strangest, most terrifying sensation she had ever known.

She cried out at the feel of his semen rushing through her, seeping into the very pores of the spasming flesh, easing the flaming lust, soaking into her womb.

She felt it. Felt each heated pulse of semen fill her, change her, complete her just before her teeth sank into his shoulder and she tasted his blood. And in that moment sensed her own defeat.

CHAPTER 3

Lance was enraged. The next morning he paced his office, scowling, his body burning as his cock throbbed in his jeans and the bite at his shoulder burned in need.

Son of a bitch. A fucking Breed. He became aware of what she was the moment those sharp little teeth of hers pierced his flesh. He had seen the mark on his cousin Megan's shoulder nearly a year before. Placed there by her mate, Braden Arness.

"I can't find anyone that meets your description in the database, Lance." Braden growled in irritation.

"Now look, dammit, I know she's a Breed," Lance snapped. "She has to be in there."

"Lance, I've been searching these damned files for an hour now. She's not in here. What the hell is this about?"

Lance drew in a hard breath.

"The bitch bit me last night, Braden," he finally snarled. "I picked her up at the bar and took her home."

"You had sex with her, and she bit you?" Braden's voice was carefully bland. "What did you say her name was again?"

"Harmony. She didn't give me a last name. Russet hair, pale green eyes, about five-seven."

"Any tattoos or distinguishing marks?" Braden asked.

Lance frowned. He barely remembered a small tattoo.

"Her right shoulder, I can't be sure, but I think it was a scythe."

Silence filled the line as the air around him whispered in warning.

"Are you certain of that? A scythe."

"A red scythe, no more than an inch and a half high. I saw it just before she jerked her shirt on. By the time she turned around with the fucking gun in her hand, I forgot about it."

She had held a gun on him. A small, snub-nosed though powerful military-issue Beretta. And those babies packed a wallop, despite their size.

"Damn. That's bad." Braden's voice was suddenly deeper; the animalistic growl of his Breed heritage only showed itself in times of anger or stress.

"The Breed part or the scythe part?" Lance asked. "You have to be a bit clearer here, Braden. My mind's not exactly working at its normal speed."

And he knew why. He knew and it pissed him off. God help her if he got his hands on her again. The first thing he was going to do was spank that pretty ass for running. The second thing he would do was fuck her until she didn't have the strength to run again.

"According to my files, the Breed with that mark is one badass you don't want to mess with. We call her by her lab name, because she never chose another that we knew of. Her name is Death, Lance. She's wanted not just by the Bureau of Breed Affairs but by several government agencies as well, for questioning in the assassinations of suspected child abusers as well as suspected Council scientists. If Death mated you, cuz, then you're screwed."

The woman in his arms had been no killer. "There has to be a mistake."

"No mistake," Braden said in denial. "No other Breed would dare wear that mark. Death is a possessive bitch. She's a class A assassin with the added rating of knifemanship. Death doesn't feel, Lance. And how the hell you could have mated with her makes no sense."

Because every instance of mating heat that had occurred in the Breed society had involved emotion. To their knowledge there hadn't been a mating that hadn't been a match of not just the physical, but the psychological and emotional as well. Lance knew that from the few explanations Megan had given him in regards to her relationship with Braden.

"Then there's a mistake," Lance grated out. "Is there a description on this 'Death'?"

"Oh yeah," Braden sighed. "The description of her hair was throwing me off. Her hair is the color of a true lion's mane rather than just a similarity. Eye color pale green. Height five-seven, age twenty-five. She escaped the labs at fifteen after killing every scientist in the facility. Including her own mother."

The air began to wail at his ear.

"There's a notation here that an op went out a few weeks ago to a suspected sighting, but no update."

"Get me her file. I want the complete dossier on her, and see what else you can find out. I'm taking the day off and going looking for her myself."

"Whoa, hold up there, man," Braden protested furiously. "Didn't you hear what I just said? This woman is one of the most lethal killers in our ranks. She hunts Coyotes for fun, Lance. And she kills them. She'll take you out if she even thinks you're going to get close."

"According to you, the mating heat goes both ways, right?" Lance reminded him.

"As far as I know. According to all the reports the Bureau has listed of mated pairs, it's always a two-way street."

"Then she's likely in no better shape than I am," Lance pointed out.

Braden sighed. "*If* the mating went both ways, she's likely in worse shape," he growled. "*If,* Lance. That's a hell of a supposition though. From what I'm seeing on the database here, this woman has no soul. You could just be swimming in hell by yourself."

"Not hardly." Lance raked his fingers through his hair, grimacing at the memory of her face, her eyes, before she left. "It has her too, Braden. I'd bet my life on it."

"Which is exactly what you are betting." Braden breathed out roughly. "Give me an hour. Wait there on me and I'll go out with you. You'll need backup on this one, Lance, and I don't want Megan anywhere near her. She still hasn't recovered from the search we did for her."

"What search?" Lance clenched his teeth at that information.

"After leaving Sanctuary last year, our first mission was to locate Death. We thought we were getting close, then she just disappeared."

"Where is Megan?" She would tell him. She wouldn't hide information she knew he would need.

"Megan flew back to Sanctuary this morning to pick up one of the new girls we're training here at the ranch. She won't be back till morning."

Now, wasn't that just perfect timing?

Lance stared out into the park, watching as the breeze swayed in the trees, the low psychic moan he heard whispering around him, a warning and plea.

"I'm heading out in an hour," he finally said and sighed roughly. "Get over here if you're going with me. I don't have all day."

Because if he didn't get Harmony beneath him again, he was going to explode with the lust ripping through him.

"I'm getting everything together now. I'll see you in an hour." The line disconnected as Lance jerked the phone link from his ear and tossed it to his desk.

Just what the fuck he needed, he scowled. H. R. Alonzo, one of the most virulent opponents of the Breeds, was already protesting city hall over the Breeds training at Megan's ranch, and members of the Blood Purity Society were streaming in. Journalists were camped out at the hotels, and the situation was rapidly escalating from a headache to a problem.

He sure as hell didn't need this added complication. And the moment he got his hands on Harmony again, he intended to make his displeasure known. In a variety ways. All of them guaranteed to make her come.

✦   ✦   ✦

Harmony was barely ready when Jonas and the Breed lawyer arrived at her hotel room late that morning. She hadn't slept, and makeup wasn't covering the results of that well. And she was in pain. Physical, aching pain from the arousal building within her.

Since when did a lack of screwing actually hurt?

Dressed in the soft black cotton uniform of a Breed Enforcer, she adjusted her utility belt at her hips and made certain her gun was comfortably holstered. Her knife was strapped to her opposite thigh, and tucked into her right ankle boot was a secondary dagger. The clothes were driving her crazy though.

The rasp of the material against her flesh was an irritation she wondered if she would survive. And she was hot. She felt as though she were burning alive from the inside out.

Her womb sizzled with need; her pussy was so wet she had given up attempting to stem the slick juices that kept her prepared for penetration, and just thanked God that it wasn't seeping through her clothing.

When she opened the door to Jonas, she avoided his eyes and stepped into the hall, slamming the door behind her. At his side, J. R. "Jess" Warden, the Bureau's attorney, watched her with a glimmer of surprise in her eyes.

"Let's get it the hell over with," she snapped as she started down the hall. "Have you informed your sheriff yet of who he's being saddled with?"

"Did you sleep well last night, Harmony?" His voice was taunting as he finally began walking to her, his nostrils flaring as her eyes narrowed on him.

The bastard. He knew. Whatever was wrong with her he could smell it.

"I slept fine, Jonas," she purred menacingly as she glanced at Jess, then back to him. "And you?"

His lips quirked, though the smug confidence was held firmly in place.

"I slept quite well." He moved slowly ahead of her. "You seem agitated this morning. Is something wrong?"

She was tempted to snarl, but restrained the urge. "Just your normal Breed psychosis," she retorted disdainfully, repeating the psychologist's profile Jonas had ordered before she left for Broken Butte.

As though her fondness for shedding blood had anything to do with her genetics. The lives she had taken after escape never weighed on her conscience. The monsters she had taken out were a disease. The world was better off with them dead.

No, it was the lives she had taken before her escape that haunted her nightmares. It was those that left her gasping for breath, a plea on her lips as she fought to escape the horrors that visited her. Harmony wasn't still alive because she loved life. Nor was she still here for vengeance. She lived because she knew hell awaited her after death.

Entering the elevator behind Jonas, Harmony turned to face the doors, ignoring the looks her brother cast her. Jonas

Wyatt, they called him. She had called him Alpha One. The leader of the small contingent of Lion Breeds at the French Labs wherein they had been created.

Even though he had been younger than several of the other Breeds there, his strength and natural dominance had assured his steady rise within the ranks. He had been created as a breeder for a few specially created females, a last attempt to see if they could create the soldier they were searching for through other means. Instead, Jonas had grown to excel in areas the head scientist, Madame LaRue, had never expected.

Deceptive, powerful, completely logical and coldhearted, Jonas had taken control of the other males from the time he reached his maturity. He manipulated them, maneuvered them and always managed to get the best out of them.

Harmony stared up at the ceiling patiently.

"Sheriff Jacobs will be your representative," Jonas informed her as the doors opened and they stepped out into the lobby, the attorney trailing behind them. "You'll live in his home, under his guidance for the time you'll be here. He'll report to the Bureau once a week on your progress. He's a fairly responsible individual. I'm certain I won't have to worry about him."

Harmony kept her pace steady as she moved along with him, tempering her opinion on his orders.

She had no idea what Jonas's game was, or how he hoped to accomplish his goals by sticking her in this little tourist trap, but she was certain she would figure it out. One thing she did know, she was not about to turn over the one thing she suspected he was after: the information she had hidden on the first Leo, the first Breed created and still living—information she had stolen when she escaped the labs.

"Are you listening to me, Harmony?" he finally asked as they stepped into the sunlit courtyard at the entrance to the hotel and he slid his dark glasses over his eyes.

"I heard you, Jonas." She smiled back coolly, reminding herself, forcefully, that she couldn't kill him. Well, she could. It would be a fight, but technically, it could be arranged. But she was fairly certain that doing so wasn't in her best interests at the moment.

He smiled, flashing his dominant canines threateningly. Drama just seemed to go hand in hand with the Breeds these days. She remembered a time when they kept their opinions to themselves and just killed. Rather like she did. The threatening thing just seemed useless to her.

"I think you're going to like Sheriff Jacobs." He finally nodded to the courthouse and Sheriff's Department on the other side of the small park they were crossing the street to. "Several of the Breed females consider him quite handsome."

Harmony barely suppressed her shudder, or the whimper that yearned to pass her lips as she kept pace with him. Walking was torturous. Agonizing. The swollen folds of her pussy rasped against her silk panties as the engorged bud of her clitoris demanded relief.

She had attempted masturbation. To her own peril. It had only increased the arousal rather than diminishing it.

As they crossed the park, Harmony fought to tamp down her growing agitation. Jonas kept a steady pace, even as his voice droned on. The do's and don'ts of how to act and react as a sheriff's deputy. As though she knew nothing but killing.

"Here we are." They stepped onto the walkway that led to the entrance of the Sheriff's Department. The building was one story, with tall, wide windows and an Old West charm she appreciated.

The door swung open as Jonas stepped aside and allowed her to enter ahead of him. She cast him a suspicious look at the move, only to receive a mocking smile in return.

"Straight ahead." He nodded to the hallway on the other

side of the reception area as he lifted his hand to the desk sergeant. "His office is at the end of the hall."

Harmony drew in a deep breath as she prayed for patience, only to flinch and jerk from Jonas's reach as his hand moved to her back.

"Okay?" He lifted his brows as his silvery eyes gleamed with amusement.

No, that wasn't okay, she thought, suddenly feeling the beginnings of fear settling in the pit of her stomach. Something was horribly wrong. The feel of his hand, even with her clothing as a buffer, had nearly made her physically ill. Even now, her flesh turned clammy as a cold burn began to build beneath the skin.

"Let's get this over with." A tremor raced down her spine as she moved for the hallway.

Jonas was up to something and she knew it. She could feel the warning tightening in her stomach, the sense of danger settling around her shoulders as they neared the end of the hallway.

Then his scent hit her. Midnight and storms. The earth, fresh and primal, pulling at her, reminding forcibly of the agonizing need building inside her.

Her steps slowed.

"Keep moving, Harmony." Jonas's voice was commanding, brooking no refusal as she felt every nerve ending in her body perking up in awareness.

Lance.

"What's his name?" she whispered, drawing steadily closer to the door, aware that there was no escape.

Getting past Jonas would be impossible.

She stopped several feet from the door, the smell of the man inside igniting her lust to a flaming height. She could almost feel his touch as the air grew heavy around her. His hands, broad and calloused, his lips, firm and heated.

"Lance."

His answer had her closing her eyes as sure knowledge rose inside her. She turned slowly, staring up at Jonas as he met her gaze coolly.

"What have you done to me?" she whispered, knowing, certain that somehow Jonas knew what was happening to her and why.

The blood tests, the saliva tests, the psychological profiles—they had been done for a reason. For this. She knew it. She hadn't survived in the world for the past ten years in her vocation and not learned when to trust her own instincts.

"Let's just say I've hedged my bets," he remarked as he reached around her and knocked imperiously on the door. "You can thank me later."

Harmony turned as the door swung open and the scent of pure, hard male lust swamped her. She felt her knees weaken and her womb clenched painfully as she stared up into surprised, then suspicious midnight blue eyes.

Lance's gaze tore from hers to stare behind her, the scowl deepening at his brow as anger lit his features.

"What the hell are you doing here?" he snapped at Jonas a second before gripping Harmony's arm and pulling her into the room.

At any other time, the fact that someone attempted to slam the door in Jonas's face would have been funny. She could have even respected the attempt if she wasn't about to orgasm from the feel of his hand wrapping around her arm.

As Jonas stepped into the room, she jerked away from Lance, only to turn and face yet another daunting figure.

Braden Arness. Husband to the empath, Megan Arness. They had tracked her to France last year and nearly caught up with her.

She stepped back, her hand going to the gun strapped to

her thigh as she moved far enough back to keep all three
men in her line of sight.

This wasn't a good thing.

"You. Stay put and get your hand off that damned gun."
Lance pointed his finger at her furiously, the raw dominance
in his voice causing her eyes to widen.

"And you can get the hell out of my office." He swung
around as Jonas closed the door behind him. "You and the
shark attorney of yours. I had enough of your games last
year, Jonas."

Jess Warden smiled, the curve of her lips holding rueful
amusement, as though his words were more a compliment
than an insult. But her eyes stayed on Lance. Soft gray eyes
that held a glimmer of interest and lust. Hell, Harmony
could smell the other female's lust and it just pissed her off.

"If I leave, Harmony goes with me." Jonas shrugged easily as he tucked his hands into his slacks and rocked back on
his heels.

Harmony's hand clenched around the butt of her gun. She
knew that voice, just as she knew how dangerous Jonas
could be when he used it.

God, he was such a manipulator. Even Harmony realized
that the emotions and lust flaring through Lance were a dangerous combination right now. Whatever the hell was going
on, it had sent so much testosterone racing through his body
that she could smell it—a dark, masculine, high-combustible
scent.

"Back off, Jonas," she growled, the hair at her nape lifting
as his gaze swung back to her.

She could hear the furious little growls rising in her
throat. She had no idea what was causing them or where
they were coming from. All she knew was that despite the
threat Jonas represented to her personally, she would not allow him to strike against Lance.

She was aware of Braden's careful, cautious stance as he watched her, but she kept her eyes on Jonas. The other enforcer might try to stop her, but not before she did some damage. Enough damage perhaps to take his mind from Lance.

"Do you really want to go back to Sanctuary, Harmony?" Jess asked her then, her voice cool as she stared between Jonas and Harmony.

Harmony stared at Jonas with cold aggression, ignoring the other woman's terse tone.

"He won't take me back." She shook her head firmly. "Not now. He hasn't milked this little exercise for everything it's worth yet."

Jonas chuckled, his expression partly approving, partly calculating as he turned back to Lance.

"She learned well, despite her time away from the labs killing petty criminals. Too bad she didn't stick to the just killing the Council soldiers and Coyotes sent after her. She might have managed to keep me from coming after her."

Yeah. Right. She really believed that one.

Lance didn't speak, but Harmony had a feeling he was all the more dangerous for it. She could feel it, like an ominous whisper on the air around her.

Braden spoke up then. "Jonas, you're pushing boundaries again. I'm going to assume this is Death." He nodded to Harmony. "Lance was pretty certain about the tattoo she carried on her shoulder and there's no doubt she's the little cat that bit him."

Jonas glanced back at her and lifted his brow mockingly.

"I should have known she wouldn't follow orders and go directly to her hotel room until I could get here." He shrugged negligently as he turned back to Lance.

Jess stepped forward at that point. "We had the papers faxed through last night. Your superiors in Santa Fe approved your representation of a Breed Enforcer within your department. As you know . . ."

"She stays with me. I'll sign the papers later. Now get the hell out of my office."

Harmony tensed at the low, primal vibration in Lance's voice.

Jonas's smile was a dare as Jess stared back at Lance in surprise. "Perhaps I should take her with me."

"Lance, stop!" Before Lance could move, Harmony jumped between the two men. Ecstatic pleasure surged through her body as her hands gripped the hard muscles of Lance's upper arms and she pushed back at him, attempting to keep him from tearing into Jonas, as he obviously intended.

"Get out of my way." The scent of his fury seethed in the air around him, despite the gentleness of his hands as he gripped her arms.

"This is not the way," she snarled up at him, fighting to stand between him and Jonas as he fought to set her aside. "Let it go. He's amused and playing with you. He's trying to antagonize you. Let it go."

"First I'll deal with him, then I'll get to you." His blue eyes flamed as he stared down at her.

"Lance, you're going about this the wrong way," Braden drawled. "Come on, man, you remember how confrontational Megan was last year. Stop and think."

"And how should he handle it, Braden?" Jonas queried then. "Have you forgotten so quickly you're an employee of the Bureau?"

"I haven't forgotten anything, Jonas." Braden's amusement was very palpable and very real. "But I also know who your boss is. Let's not go there, okay?"

Jonas's eyes narrowed a second before his lips tilted with mocking approval.

"You're learning." He nodded abruptly to Braden as Lance placed her back flush against his chest, while his hands gripped her arms firmly.

"Get the hell out of here." She could barely speak for the need whipping through her.

"Not yet," Lance said. "You're forgetting something here."

"And that is?" Jonas tilted his head curiously.

"The hormonal treatments," he snapped. "I know what's going on here, Jonas. Don't try to screw me around."

Jonas's eyes narrowed on Braden. "It's illegal to give out that information, Braden."

Braden shrugged. "I didn't say a word. Maybe the wind told him."

The wind?

Jonas's lips thinned in irritation before he brought his gaze back to Lance. "I didn't completely expect this," he lied smoothly. Harmony knew he was lying. "I'll have to contact Sanctuary and get Ely to make time to fly in. It could be a few days."

"You son of a bitch. You're going to let her suffer through it." Sheer, amazed fury colored Lance's voice as Harmony fought to understand exactly what they were talking about. "You know what will happen."

"I think she'll make a lovely mother," Jonas crooned as he turned the doorknob and opened the door. "Maybe it will tame her down a bit. If she's lucky. Are you ready, Jess?"

"We need the papers . . ." Jess protested again.

"He can fax them to my office." He held the door open for her and the attorney did as she was told, but Harmony had a feeling she wasn't nearly as submissive as she was letting on.

Before anyone could respond further, the door closed behind them and Harmony turned to Lance slowly. She hadn't missed Jonas's parting shot in any way. Though it made no sense. A female Breed could not conceive. It was proven.

Hell, they had tried for years in the labs with no success. But then again, she had never heard of the strange sexual heat attacking her either.

"What's he talking about?" She felt dazed, off balance. She wanted nothing more than to crawl up his body and beg him to take her, but the sudden fear, that Jonas may have found the perfect revenge against her, held her grounded. "Breed females can't conceive."

"Under the right circumstances, they can." Lance grimaced.

"What circumstances?" She could feel an edge of panic beginning to build within her now. As though the emotions churning wildly inside her weren't enough. This was one worry she didn't need.

He turned back to her slowly, crossing his arms over his chest and watching her with heated, barely restrained lust.

"Mating heat. We mated last night, Harmony. We didn't just fuck. If it continues without the hormonal therapy the Breeds have produced, then you'll conceive. And most likely rather quickly. Now, what makes me think Jonas knew that?"

◆ C H A P T E R   4 ◆

The blood tests and saliva swabs—that was the only way to know. Harmony stared back at Lance in shock before slowly turning to Braden.

"This can't be true." She stared back at him, desperate for his agreement.

Braden sighed roughly. "It's true. I'm betting the glands beneath your tongue are swollen even now, and hot. Within twenty-four hours the arousal will be so intense it'll become physically painful. The womb begins to convulse, spasming as the hormones attack it, and your nerve endings become so sensitized that a female can literally feel the air around them. Megan describes it as PMS times a thousand. The only thing that eases it is male semen. A mate's semen. Any other male's touch is extremely painful. So much so that it's un-bearable."

He wasn't lying. Harmony could smell a lie as easily as she could smell Lance's lust.

She moved unsteadily to a nearby chair before sitting down heavily and pushing her fingers through her hair in frustration.

"There's a cure?" She stared up at Braden for the answer. "This hormonal therapy stuff."

He shook his head slowly. "There's no cure. The hormonal therapy merely eases the worst of the symptoms and prevents conception."

She turned back to Lance.

"I can't conceive." The thought of it was horrifying. No child of hers would ever survive those who sought to take her, to kill her. "You don't know who I am, Lance. You don't know what I am." Fear rushed through her mind, tore through her soul.

She felt the emotion, so unknown until now, explode inside her being until she knew nothing but the horrifying realization of what would happen to any child of hers.

"Jonas. He has to stop this." She jumped to her feet, stumbling before she managed to right herself and rush for the door.

"Harmony, wait. You can't go after him." Lance grabbed her around the waist, pulling her to a stop as she struggled against him, rough growls falling from her lips. "Harmony, dammit. He's gone. You know he's gone."

"No!" she screamed, striking back at him as she tore loose from him. "No. He can't be gone. He has to fix this."

He stared back at her, his gaze rife with pain as his chest rose and fell with his breaths. She was breaking apart inside. She could feel it. In all her life she had never known a pain so intense, so blinding as the one whipping through her mind now. A child. She couldn't have a child, because she could never keep it safe.

"You don't know what I am, Lance." Shudders whipped through her body as she stared back at him in horror.

She would be damned. Jonas had finally found a way to destroy her. Slowly. Painfully. She should have killed him when she had the chance ten years before.

He was her brother. Her blood brother. They shared the mother she had killed. And now he would see her child destroyed. A child she was never meant to have.

"I can't do this," she whispered miserably. "Let me go, Lance. I'll leave. I don't care what he does . . ."

"He'll have her killed, Lance."

"Shut up!" She turned on Braden, instantly noticing that he had placed himself against the door. No escape there.

"If you destroy yourself, you destroy your mate, Harmony," Braden snapped, his golden eyes narrowed on her. "I saw your need to stand between him and Jonas. You feared for him. You were determined to protect him. Run from him and you'll condemn him to the same agony you'll suffer as well. You're not in this alone."

"I am always alone," she snarled back at him. "They call me Death for a reason . . ."

"And if you've already conceived?" Lance asked quietly then. "Would you deny me the right to help protect my child? And trust me, Harmony, I can and will protect both my mate and my child."

He honestly believed he could. Harmony felt the hard sob that clenched her chest as hopelessness filled her.

"No force on this earth can protect a child of mine," she sneered. "You don't understand. You don't know the lives I've taken, the blood I've spilled or the monsters that would attack. There's no way to save either of us now."

Lance watched the pain-ridden features staring up at him. Fear filled the eyes of a woman whose file stated she knew no fear. No, it wasn't fear, it was complete terror, and it was destroying his soul.

The air was heavy with her pain, wailing at his ear like a distant scream rife with torment. Harmony *was* tormented. He could see it in her expression, in her tears. In her confusion as she wiped at the dampness.

The need to protect her, to reassure her, rose inside him like a tidal wave. It was more than just a need; it was an impulse, an instinctive response to the pain tearing her apart.

The thought of a child, and a woman that completed him, couldn't distress him. And protecting that woman and child would be his main focus.

"Braden, can you contact Ely without Jonas knowing?" Lance kept his eyes on Harmony as he spoke.

"That would be easy enough," Braden answered.

"Get her out here for the tests Harmony needs. I want that hormone therapy. Get her out here fast."

"Jonas's scientist?" Harmony's question had his gaze swinging back to her.

"She's the Breeds' scientist," Lance corrected her. "She heads the department working on the mating phenomena."

"She took the blood and saliva samples while I was at Sanctuary . . ."

"You haven't been at Sanctuary," Braden growled. "I pulled your file this morning, Harmony. Jonas would have had to log you in."

Lance watched as the bitter mockery twisted her lips.

"That's a nice little underground cell system you have below the main detention building," she said softly, sarcasm thickening the slight French accent that he hadn't noticed the night before. "I was there for two weeks, Braden, while your Ely poked and prodded at me. I was slipped out at night and put on a heli-jet to Carlsbad. Check with your precious Ely and see if she can tell the truth any better than Jonas can."

Lance stared back at Braden, seeing the surprise as Harmony described the cells.

"Shit. He's going to get himself killed at this rate." Braden swiped his fingers through his unbound hair as he stared back at both of them in acknowledgment. "I'll contact

Ely the moment I get to the house. I want a completely secured line for this one. Jonas is no doubt tapping yours, as
well as your home line. So watch that. Check the house and
this office for bugs while you're at it."

"That was done when I first came in," Lance snapped. "I
take nothing for granted in this office, Braden."

Braden nodded firmly, his gaze touching on Harmony in
compassion as she wrapped her arms across her chest and
paced to the window across the room.

"You're his sister," Braden finally announced. "The same
one who killed his mother. Why is he giving you a chance to
redeem yourself?"

Lance watched as she turned, her body tense with the obvious results of the unnatural arousal tearing her apart.

"You'll have to ask him that one." Her teeth bared in
anger. "According to Jonas, he would give any other Breed
this same chance." Her lips twisted into a sneer. "The re-
demption offer was a trick. He knew this would happen,
somehow; he knew the reaction that would result from being
with Lance. He knew and he used it. He found the perfect
way to destroy me."

Braden cursed as Lance felt a killing rage echo inside
him. God help Jonas if he got hold of him anytime soon.

"Can we lodge a complaint with the Breed Ruling Cabinet?" He turned to Braden again. "They could leash him."

"You do that and you reveal Death's whereabouts to whatever spy is still spilling secrets at Sanctuary." He sighed. "It
poses more of a danger than a solution at this point. Until the
heat dulls, she's at her weakest, Lance. If another male
touches her, he'll debilitate her. Right now, Death is as vulnerable as any babe. The hormonal shifts and changes tear down
the defenses, physical and mental. She wouldn't survive it."

"I won't let this happen!" The rage and fear in her voice
sliced through his soul.

Lance swung around, rushing to her as he watched her crumple. The mating heat was building in her, her expression distorted with pain as her hand clenched at her stomach and her face paled.

He caught her in his arms, burying his face in her hair, crooning to her, lifting her against his chest as he turned back to Braden.

"Contact Ely," he snapped hoarsely. "Now."

Braden nodded and left the office. The door slammed behind him, clicked and locked, sealing them safely within the office.

"Sit." Lance deposited her in the chair as he strode to his desk and hit the intercom link.

"Lenny, I'm not available until I inform you otherwise," he snapped into the desk sergeant's link. "Do you understand?"

"I figured," he grunted. "I saw that damned Jonas striding out of here grinning like a polecat. I got your back, Sheriff. No one will bother you."

It was no secret that after one of Jonas's surprise visits, Lance normally disappeared for hours to fortify his patience.

Disengaging the link, he turned back to Harmony. She was pacing now, her head lowered, auburn hair covering her face as she fought the obvious effects of the mating heat.

It was killing him too. His balls were drawn up so damned tight he swore they were going to implode. His cock was like living steel behind the fly of his jeans and pressing painfully into the zipper.

Dealing with this was going to be impossible until the more pressing physical needs were taken care of. Namely, bending her over and fucking her past her tears and her hunger, until they could both stand to breathe without the agony of need torturing them.

God help them both if she let out one of those animalistic little roars when she came, though. If she did, the entire department would know he was spending on-duty hours screwing the hell out of the little cat.

"Harmony, we'll find a way to fix this." He breathed out roughly as he moved toward her. "Until then, baby, before we can leave this office, we have to take care of this arousal. It's killing both of us."

Her head whipped up, her expression blank with shock.

"No." She shook her head emphatically. "We can't take that risk, Lance. You know we can't."

Her hand pressed against her lower stomach as she breathed in roughly.

"We don't have a choice," he bit out. "I can't think for the remembered taste of your kiss. It's killing me. You might have the control to withstand it, but I don't."

She shook her head again as he moved to the utility cabinet at the side of the room. Opening the doors, he pulled a clean ball gag from its cellophane wrapper and turned back to her.

Her eyes widened as they dropped to the device, and he grinned wickedly.

"A little present from one of my depraved cousins. She thought I should keep them here in case I wanted to play on the job."

He liked the little frown that creased her brow, the glimmer of jealousy in her eyes. Yeah, he liked that a lot. He stepped into the bathroom beside the cabinet and quickly cleaned the rubber device before drying it and moving back into the room.

"You are crazy if you think I'm going to let you gag me," she snapped.

"Would you rather my men hear you screaming?" He arched his brow curiously. "I don't care, but you will have to work here once we have a handle on this, baby."

"No."

"I could cuff you too." He pulled the old-fashioned metal cuffs from the cabinet and jangled them at her.

Her breath caught, her hand pressing tighter to her stomach.

"Oh, you like the idea of that, don't you, baby?" he crooned, as her gaze became hotter, hungrier . . .

Oh yeah, he could grow to like this mating shit. He had a feeling Harmony would have never let herself go enough to allow him this much control over her otherwise. He had read her file; he had seen the weapon she had built herself into. The weapon that was quickly eroding beneath the needs of the woman.

"There, little cat." He moved behind her, slowly pulling one wrist to the small of her back before capturing the other and snapping the cuffs on them.

She flinched at the sound, jerking in his embrace as a little whimper left her throat.

"You know what this gag is going to do?" He bent close to her ear as he moved her toward the dark bathroom. "It's going to trap all that sweet aphrodisiac spilling from your tongue inside your mouth. It's going to flow into your system like lava and make you hotter than hell."

He pulled her to a stop at the small sink.

"This is not a good idea," she whispered roughly as she stared up at him. "Don't do this, Lance. I can't fight you. It's not fair when I can't fight back."

"But, baby, it's not a battle." He lowered his head until his lips could touch hers. "Come on now, give me that sweet taste. Make me as crazy as you are."

Harmony tried to fight, to resist. But how do you resist what you can't understand? A weakness for one man that made no sense. She tried to assure herself it was this mating heat stuff he and Braden had explained earlier. But a part of her knew better. She knew that even without the heat, fighting against him would have been a battle she might not have won.

So when his lips touched hers, her senses flamed and her will crumbled. Her lips parted to the incredible gentleness of his touch, the stroke of his tongue, the sips he took of her kiss. The small, shorter kisses had her reaching for him, needing more as her fists clenched behind her back.

Why had she been so insane to let him cuff her? She needed to touch him.

"Easy," he whispered against her lips as she strained to get closer. "It's okay, baby. I'm going to have all your sweet kiss in just a minute."

Another sip of her lips, his settling against hers, his tongue licking over her lips until hers followed. Then he had her. Before she guessed his intent, he drew her tongue to his mouth, his lips closing on it as he kissed her deeper, harder, suckling the sweet taste of the hormone from its tiny glands.

The pleasure was indescribable. Harmony rubbed against him, fighting to ease the ache in her nipples, in the saturated folds of her pussy. She was on fire and burning hotter by the second.

"God, the taste of you," he whispered. "Come here, let's gag those sweet cries of yours. I'm a damned possessive man. Those little screams are for my ears only."

He slipped the small rubber ball into place before securing the ends. She was cuffed and gagged, helpless before him. Death had never been helpless. But it wasn't Death standing before him, she realized. It was Harmony. The woman who had never been a woman.

"Oh, that's pretty." His smile was tight, hard as his hands lifted the snug shirt from her pants and over her breasts. "But, baby, this is a work of art."

The front clasp of her lacy bra was loosened, the cups peeled back to reveal the tight tips of her breasts. The cry that tore from her throat as his lips covered a sensitive peak would have alerted the building to what was going on. The gag effectively silenced her, but nothing could halt the incredible pleasure that ripped through her.

Lips and teeth tugged at a tender peak before his tongue curled over it and he drew it into the hot depths of his mouth. Firm, heated draws sent her racing toward an edge that would have been terrifying if she'd had enough of her senses left to consider it.

Her eyes closed as she struggled to keep her legs beneath her, to bear the agonizing pleasure tearing through her. It was so good. It was past good.

She tried to cry out his name, to beg for more as he took his time, moving from nipple to nipple as his hands cupped her breasts, plumped them, massaging the swollen curves. The rasp of his tongue over the violently sensitive tips sent searing arcs of sensation tearing into her already tortured womb as she arched closer, searching for relief.

Lance's leg slipped between her thighs, the hard denim-covered muscle pressing tight against her pussy as he began to move her on him.

Her strangled cries were animalistic, desperate.

"Such pretty, tight little nipples." He kissed each in turn before tugging at the soft material of her pants. The comfortable band at her waist lowered, sliding beneath the wide black belt strapped on her hips.

He didn't bother to release the utility belt, or her weapon. He left them on her as he worked the waist of her pants beneath them until he bared her thighs. Harmony stared up at him in surprise as he straightened and began to loosen his pants.

"I've been so hard since you left last night I could drive spikes in railroad ties," he growled as he freed the raging length of his erection, pushing his jeans and briefs below his thighs. "All I could think about was fucking you, Harmony. Tying you to my bed and making you scream for me. Making you beg for me."

She whimpered as he turned her, one arm wrapping around her waist to brace her as he moved behind her, nudging her feet wider. Harmony stared into the mirror, watching him through the dim light that fell from the office. His cock tucked against the desperately wet folds between her thighs before he paused.

Heat seared her, the feel of the heavy crest parting the juice-laden folds and sending sizzling arcs of sensation racing from her vagina to her engorged clit.

"I remember how tight you were." He grimaced, his expression growing heavier with lust. His eyes were heavy-lidded, his lips swollen, sensually full. "So tight I wondered if I would die of the pleasure before I could ever come."

His hips shifted, the thick crest parting her, working inside her, stretching tender tissue to its furthest limits as she screamed behind the gag.

"There, baby," he crooned, his free hand hooking into the leather belt that still cinched her hips. "There I am. Let's see how much you can take. Can you take me, little cat?"

Harmony went to her tiptoes as he began stroking inside her, pulling back, pushing in deeper, impaling her inch by straining inch on the thick cock burrowing inside her.

It was agony. It was more pleasure than she could bear. She bucked backward, fighting for more, relishing the pleasure-pain screaming through her nerve endings. The slick juices of her response eased his way, but nothing could ease the extreme snug depths of her vagina. Little used, rarely aroused, her flesh was now making up for the years it had gone without Lance's touch.

"More, baby." He slid in deeper. "God, your pussy is so

sweet. So wet and tight. I could fuck you like this forever, Harmony."

He pulled back, the hard length of his erection nearly sliding free of her before he paused.

"Look at me, baby. Open your eyes."

She struggled to force her eyes open. He was a weakness. She had sworn she would never allow herself to be weak, but had Coyotes attacked in that moment they would have to just kill her, because she didn't have the will to tear herself from Lance.

"I want to see you when I take you. I want to see how much you love it, since I can't hear it. Do you like this, baby?"

One hard, fast thrust sent him to the very depths of her. Searing, white-hot ecstasy tore through her as she felt her flesh struggle to stretch, to accommodate the length and width penetrating it. Darkness washed over her gaze, though her eyes remained open, directed at the mirror, fighting to focus.

"Hell yeah, baby. Move your hips just like that."

She was moving her hips? She was. She could feel it now, writhing against him in tight little circles that stroked him inside her and caused her pussy to ripple in pleasure.

"There, baby, suck at my cock just like that. Keep that up and I'm going to give you exactly what you need to cool those fires until I get you to my bed."

He moved then, a slow retreat and return, thrusting inside her, stroking violently sensitive nerve endings and throwing her deeper into the quicksilver arcs of pleasure tearing through her.

Harmony was losing herself. She could feel it happening, the layers of defenses she had built between herself and the world were crumbling beneath his possession. Nothing in the world mattered but this. This man, his touch, his hunger, his cock filling her until she was certain she could take no more.

Then she took more.

He fucked her like a man taking possession, a claiming. One hand held to her belt, pulling her back on his hard length, driving inside her deeper, harder, with each stroke as she began to tighten.

"Yeah, baby, tighten like that. Work my cock with that sweet pussy. There you go, sweetheart." His voice was heavy, dazed, the pleasure infusing it, as it infused the shattered cries that escaped her gag.

The hard, steady rhythm began to quicken then. Behind her, Lance's breathing grew ragged, heavy, filling the room with the scent of power and lust as he began to take her with hard, driving strokes. He thrust inside her, holding her firm by her own belt as she felt the world dissolving around her.

She was trembling. Shaking. She couldn't make her legs hold steady, she couldn't fight the vortex swirling within her. Emotion. Sensation. They clashed and burned in her mind and in her body, and she was lost within it.

When her orgasm hit, it destroyed her. She felt her legs weaken, her back arching violently as she strained to scream past the burning, tearing pleasure. It rushed through her like violent forks of lightning, detonating in her womb, convuls ing her body as she felt Lance tense behind her.

A second later, he bent over her, his teeth clenching on her shoulder, biting her as she had bitten him, as the first pulse of semen began to fill her greedy vagina. Hard, des perate pulses of heated warmth that shot to the entrance of her womb, burned with agonizing pleasure and threw her into another desperate, mind-numbing release.

She was sensation only. Shuddering in his arms, twisting in his grasp, with the spasms that threw her higher, then exploded in a white-hot haze of ecstasy.

Harmony was lost. Death didn't exist. There was only this. This blinding pleasure and the pure sensation, emotion and desperation that whipped through her soul. A distant part of her recognized that the fallen shields, the defenses she had relied on all her life, lay as dust. And Harmony, past and present, collapsed weakly against the arm holding her steady, and gave herself to what nature had intended all along. To her mate.

CHAPTER 5

Harmony was unable to even fix her own clothes. Lance helped her dress, his touch gentle after he released the cuffs and the gag from her mouth.

She avoided his eyes, keeping her head down as tremors shook her body. This wasn't the woman they called Death. The woman who trembled beneath his touch wasn't the killer portrayed in the file Braden had given him.

Lance carried her to the office couch, then fixed his clothes, strode to his desk and picked up the link. Attaching it to his ear, he clicked the inner office link and waited for Lenny to pick up.

"Blanchard." Lenny's voice was quiet as he answered the summons.

"Lenny, I'm slipping out the back entrance and heading home. I'll be there if anything important comes up."

"Gotcha, Sheriff. Everything's pretty quiet for now," Lenny answered. "But Alonzo's been stomping around town again, trying to stir up trouble."

Lance grimaced. H. R. Alonzo had been a thorn in his side since the day Megan had opened her home as a halfway house for the Breeds selected for the National Law Enforcement Induction.

The six men and women were spending the next year at Megan's home, learning tactical maneuvers and command situations from several members of the family who worked in law enforcement. There were a lot of them.

"Keep an eye on him and let me know if the situation begins to heat up."

Lance turned as Harmony lay across the couch, her eyes closing. Her face was drawn and pale, exhaustion marking her features as she curled into herself.

"I gotcha, Sheriff. We'll see ya in the morning," Lenny drawled. "And I don't blame you, dealing with that Wyatt dude would wear me out too."

Lance grimaced. Jonas was well known in Broken Butte by now. And not well liked.

"I'm out then. Keep me updated." Lance severed the link before breathing out wearily and smothering his own yawn.

He hadn't slept a wink last night after Harmony left. Hell, he had been in the office before daybreak searching for information on her. He strode across the room and knelt by the couch, gently brushed back the hair that had fallen across her face.

"I have to leave," she whispered, her eyes struggling to open as he stared down at her.

His little cat was thrown off balance, shaken. The mating had thrown her into a reality she was ill equipped to deal with.

"Come on, let's take you home and get you to bed, baby." He helped her sit up, before lifting her to her feet. "You won't have much rest before it builds again."

He wrapped his arm around her waist as he led her from the office to the back door.

Sliding the electronic key through its slot, he waited for the click of the lock before opening the door and moving quickly from the exit.

His Raider was parked in front of the door, so getting her into the passenger seat was accomplished without a problem. She slumped into the comfortable seat, her eyes drowsy, her body nearly boneless.

Lance allowed a grin to quirk at his lips as he buckled her in, pressing a kiss to the top of her head.

"Go ahead and nap, baby, I'll wake you when we get home."

He brushed the hair back from her face, his fingers lingering against the incredibly soft skin of her cheek as she stared up at him. Exhaustion marked her face, glazed her eyes. How long had it been since she had slept?

"I have someone trailing me," she whispered.

He frowned down at her before scanning the parking lot, knowing instantly what she was talking about.

"Have you identified him?"

She shook her head slowly. "I'm weak," she said then, distress filling her eyes. "I can't be weak, Lance."

"It's okay, baby, I've got your back. You rest, I'll keep an eye out for your tail."

She shook her head, drugged with the exhaustion overtaking her.

"I can't be weak," her voice slurred. "I can't be . . ."

Between one second and the next she was asleep. Lance sighed as he closed her door gently before loping to the driver's side. After closing his door, he set the radio to link into Lenny's line.

"Lenny, I'm setting security protocols on the way to the house," he told the sergeant as he activated the energized shields around the vehicle. "Track GPS and see if I have a tail on the way."

"You got problems, Sheriff?" Lenny's voice was concerned.

"I don't know yet. See if you can detect anything suspicious from the public GPS and let me know."

GPS protocols were required on all vehicles, though they could be disconnected legally in many areas. He didn't have high hopes of Lenny catching anything, but it was worth taking the chance.

"I got you, Sheriff," Lenny answered. "I'll let you know if we catch anything."

He pulled out of the parking lot, hitting the main street as he headed home. Lance cracked open his window, and for the first time in his life, he deliberately opened his mind to the whispers flowing on the wind.

A world of secrets, of pain, happiness and fears could be heard in the winds, his grandfather had once told him. If he listened close, then the wind would bring him what he needed, but only if he was willing to hear what it had to say.

He had never been willing before. Lance had fought the secrets of the wind, and his place as its chosen child. He had believed he could live without it, and perhaps he could, but he knew that saving Harmony was more important than his reluctance to follow something as unseen as the air around him.

As he drove, he let the wind blow around him, curling around his body, and Harmony's, before he detected the whisper at his ear. There were no words, there was the whisper of her cry, but he had heard that before. Behind the cry, though, was the secret he searched for, the whisper of deceit. And the warning.

He was being watched. Lenny hadn't reported on the GPS, which meant control wasn't picking up the tail, but the winds whispered the knowledge.

He grimaced at the illusive whispers. There were no answers, and that was the part that had driven his reluctance over the years. There were no answers, no proof, nothing to hold on to to give him what he needed to solve the problems he faced.

He was a sheriff. He dealt in facts, in proof. A whisper of danger, or a ragged cry that only he could hear, and a strong intuition weren't enough to arrest a man. They weren't enough reason to pull the trigger.

He had learned that years before in Chicago, deployed with the highly advanced SWAT team. His scope centered on a suspect, he had ignored the demand that he pull the trigger. He had fought the winds whispering at his ear, tugging at his trigger finger. Seconds later, a mother and her unborn child had died. A casualty to a bastard terrorist determined to take out as many innocents as possible.

And now the winds were at his ear again, a subtle scream of horror, pain and warning. And in those winds he heard Harmony's name.

Glancing over at her, he sighed heavily. She was slumped against the door, boneless, nearly unconscious with exhaustion. That depth of weariness wasn't caused by the heat alone. She had been running on nerves and sheer will alone for too long.

Did she ever sleep?

He heard the answer in the wind. She ran, she fought, and even in sleep she was on guard. Until now.

She was weak, she had whispered. Unable to fight, and she was scared by that weakness.

As he drove to the edge of town and headed for home, Lance knew that protecting Harmony would mean more than just protecting her from whatever danger now followed them. It would mean protecting her from herself. Because Harmony would try to run. Once she awoke, once the heat had settled down, fear would tear her from him, no matter her desire to stay.

Was this the reason Jonas had brought her to him?

Lance frowned at the thought, wondering how the hell the other man could have known there would be a chance of this happening.

He felt the wind curl around his arm then, a whispery stroke that reminded him of the blood and saliva samples the Breed scientist, Elyiana, had taken from him the year before, after Braden had worked on the force. According to her and Jonas, it was required by any law enforcement official working closely with the Breeds.

It was a ruse. He sensed it, heard the whispered affirmation at his ear. Jonas had been planning this for a while, but why?

There were no answers there. There was only the cry, shattered, broken, a wail of soul-deep agony that caused his heart to clench, and his spirit to ache. It was Harmony's pain.

· CHAPTER 6 ·

"She was better off sleeping through it . . ."

"Exhaustion. She hasn't slept in two weeks that I know of . . ."

"Goddammit, no one sleeps twenty-four hours . . ."

The voices slid through Harmony's consciousness as she felt a cold burn building in certain parts of her body. Her thighs. Arms. Along her neck. Her tongue. Which was odd as hell.

It felt as though an icy fire were building beneath the flesh in those areas. It was drawing her slowly from the heavy sleep she was encased in, forcing her to reality despite the obvious reluctance of her body to awaken.

But it was becoming irritating. That cold burn. Irritating enough that she frowned and forced her eyes to open.

Her gaze focused on the Breed scientist Elyiana Morrey, and Lance. Lance looked haggard. Ely, curious.

She stared around Lance's bedroom.

"It's about damned time you woke up," Lance snapped. "Don't you have to use the bathroom or something?"

The incongruous question had her blinking up at him.

"Why am I here?" She turned her gaze to the scientist. "Why are *you* here?"

Ely's lips twitched.

"I'm here because Jonas ordered me not to be." The smug satisfaction in her expression brought a frown to Harmony's face.

"*Why* are you here?" she asked again.

"She's here to begin the hormonal treatments you need to keep from conceiving," Lance finally answered for the doctor. "She stayed when you hadn't woken up through her examination."

Harmony's fingers curled in the blanket at her side.

"You examined me while I slept?" And she hadn't known it? Hadn't sensed it?

She swallowed tightly as she stared up at Lance. He was watching her with tormented eyes, his expression heavy with worry.

"It was easier for you that way," Ely answered. "The examinations are very painful after the mating heat begins. This way, you didn't suffer."

"I would have been fine." She couldn't remember any dreams. She looked at Lance again, but she couldn't tell from his expression if she had spoken in her sleep or not.

"Either way, the tests are completed." Ely shrugged. "You seem to be in fine shape other than a bit of anemia that you're still suffering from. You haven't been taking the vitamins I gave you, have you?"

"Sure I have." Yeah. Right.

Ely snorted. "I found the bottle in your bag, Harmony. They've been untouched. But no worries, the hormonal therapy will set that to rights."

She moved to the black bag sitting open on the dresser across the room. "One of these a day for this first month. The mating hormones are showing up in high concentrations in your blood and fluids." She lifted the vial of pills where Harmony could see them before moving back to the bed. "You've been on injections for the past twenty-four hours, which probably explains why the heat allowed you to sleep. These will prevent conception and allow you to function through the more debilitating symptoms. Though hiding from another Breed will still be impossible."

Harmony watched as the doctor set the vial of pills beside the bed.

"What is the mating heat?" she asked then. "Why is it doing this?"

Ely glanced at Lance, as though needing his permission to reply.

"He didn't ask you." Harmony tried to insert strength into her voice, but she felt as strong as a wet noodle at the moment.

Ely's lips twitched. "You remind me of Jonas when you use that tone. And that's not a compliment."

"It wasn't taken as one," Harmony growled. "Answer me."

"It's a bonding." Ely tucked her hands into the pockets of her white lab jacket as she stared down at her. "Nature's way of ensuring that you stay with the male she chose for you. From what we've been able to figure out, it's an emotional and pheromone-based reaction. We're still working on it." She shrugged again as a regretful smile curved her lips. "There is no cure, and no way to escape it."

So Harmony had heard.

"I need to get up." She was naked beneath the blankets.

She glanced back at Lance as he moved across the room and picked up her silk robe.

"I picked up your clothes at the hotel. And your weapons." He turned back to her with a frown. "Do you know that half of what you carry is illegal?"

She stared back at him silently.

Lance breathed out heavily. "Here's your robe. Are you strong enough to get up on your own?"

She took the silk from his hand.

"Leave." She didn't bother to voice it as a request.

His gaze narrowed on her.

"Ely stays," he ordered as he headed for the door. "I'll see about getting dinner together."

Harmony flipped the blankets from her nude body and swung her legs over the side of the bed before struggling into her robe.

"You touched me with your hands?" she asked the doctor coldly.

"I was gloved." Ely crossed her arms on her chest as she stared down at her.

"Find better gloves," Harmony snapped. "My skin is burning where you touched me."

"Burning?"

"A cold, deep burn. Thighs, arm, neck and tongue."

"No one has ever mentioned a burn. Pain, but no burn."

"It happened when Jonas touched my back after the first night with Lance as well. It's highly uncomfortable."

"Which means painful as hell," Ely grunted. "You're one of the most willful Breeds I've ever met. Do you ever feel pain, Harmony?"

"Not if I can help it. I need a shower. Where's my overnight bag?"

"You mean the lotion boutique?" Ely laughed. "Lance couldn't pronounce half the names on those bottles. Quite a collection you have there."

"Where is it?" She wasn't in the mood to talk.

Ely sighed heavily as she moved to the closet and pulled the large overnight bag from the depths of it.

"You can talk to me, Harmony. I'm not your enemy."

"Anyone not a friend is an enemy." Harmony stared directly into her eyes. "And I have no friends."

"Well, that puts me in my place." Ely carried the bag to the bathroom, sitting it on a counter before turning and reentering the bedroom. "There you go. Can you walk to the bathroom?"

"I can walk." Or she would die trying.

She was weak. Terrifyingly weak. Her legs shook as they took her weight, but they held her up. For the moment, that was all that mattered.

"Harmony, I have to leave tonight," Ely announced as Harmony made her way across the floor.

"Good-bye." What the hell did the woman want her to say? The doctor had helped hold her captive for two weeks and had helped take enough blood to refill another human body.

"You can't run from him, Harmony," Ely retorted as Harmony reached the doorway. "The hormonal treatments only work if you're having sex regularly with your mate. If you leave, the mistake could be fatal."

Harmony lowered her head, staring down at her feet as she gritted her teeth furiously.

"Jonas knew what he was doing, didn't he?" she whispered. "This was planned."

"I can't verify that." Ely's voice chilled, assuring Harmony that Jonas had indeed known exactly what he was doing.

"This is a dangerous game you're letting him draw you into, Doctor." She turned her head, staring back at the other woman bitterly. "I won't be the only one to die if this turns out the wrong way, I promise you that."

"Who will avenge you, Harmony?" Ely asked her. "The same people who have pulled your ass out of the fire before. I read Jonas's file on you, and it's vastly different from the one in the Breed database."

"As I said, you don't want to get caught up in this." Har-

mony smiled tightly. "If he hadn't played his little game, if
he had left it with merely attempting to reincorporate me
into the Breed society, we would have all been safe. But
this . . ." She waved her hand down her body. "This just
changed the stakes. If I'm taken out, trust me, Jonas won't
escape unscathed. And neither will you."

◆   ◆   ◆

"How is she doing?" Lance asked Ely as he stood over the
pot he had poured the chicken soup into, letting it come to a
slow simmer as his aunt had instructed.

She walked slowly into the room, her hands tucked into
the pockets of her lab jacket, her shoulders hunched.

"She's frightened, but hiding it well." She shrugged, her expression concerned. "She has a few symptoms no others have
mentioned. A cold burn where I touched her while examining
her, but other than that and being a bit weak, she seems fine."

Lance nodded before turning back to the soup, watching
as the slow curl of steam began to build at the top of it.

"Jonas called again," he said. "He says he needs you back
at the labs."

"I'm surprised he waited this long." Her expression was
wry as she stared back at him. "At this point, I've done all I
can for your mate. She won't conceive, and I was expressly
forbidden to add that particular hormone to her treatments.
For some reason, he believes conception will ensure she
stays with you."

"You disagree?" He watched her narrowly.

"My only purpose is her survival—period. Your first pri-
ority is her protection and the bonding building between the
two of you," she informed him harshly. "Listen to me,
Lance, if she runs, for whatever reason, then she's lost to you
forever. She'll go on the Breed registry as a rogue. Kill on
sight. We can't allow that."

"And why do you care?" Lance watched the young doctor, saw the compassion in her eyes, but he sensed something else. She wasn't completely selfless in her desire to help Harmony.

"Because Jonas is so determined to have his own way." She smiled mockingly. "At this point, that's enough for me."

"And when it's no longer enough?" he asked sharply.

"Then I'll take it up with Jonas." She shrugged again. "But I do have to leave now. I don't want to give him reason to order more tests on her, with another scientist. It's best that he never learn of my deception here."

"Braden will take you back to his place." He nodded rather than questioning her further. "Jonas is having the heli-jet dispatched there."

"Lance, I couldn't strengthen the hormone as I could have if she were at the labs. She needs a more precise adjustment that can't be accomplished as long as Jonas is playing his game. What I gave her will help; she won't be completely helpless against the arousal, but it will still be severe. I'm sorry about that."

"You took care of the most pressing problem." He sighed. "She won't conceive. I won't have that choice taken away from her."

"And I agree with you, obviously." She shook her head wearily. "I'll be leaving now. Make certain she gets plenty of fluids, but no caffeine. And rest. Right now, she needs that more than anything."

God, could he handle another of those deep sleeps? She had cried as she dreamed. Streams of tears as she begged Alpha One, Jonas, to help her. To save her. Pleaded with him for forgiveness.

Twenty-four hours she had slept. Torn between silent tears and nightmare battles, Harmony had faced demons that Lance had been unable to fight for her. He had only been able to hold her, to croon to her. At times, it had seemed to ease her a bit; at others it had seemed to only frighten her further.

As Ely left the house, Lance moved to his bedroom and strode quickly to the small safe hidden in the back of his closet. There, he removed the small electronic bug detector Braden had brought in that morning.

Twenty minutes later he found two of the listening devices in his bedroom and three more throughout the house. As he stared at the small devices, he shook his head in resignation. For all her help, Ely had obviously been there for her own reasons as well, perhaps even Jonas's. He stored them in the safe along with the detector, snapped it closed and moved for the bathroom.

"Harmony?" He knocked on the door before easing it open.

She was sprawled back in the large tub, hair wrapped in a towel, a blissful expression on her face as the water frothed around her.

"Comfortable?" He smiled as her eyes peeked open.

"Go away and I might let you live," she retorted drowsily.

"I have some homemade soup on the stove. It will be ready when you're done." He paused. "When will you be done?"

She rolled her eyes. "When you see me coming into the kitchen. Now go away. I need to recuperate." She closed her eyes again and settled back into the tub.

"And here I thought cats didn't like water," he commented, failing to hold back his amusement.

"This cat does. Now go away." She didn't bother even to glance at him.

Lance chuckled before moving from the bathroom and heading back to the kitchen. When she managed to recuperate, he was certain he'd have the wildcat back. For now though, while she was weak, he'd press his own advantage.

He had very little time left in which to make Harmony Lancaster, aka Death, fall in love.

◆　　◆　　◆

What had she done?

Harmony sat up in the water after Lance left, lifting her knees until she could rest her forehead against them, and fought for control.

She had slept for twenty-four hours, so deep that she hadn't even known she had been examined. There was no doubt in her mind that she had dreamed. But what had she dreamed?

She closed her eyes and swallowed back the bile threatening to rise in her throat. She knew what she did when she slept so deeply, when the exhaustion finally overtook her and her body overrode her control. She cried and she begged. Fear filled her voice and horror whispered past her lips. She knew, because before she had always awakened to the sound of it, to the memory of the nightmares that haunted her.

She only prayed that she hadn't given her secrets away.

God, she was going to have to find a way out of this. There had to be a way to defeat this need, to still the hunger that ate at her and escape this situation. Nothing good could come of it. Only death could result. Her death.

But to leave, she had to walk away from Lance. She lifted her head then, her eyes still closed, and breathed in the scent of him. His home was infused with the smell of him. Strong and male, filled with a powerful sense of warmth she hadn't known she needed.

But as she sat there in his bathtub, the heated water swirling around her, she realized that was what had drawn her to him that first night. That sense of warmth, of his body heat flowing from his hand into hers, swirling inside her soul and creating a bond that made no sense.

She couldn't do this. She blinked back her tears, realizing

that the shields she had used to keep herself hard, to keep
her emotions cold and unfeeling, were gone. She was vulnerable now, and she had no idea how to fix it. Hell, she
didn't even know how it had happened.

The man had no idea what she was. He couldn't. If he did,
he would have reviled her, just as Jonas so obviously did.

Six months. She sighed wearily as she leaned back and
stared up at the ceiling, a frown pulling at her brow. She just
had to make it six months, that was all. By then, this heat
stuff, whatever it was, would surely dissipate. She could find
a way to control it, to walk away as she needed to.

Ely said she had given her the hormonal treatment to prevent conception, and she hadn't been lying about that. Harmony could smell a lie a mile away. She could read it, even
in Jonas; the doctor hadn't been deceiving her.

Okay. She straightened her shoulders. Six months. She
could do this. She would be free then. Free of Jonas and of
Lance.

She ignored the prick of regret at the thought of ever being free of Lance. It wasn't emotion, she assured herself; it
was the thought of losing something she had never had and
always wondered about. The warmth. The pleasure in touch.
That was what she would miss.

Not the man. Never the man.

She flipped off the jets, pulled the plug to drain the water
from the tub and stood carefully. She was still weak, but it
would go away soon. The inactivity and lack of food had
caused it, not anything serious.

Pulling the towel from her head, she shook her hair out,
then moved to the counter and the overnight bag sitting there.
Ely's voice had held some disdain when she spoke of the lotions inside. Lotion, hair products, makeup, oils and the
tools needed to keep every inch of her body clean, soft and
gently scented.

Not like it had been that first year of her escape. Her skin dry and flaky, the filth of the labs lingering on her, drawing in every Coyote sent to look for her. Tracking her had been easy then. Hungry, living on raw nerves and what scraps of food she could steal, Death had been close to succumbing to her own curse.

Not anymore.

An hour later, she shook her dry hair around her shoulders, feeling the thick, silken strands caress her satin-soft skin. It shimmered with life as the subtle morning dew scent of her lotions blended with the scent Lance had left on her body.

She was no longer the scrawny, dirty animal who had been yanked from the gutters and dragged into the world of the living. She was Death when she killed. A dark shadow of vengeance, unstoppable in its resolve. As a woman, she was Harmony. Serene. Calm. And she would survive this.

Maybe.

CHAPTER 7

The only advantage of the hormonal therapy was prevention of conception, Harmony thought as night fully descended over Lance's home. Because it sure as hell wasn't helping with the arousal.

Well, the pain wasn't there. She could feel the building hunger growing inside her without the white-hot flames exploding in painful awareness of the need. But she ached. She was wet. And she wanted nothing more than to lick Lance from head to toe.

Sitting in the open living room, Harmony tried to keep her attention on the news program showing on the widescreen television hanging on the wall across from them. Sitting cross-legged in one of the broad, comfortable chairs as she worked on her nails, she could see Lance from the corner of her eye.

He was slouched back in the corner of the couch. A large pillow rested behind his back and he held the remote with firm possession at his side.

The position gave Harmony the advantage of tracking every hard muscular line of his body. Long, powerful legs were encased in denim that did nothing to hide the absolutely luscious muscle beneath. He shifted a bit, stretching out more comfortably, drawing her attention to his thighs as they flexed. And she had no business letting her eyes wander to that area, because keeping her gaze from the hard bulge between them was damned impossible.

He was hard. His erection was like a thick wedge beneath his jeans, reaching toward his lower stomach. She jerked her gaze back to the television, but the pretty boy charm of the newsman had nothing on the rough-around-the-edges, earthy draw Lance projected.

Within seconds her eyes shifted again, moving back to the temptation of the body stretched out in abandon on the couch.

He looked half-asleep. Drowsy-eyed, relaxed. Unthreatening. It was hard to believe this was the man she had allowed to cuff her, to gag her. The man who had kept her belt on, her pants around her thighs and fucked her to dizzying heights.

Her vagina clenched at the memory. She could feel the dampness growing between her thighs as her nipples began to press tighter against the loose tan cotton sleeveless shirt she wore with the wide-legged matching pajama bottoms.

If she sat there much longer, she was going to end up crawling up his body like the cat he called her. And God, wouldn't that feel good Stroking along his body, licking at every delectable inch of male flesh as she went.

"Is it working?"

His voice jerked her out of the daydream, causing her eyes to widen as she jerked her head around to stare at him more fully.

"What?" Had he known how she was watching him? Hungering for him?

"The hormone therapy." He lifted his hand, still gripping the remote, and waved it toward her. "Is it working?"

The need to taste him was killing her.

"It's working fine." She nodded before ducking her head and pulling her gaze from him.

She lowered her head and concentrated on buffing her nails.

"Hmm." The low, dark murmur had her eyes lifting as they narrowed on him.

"What does that mean?"

She expected another of those wicked smiles, or at least a heated look. He was watching her with a slight frown instead, his expression much too serious.

"You're a strong woman," he finally said softly. "Megan said the heat is impossible to ignore, even with the hormones."

"What do you want me to say, Lance?" She swallowed tightly. "This isn't a comfortable situation for me."

"Why? You were comfortable enough that night in the bar to come home with me. What's changed, Harmony?"

"A one-night stand . . ."

"Have a lot of those, do you?" he asked mildly.

"No." She shook her head, confusion tearing through her. Where the hell was her self-control, her ability to smack a man in place with no more than a look?

She stared back at him, his scent wrapping around her, affecting her senses in a way that threw her system into chaos. Nervous awareness sizzled along her nerve endings as her breathing began to roughen and the arousal began to grow.

"So why should it be different now?" he asked her.

"You weren't a weakness then," she snapped, jumping to her feet as she wrapped her arms over her breasts and paced to the doorway. "You're a weakness now."

He didn't move; he just lay there.

"Running away, Harmony?" he asked as though she intended to do just that.

"This conversation is pointless."

"You can't run away from yourself forever. Aren't you tired of running by now?"

Harmony turned back to him, knowing she wasn't hiding the effect his accusation had on her.

"Hiding is the only way to survive," she whispered. "Do you believe Jonas was the only person searching for me the last ten years, Lance? Or the only one to get close? Eventually, my enemies will find me. When they do, they'll strike where I'm weak."

"Chemistry doesn't bind you to another person, Harmony. Emotion binds."

She stared back at him in shock. Emotion?

"I have no emotions," she snapped. "Unless you count vengeance."

"Then you have no weakness." He shrugged. "Your enemies can't use what you care nothing about."

She stared back at him, pressing her lips together as she clenched her teeth on the furious words threatening to fall from her lips.

"A one-night stand does not a lover make, darling." His smile was faintly sardonic.

"So I should just become your little bedmate and forget the danger in it?" she snapped.

His brow arched slowly. "I wasn't asking you for sex, Harmony. I was trying to get to know *you*. I was pointing out how stubborn and willful you are. Not trying to find out how easy you would fall into my bed."

"I've had to be stubborn. Strong," she bit out. "I would have died that first year I escaped if I hadn't been."

The year Dane Vanderale had found her, broken, all but dead. He had saved her, just as he had saved her many times since.

"Yeah, there were a few notes in your file concerning that

first year." He nodded as though the information were general knowledge. "The Coyotes sent after you reported you were wounded, severely. They would have caught you if they hadn't been diverted by an unknown team of men."

One of the Coyotes must have lived. She had hoped she had taken them out. There had been two, merciless and bloodthirsty.

"I don't know about that." She shook her head firmly. "I just know I escaped. That was all that mattered to me."

"You were fifteen years old, severely wounded and alone," he pointed out. "Yet you survived."

"What's your point?"

Harmony watched Lance warily now. He was fishing for information, which meant he knew something. Something more than her file had provided for him.

She remembered well the fight between those two Coyotes. Running on nerves alone, hungry, exhausted, they had nearly taken her. Instead, she had escaped when two shadowed figures had jumped into the fray.

The knife wounds she had carried had nearly been fatal once infection and fever had set in. The wounds had been too deep, and her body too weak to fight. She would have died if Dane hadn't found her.

He was the son of an African industrialist, a rogue and a man who followed his own rules. At that time, he had been tracking the Coyote Breed who had been sent to kill a friend of his, a young man who knew more than he should have. His death had not been easy. And neither had the Coyote's after Dane had caught up with him.

The secretiveness of his work was imperative for him to succeed in his goal of helping the Breeds destroy the Genetics Council. If it were ever learned that the heir to the vast holdings of Vanderale Enterprises was no more than a vigilante, it could destroy all his family held. It was a secret Harmony had sworn to carry to her grave.

"How did you escape, Harmony?" He lay there asking the question as though the subject meant no more than the weather. He wasn't demanding answers, he wasn't interrogating her. He was asking.

"I had help," she whispered. "Two men heard the fight. I ran while they distracted the Coyotes."

"Why did the Coyotes say they didn't have a scent?" A light frown furrowed his brow. "The interrogation reports stated that the Coyotes swore there was no identifying scent. Does everyone have a scent to the Breeds?"

"Yes." She nodded slowly. "Everyone has a scent."

"Is it unique, or can it be disguised by perfumes and whatnot?"

"It's unique," she answered carefully, watching him warily.

She knew where this was going and was helpless to prevent it.

"So, why would the two men who saved your butt have no scent?" He frowned as he laid the remote on the floor and scratched, rather absently, at the hard, well-muscled flesh of his abdomen.

The movement lifted his T-shirt, flashing the dark tough skin before he allowed his hand to rest there. Harmony fought to drag in enough oxygen to make her brain work again.

Dammit, she was a cold-blooded assassin, not his sex kitten. But at the moment, the sex kitten was definitely making itself known.

"I'm not certain." She really didn't understand the process, so she wasn't technically lying to him. Right?

"But you have an idea?"

Harmony stared back at him suspiciously.

"Why all the questions? What does this have to do with the fact that a mate is a weakness and I'm not willing to play the sex kitten for you?"

"Sex kitten?" Wicked amusement lit his eyes then. "I hadn't thought of that one, but I like the idea. I like it a whole lot."

"You are not making sense." She held her hand up to halt the words his lips were parting for. "These myriad little subjects of yours are not going together well, Lance."

"Hey, you brought up the sex kitten thing, not me. It just happened to interest me, that's all. Tell me." His brows lifted then lowered suggestively. "How does a Breed sex kitten do it?"

"With claws?" she suggested in irritation.

His lips pursed as his eyes gleamed with playful lust.

"I like claws," he whispered as he raised his hand to rub absently at his shoulder, the area next to his neck. The exact area where she had bit him. "You could come over here and show me how it's done."

She actually moved to go to him. Harmony stared down at her feet in alarm when she took that first step; then she stopped and glared back at him furiously.

She hissed.

Without thought, without realizing the sound was moving through her chest, she really hissed. She had never hissed in her life. Not the catlike, growling hiss that came out of her mouth now.

She stared back at Lance in shock.

"Keep that up and you're going to make me come." His voice had lowered, thickening with arousal as his eyes gleamed with heated hunger.

"You are insane."

"I'm so fucking horny I'm about to come in my jeans just

listening to you hiss." He grunted in irritation. "Insanity is probably closer than you think it is."

The pain of her arousal before the doctor had begun the hormone treatments had been horrible. Did he suffer too? She frowned, drawing in the scent of the room deeper than she had allowed herself to this point.

The smell of male arousal was intoxicating and thick. It permeated her senses, rushed through her brain, and sent her heartbeat to a thundering speed as she felt her mouth fill again with that strangely sweet taste.

"Does it hurt?" she whispered, fearing the answer. Knowing the answer.

"No, baby, it doesn't hurt." Lance sighed heavily. "It's just aggravating as hell."

And he was lying. Why was he lying when telling the truth could guilt her into giving him what he wanted? He could have easily played the wronged male and had her in his bed hours ago.

"Then why aren't you moving?" she asked him then. "You've been in that same position for more than an hour. Sit up."

She could see his erection outlined by his jeans, pressing hard against the material.

"I think I'll just lie right here for a while." He chuckled instead. "Did I mention I'm a little low on rest myself?"

He hadn't slept in two days, not enough to matter. He had watched over her, protected her when she couldn't protect herself.

Harmony licked her lips nervously. "When I was wounded, the men who fought off the Coyotes found me a week later. I was very ill."

His gaze sharpened on her.

"They had known then about the Coyotes. They hunted them; I wasn't certain why." She hadn't known then, though

she knew now. "They nursed me back to health and protected me. They never told me exactly why they had no
scent. But sometimes, if I'm in trouble, they know it, and
they show up."

"Does Jonas know about them?"

"The information contained in the Breed database on me
isn't everything the Council had," she revealed. "I don't
know why Jonas has hidden the files on the few times the
Coyotes actually managed to capture me, but those reports
aren't in there. Just as the reports reveal that each time I was
captured, the same two men rescued me."

"Who were they?"

She glanced away for a second before turning back to him.
"I can't reveal their names to you, Lance. Their lives . . ."

He held his hand up. "I don't want names. Why do they
watch you, Harmony? What do they want? What does Jonas
want?"

She shook her head, a frown creasing her brow.

"Jonas wants me dead, Lance. But he can't kill me without giving me a chance to redeem myself first. But make no
mistake, he hates me."

"Why?"

She inhaled painfully at the question.

"I killed his mother. The only person at those labs who
cared anything about Jonas, besides me. And I couldn't show
him how much I cared, or I suffered for it. Madame LaRue
was very possessive of her personal creation. As for why the
others help me, it benefits both of us. They help me, I help
them. It's enough that they've been there."

"So why tell me this much now?" he asked her, rather
than pursuing the information further.

"You protected me while I slept," she whispered. "You
didn't have to do that. You deserve to know what you're facing."

"You're my woman, Harmony," he growled. "I always protect what's mine."

She shook her head slowly. "I can't belong to you, Lance. Not ever. In six months, when this is over and I've redeemed myself by Breed Law, then I'll leave. If I can manage to keep my enemies from finding me that long. You can't afford to take me as your woman, any more than I can claim you as anything of mine. Doing so will only get us both killed."

"How much longer can you fight alone? How much longer, Harmony, before Death gives up because she can't kill enough monsters or save enough children?" he asked as she moved to turn away from him.

"Why are you doing this?" It was a question she had fought for too long now herself. "Why can't you just let it go, Lance?"

"Come here." His voice gentled.

"What?"

He lifted his hand, crooking his fingers in a wave back toward himself.

"Come here," he repeated.

She moved toward him slowly, hesitantly. He didn't know what it did to her to be too close to him, how much he made her want. It rose inside her like a hungry beast, tearing at her soul with a need she had pushed back all her life.

"What?" she asked again as she paused by the couch.

"Touch me, Harmony."

"I told you . . ."

"I didn't say fuck me, dammit, I said touch me," he growled. "Right here." He thumped his chest. "Just touch me."

She bent and placed her palm on his chest.

Heat. Harmony felt the weakness that flooded her as she went to her knees beside the couch, feeling the incredible heat of his body moving into hers. The phenomena was unlike anything she had ever known with another person. She had touched others, she wasn't a virgin, but she had never experienced this.

"This is why, Harmony." He brushed her hair tenderly back from her face, his thumb caressing her cheek as she stared into his eyes. "Feel my body giving to you. I've never done that before. As though my soul knows what you need, just as my body knows, and it gives to you selflessly. That's why I can't walk away. It's why I claim you as mine, even knowing that isn't what you want. Because that bond is already there. It was there when I pulled into the parking lot of that bar when all I wanted to do was head home. It was there the second my eyes met yours, my skin touched yours. Run away if you have to, but at least be aware of what you're running away from, baby."

He looked so sincere. His eyes darkening, his expression pulled into lines of worry and concern. As though he cared.

"Why?" She couldn't stop the question from passing her lips even as the heat of his body poured through her palm. "Why do you care, Lance? I kill . . ."

He shook his head slowly. "What the child was forced to do is not her fault," he whispered. "What the woman has done to survive, and then to wreak vengeance, can be forgiven. It's where you go from this point that matters. Learning the difference between what is just and what is justice could mean the difference in your freedom or your own death. But what's between us goes deeper than life or death."

"It's a chemical reaction," she snapped, attempting to jerk her hand back.

His hand gripped hers, forced it to flatten against his chest once again as his gaze turned fierce.

"How many one-night stands have you had, Harmony? How many men have you picked up in bars and spent the night fucking?"

"Stop!"

"Answer me. Or should I answer it for you? None." His voice lashed at her as his anger, lust and need seemed to lie in the very air around her. "You've never done it before. Why?"

"It's none of your business."

"Why, Harmony?" His voice rose, trapping her in place as effectively as his hand trapped hers against his chest. His arm had come down from the pillow behind him as his free hand shackled her other wrist, keeping her in place. "Answer me."

"I didn't want to."

"The truth, damn you!"

"Because their touch didn't matter." She tore away from him then, the memory of her first night with a man, a man she trusted, lashing at her brain.

She had forced herself to go through with it, forced herself into an intimacy she knew she didn't want. Dane was her friend; he had helped her, had given her a place of safety to hide. His touch hadn't sickened her, but neither had it heated her, drawn her.

"My touch mattered then." There was no smugness in his voice as she heard him rising to his feet. "Just as your touch matters to me, Harmony. You matter to me. Hiding isn't going to help you, or me. If your enemies find out you were here, whether you've been gone a week or two years, they'll find me."

Harmony stared back at him, her breathing rough as fear began to race through her mind. He was right. It wouldn't matter; the Coyotes and Council soldiers still stalking her wouldn't care. They would strike for the hell of it.

"Run now, Harmony." He waved his hand toward the door as she turned back to him. "There's the fucking door. Do you think it's going to make a difference?"

"Why are you doing this?" she cried out desperately, her

fists clenching at her sides. "Why can't you let it go? Let me go?"

"Because you fucking belong to me!" he yelled back, his voice furious, his blue eyes blazing. "Mine, by God, just as much as I belong to you. Deny it. Go ahead, Harmony, look me in the eye and deny it."

"Where do you get these insane ideas?" she screamed back, pushing her hands through her hair as frustration began to tear through her. Frustration and anger. "Why are you doing this?"

"You want to know why? Why?" he snarled. "Try this, Harmony."

Before she could fight him, his arms were around her; one hand clasped her head, the other wrapped around her back as his head lowered. His lips, heated and possessive, covered hers as his tongue swept possessively into her mouth.

The glands along the underside of her tongue flared to life, spilling the sweet taste of arousal. Lifting her arms, she twined them around his neck, as desperate to be close to him as he was to pull her against him. Desire raced through her nervous system as her objections, her fears, were swept away.

Lance devoured her, took her kiss and gave in its return a pleasure that should never be so intense, so fiery from such a simple caress.

Tongues dueled, battled, as moans began to fill the silence of the room. Harmony strained against him, feeling his erection grinding against her lower stomach, fueling the heat building in her vagina.

This was perfect. His kiss was perfect. His lips matched hers, his tongue stroked hers in a caress too heated to deny. As though every cell of his body, every breath, every touch had been created just for her. At each point that their bodies touched, his heat sank into her, warmed her, bound her.

"No. Dammit. I won't take you like this."

Before Harmony could protest, Lance broke the kiss and set her carefully away from him. His hands swiped through his hair as his expression tautened with the effort at maintaining his control.

"What? What did I do?" Harmony shook her head in confusion.

"I won't take this choice from you," he growled, grimacing painfully. "I won't take anything from you by force, Harmony. If you want me now, then you have to come to me."

Lance shook his head, his frustration evident on his face as he propped his hands on his lean hips, lowered his head and shook it slowly. When he lifted his head once again, a wry smile crossed his lips.

"I'm going to bed, baby." He sighed. "I need some rest. We have to go to work tomorrow morning. I'll see you in the morning."

He leaned down, kissed her cheek gently then walked away. Harmony stared at him in shock as he just walked away.

Her hand lifted to her cheek as she turned and stared at the doorway he'd disappeared through. Why had he done that? He could have had her. He was obviously painfully aroused, hungry, why walk away when he could have what would ease him?

God, he made no sense.

She growled in frustration then grimaced at the animalistic sound. Damn him, she was starting to sound like Jonas now.

"Men!" She stomped to the kitchen, certain she had seen ice cream somewhere in that huge freezer he kept in the pantry. Aggravation like this definitely called for ice cream.

CHAPTER 8

He was trying to protect her.

Several hours later Harmony stood at the open bedroom door staring into the room and watching as Lance slept. The blankets were kicked back from his long, muscular body, the dim light from the hallway shadowing his form.

Nothing could shadow his erection rising from between his thighs.

Harmony inhaled slowly as she dipped her spoon into the pint of butter pecan ice cream she had tried to stay away from. She brought the frozen confection to her lips. It eased the swelling in the glands beneath her tongue, stilled the hormone wanting to spill from them, but it did nothing to ease her arousal.

As she paced the house over the hours, she had assured herself she had to be imagining things. She protected others; she wasn't used to being protected.

She licked the spoon as Lance shifted on the bed, his legs spreading, the fingers of one hand curling around the width of his cock for a second before a frustrated groan left his lips. His hand fell back to the bed.

The spoon dipped into the carton again, bringing back another spoonful of sweetness to her lips. She let the icy flavor melt in her mouth as she watched him. As tasty as the ice cream was, she knew it was nothing compared to the taste of the man attempting to sleep through his arousal.

Her lips quirked into a smile. There was one thing she could do for him. She remembered once, several years past, when she had watched a very naughty movie. Just out of curiosity. The movie involved a very vampish female, an aroused male and ice cream.

Lance was very sexual. A sexual creature with the experience to please any female. Her experience was lacking, but she knew he enjoyed her touch. Would he enjoy ice cream?

She licked her lips as she moved, dipping the spoon into the ice cream again as she placed her knees on the bed and moved into position.

◆　◆　◆

Lance came awake awash in pleasure. A chilly, sensual, exquisite pleasure that had his balls tightening and his body rearing as his hands reached out to hold the pleasure in place, to keep it from retreating.

"Stay. Or I stop." Harmony's voice was silky smooth, dark and aroused.

He watched as her mouth rose from the aching length of his erection. She lifted a pint of ice cream from the bed beside her, dipped the spoon in and brought a healthy chunk to her lips. Lance tightened, watched, waited. Her head lowered as one hand gripped the base of his cock and tucked it at her lips. Then she flowed over it.

"Oh fuck!" His hips arched from the bed as she began to suckle at his flesh with greedy hunger.

The cold cream washed over his cock, sending a riot of

icy sensations to attack his overheated flesh. Her tongue flickered over the violently aroused flesh, stroking and caressing as her mouth suckled at the engorged head.

Lance fisted his fingers in the sheet beneath him, his hips arching, his head grinding into the mattress as ice and flames battled, dragging a tortured groan from his throat as he felt sweat begin to bathe his body.

Son of a bitch, this was good. So fucking good he wondered if he would survive it. He fought to stay still, to keep his hands at his sides and to let Harmony choose. Oh hell, if she didn't hurry and choose to let him fucking come then he was going to have a stroke.

"Harmony." Fuck, he was panting. "Baby. Hell." She was teasing him again. Her tongue licked around the engorged head before she sucked it deep into her mouth again, her tongue working on the underside like a silken flame.

She moaned around the swollen crest. The vibration of the sound nearly sent rockets exploding in his brain. Clawing fingers of sensation gripped every vertebrae of his spine and tautened every muscle in his body.

He blinked, trying to clear his vision as he felt his cock swelling. Son of a bitch, as though it weren't swollen enough. Her hands were stroking the shaft, from the base to where her lips covered, up and down, as she sucked, licked and then moaned again.

And he exploded.

The growl that tore from his throat shocked him, as did the exquisite ecstasy that began to race through his balls, up his spine, and struck his skull with resounding force. A second later the feeling of his semen exploding in her mouth sent his mind into complete chaos.

His hips arched as spurt after spurt of semen blasted into her mouth, relieving only the worst of the hunger clawing at his belly. It took the edge off, yet it did little to relieve the stiffness of his erection.

"I hope you know what the hell you've just done." He groaned as his hands reached out for her, gripped her arms and tossed her back on the bed.

He lifted himself up over her, his knees spreading her thighs as she stared up at him with a sultry, heated gaze. Damn, she was sexy. Her eyes were slightly tilted, the brilliant green gleaming up at him as he stared down at her. Her swollen breasts were tipped with hard, cherry nipples. Sweet, sweet nipples.

He lowered his head, drew one into his mouth as a cry tore from her throat and he tucked the head of his cock between the luscious folds of slick, soft flesh.

"Oh yeah," he mumbled at her breast before licking at her nipple again. "Oh, this is good."

He pressed forward slowly, fighting to breathe as he felt the incredibly snug muscles of her vagina grip his dick. Sweet mercy, she was so tight it was all he could do to live through the pleasure.

It was like taking a virgin. Every time. Working his cock slowly inside her, feeling her milk him in, hearing her startled little cries of pleasure.

"Harmony . . . baby." His hands moved to her hips, holding her still as she arched beneath him. "Hold still, baby. Let me be easy. Let me take you easy."

"Who needs easy?" Her voice was rough, desperate as her hands gripped his hair.

He would have chuckled if he could have caught his breath. He was halfway inside her when the muscles of her vagina began to do that *thing*. Shit. Hell. How was he supposed to keep his control with a thousand tiny fingers working over his cock, pulling him inside her. That was what it felt like. The muscles working against his cock, stroking and sucking at him until he felt as though his head was going to explode from the need to come.

"Baby. I'm trying." He retreated. Pressed. Retreated.

"I don't need . . . easy." Her cry echoed with hunger. "I need it all. Now. Now, Lance." She arched to him again, her thighs widening, her body straining against him.

And as he had twice before, he lost control. With a ragged groan he pulled back before surging inside her in one hard, long thrust.

Fucking her was so incredibly hot, so much pleasure he swore each time he would never survive it.

"Kiss me, baby." His hands moved from her hips as he penetrated her to the hilt.

His fingers speared into her hair, clenching into the silky strands as his lips covered hers. The taste he craved was there instantly. Honeysuckle and spice. Ambrosia. He kissed the taste from her lips then drew her tongue into his mouth and suckled more.

God, she was sweet. From head to toe. Every soft pore she possessed, and it was his. She was his.

Holding her to him, he began to move, his hips shifting, drawing back before plunging his cock inside the hot, tight depths of her pussy. He fucked her with desperation, because he was a desperate man. He fucked her with imperative need, because she made him ache, made him long, made each possessive impulse in his soul desperate to bind her to him.

He took her with his body, then he took her with his soul. Deep, driving strokes, and shafted inside her powerfully, satisfaction surging through him as he felt her tighten.

"There you go, baby," he growled against her lips. "Come for me, sweetheart. Let me feel that sweet pussy exploding around me."

"Damn you." Her cry was filled with hunger. "Harder. I need you harder."

"Harder," he groaned. "Hell, baby. I don't want to hurt you. I can't hurt you."

It was all he could do to slow his thrusts as much as he was. He wanted to drive into her. But she was still so fucking tight, gripping him with exquisite strength, with tender muscles. He couldn't hurt her.

"Do it." She tore her lips from beneath his. "Do it now."

She set her teeth in his shoulder and she bit him. It wasn't a delicate little bite. Sharp canines sank into his flesh, sending a spear of heat and pleasure-pain exploding inside his skull.

He took her harder. Holding her beneath him, he drove into her over and over again, until she arched under him, tore her mouth from him and screamed.

As though that sound were the catalyst he needed, Lance felt his balls tighten violently before he exploded inside her.

He came as though he had never come in his life. Violent pulses of semen erupted inside her as he drove into the very depths of her. His body jerked as hers shuddered beneath him. Convulsive spasms tore through them both as the explosions began to ease and then slowly faded away.

Lance lay against her, fighting to breathe for long seconds before he finally collapsed to her side and drew her against his body. The violence of his release had sapped the last remaining strength of his body, and he knew sleep was only seconds away. Peaceful sleep.

He heard the soft call of the winds outside his home, the promise of protection as he surrendered to his need to rest. He didn't have to worry about protecting Harmony for now. The land would protect them both.

"Sleep now," he whispered at her ear. "You're safe."

"Good night, Lance," Harmony whispered, allowing him to tuck her closer to his chest as his chin rested against her head.

Here. This was life, he thought as his eyes closed and sleep overtook him. Right here. And the small breeze at his ear whispered its affirmation. This was life.

◆   ◆   ◆

Harmony dozed through the night, her senses always aware, her sensitive ears picking up each sound outside Lance's home, listening for any change to the sounds of the night.

When danger neared, the wildlife would pause. It was a part of nature. They would watch and listen to see if the danger was to them or to others. There was no pause, no change in the symphony outside the windows.

That symphony allowed her to find partial rest. To lie against his chest, sheltered in his arms as he slept deeply, helplessly. She protected him as he had protected her. Allowing him the rest he needed before a new day began.

The last three days had been exceptionally hard on them both perhaps. It couldn't be easy for Lance either. His life had to have been thrown into as much disarray as hers.

As she dozed in his arms, at times she imagined she felt parts of his soul in the heat of his body that soaked into her own. Why he would allow such an intimate part of himself inside a being as dark as herself, she couldn't fathom.

She didn't mean to sleep, not really. She had learned the fine art of dozing long ago. But for the first time, Harmony found peace. Cradled within his warmth, her soul rested.

CHAPTER 9

Keeping distance between her heart and Lance wasn't going to be easy, Harmony admitted two days later as she drove through town in her assigned Raider. The spare Raider was normally kept in case one of the others was down for repairs, Lance had explained the day before, almost apologizing for the sad shape of the vehicle.

It wasn't the best of the lot, she admitted, and it definitely wasn't fit for desert patrol, but once she learned its quirks, maneuvering it through town was easy.

Tourist season was in full swing in Broken Butte. The desert, canyons and cave formations outside town made it a regular attraction for summer travelers. The town itself had an Old West flavor, from the boutiques, cafés and specialty shops that lined the main thoroughfare, to the bars, restaurants and hotels that rimmed the edges of the city.

There was a clinic, hospital and medical pavilion on one side of town, then along the western edge was a small industrial park and the stockyards to accommodate the ranchers.

It was a charming town, she admitted as she made her way along the industrial area she'd been given to patrol.

There were a few homes on the outskirts of town here, a trailer park as well as a few apartment complexes, but she had heard from the other deputies that it was considered the quietest part of town.

It was boring as hell, but she contented herself with the fact that as long as she wasn't in town, then she wasn't likely to run into H. R. Alonzo. Or get into any more trouble.

Good ole Reverend Alonzo was going to keep pushing buttons until some enterprising Breed decided they had heard enough of his propaganda and capped a bullet in his brain.

He was the scourge of the Breed community, rallying the Blood supremacist and purist societies to protest every advancement the Breeds made in society. At present, he was once again applying for a permit to protest Megan Arness's ranch and the Breed halfway house she had set up there.

Megan Arness was another problem, and Harmony did not want any part of the empath and her Breed husband. They had nearly caught up with her in France last year. Why they had given up the chase she had never been certain, but before they did, she had wondered if outrunning them was a hopeless cause.

Megan Arness could blow her secrets faster than anything or anyone alive if she got close enough. Harmony knew her shields were strong, but she also knew the rumors of that woman's power to detect emotions and secrets. And Harmony had too many secrets to hide.

And then there was the fact that sometimes tourists were just strange. She had stopped a mugging the day before— wrestling with the little SOB who had snatched a young mother's purse had been irritating as hell. He had been hyped on drugs and stronger than normal; she had been forced to slam his face into the pavement to disable and restrain him.

Unfortunately, she had broken his nose. She hadn't meant to. Hell, she wasn't used to wearing kid gloves. The little twit should have felt lucky he was alive rather than scream police abuse. Which was what had gotten her assigned to the town's outer limits.

"Harmony, your GPS is blinking again." Lance's voice came over the Raider's communications link, suggesting a thread of irritation. "Have you been messing with it?"

She rolled her eyes. She had fixed it to begin with.

"I haven't touched it, Sheriff," she drawled as she reached to the dash and tapped at the GPS display. "It appears to be working fine on this end."

She checked her mirrors before pulling into an empty lot and adjusting the tracker module set in the dash.

"Don't start working on it." Lance's irritation was coming across loud and clear. "When you come back in, check with Davy in the garage; tell him I said to check it out."

"Davy worked on it the first time," she informed him as she unclipped her seat belt before leaning to the side to look at the wires under the dash. "You should let me take it back to the house. I could get it together in a few hours on my own."

"A terrifying thought," he remarked. "Turn it in to the garage. And stop fooling with the wires."

She jerked her hand back from under the dash guiltily as she glared at the receiver.

"If the GPS is down, you can't track me," she snapped.

That wasn't going to work. She was a little too paranoid for that scenario. Jonas's terms for placement on the force was that she be trackable at all times. The bastard.

"It's fading, not offline," Lance assured her. "Go ahead and call it a day and head in to the garage. Maybe Davy will let you help him work on it."

She grimaced at the thought, then rose in her seat and

sighed in frustration. Her gaze lifted to the rearview mirror and she froze in shock.

The navy and white SUV had parked close behind her, and the familiar form sitting in the driver's seat had her checking around the area quickly for witnesses.

Damn, she didn't need this.

She flipped the comm link back on, speaking as she kept her eyes on the vehicle behind her. "Control, I'm going to need to take a personal break before heading in. There's a station just ahead."

"Roger that." Lenny Blanchard's voice came over the link. "I'll inform the sheriff."

Which meant she had only a few precious minutes.

Pulling out of the vacant lot, she headed for the station ahead, where she turned in and drove around to the back of the building.

Dane.

Harmony parked the Raider, watching as he stepped from the SUV before lounging against it with deceptive laziness.

"I don't have time for this." She stopped a few feet from him, watching him warily.

He was as savagely hewn and intrinsically handsome as ever. White-blond hair framed his darkly tanned face as he stared back at her from emerald green eyes. He was a few inches taller than Lance, easily six-five, with a powerfully corded muscular body that made most women pant in lust.

"I received a report you were captured." His gaze raked over her.

And here was the part that always confused her most about Dane. How had he known she had been taken?

"Yeah, well, let's say I'm on parole," she quipped. "And meeting with you is going to cause problems. What the hell are you doing here?"

"I'm here to rescue you." White teeth flashed dangerously. "Are you ready to leave?"

Harmony stepped back quickly. He was more than capable of making her leave; he had done so before. She stared around the deserted area, searching for his backup. Dane always had backup.

"I can't leave, Dane." She finally shook her head firmly. "I'm sure you know exactly why I'm here by now."

Dane always seemed to know everything.

He crossed his arms over his chest as he watched her silently for long moments.

"Of course you can." His eyes finally narrowed on her assessingly. "I have a heli-jet waiting outside town. We can be out of here in half an hour."

"I told you, I can't leave." She gritted her teeth over the words as she felt her mind rebelling at the idea.

God, what was wrong with her? The mating heat was supposed to affect her body, not make her stupid. Of course she could leave; she just didn't want to. That was all. Freedom was a powerful lure.

"I just have to stick this out six months . . ."

"You won't make it six weeks before your enemies find you," he bit out. "The change in hair color is a nice touch. The makeup is nice. But you'll be found, Harmony. Eventually."

"Not if I'm careful." And she did know how to be careful.

Dane grunted as he watched her closely.

"We can get you out, Harmony. In a matter of months we can figure out how to hack the Bureau's computers and delete your files . . ."

"Jonas won't let me go that easily. It's better to play this game out and have it done with."

"He's set you up to fail, sweetheart . . ."

As though she weren't very well aware of that.

"I don't have time for this." She shook her head quickly. "I have to head back to the department and get that stupid GPS fixed. I can't run this time, Dane. If I stick it out, then he'll wipe the records."

"You're fooling yourself, Harmony." His smile was knowing. "He's trapped you. I can get you out of it."

She took another step back. For years he had always been there, pulling her ass out of the fire. He had rescued her, saved her life more than once, and always seemed to know exactly where she was, and what she was doing at any given time.

And she had never known why. She had never really questioned why until lately.

Suddenly the haze of hormones, hunger for Lance and confusion cleared from her mind. She stared around the deserted area, the hairs at the back of her neck lifting before her gaze returned to him.

"You know I'm being watched," she said, certain of that fact.

"Of course." His smile was supremely confident. "But not at the moment. Go on, little girl, run back to your sheriff. I'll hang around awhile and watch your back. Just like I always have." It sounded like a threat.

"I'd prefer you leave." She had a feeling things were about to get a hell of a lot more complicated.

"I'm sure you would, baby." He smiled again as he swung into the SUV. "I'm sure you would. Unfortunately, I think my curiosity has been aroused."

With that, he closed the door, engaged the engine and drove away.

Not for the first time in the past week, Harmony cursed.

Davy wouldn't let her touch the Raider.

Harmony strode briskly from the department's garage, along the sidewalk that led to the Sheriff's Department, as irritation began to surge inside her.

The aging excuse for a mechanic was a prime candidate for an ass-kicking with his smarmy smart-assed comments and smug smiles. She had a feeling he was deliberately screwing with the GPS, and if she found out he was, she was going to clean that excuse for a garage with his ponytailed head.

Dumb twit.

She was at the edge of her patience for the day and she knew it. Dane's arrival was a complication she could ill afford, and the implications of it were worrisome. Dane could cause problems. And she couldn't figure out why he was there.

She turned the corner and strode quickly to the steps that led to the single-story adobe building that housed Lance's offices. She took the steps two at a time, ignoring the looks she received from several bystanders. It was the uniform. All black, with her holster lying low on her thigh and the Bureau of Breed Affairs insignia on the sleeve, it was guaranteed to draw attention. Attention she really didn't need.

She strode through the lobby, waving at Lenny Blanchard as he shot her a smile; then she moved purposefully for Lance's office.

She gripped the doorknob and pushed her way inside.

"Lance, that excuse for a mechanic of yours is going to get on my last nerve," she snapped as she directed a fierce glare across his desk at him. "And the next time he calls me kitty, he's going to be missing a ponytail."

The new scent hit her then. It took a minute, because Lance's scent seemed to overwhelm everything else at first.

Her hand fell to her weapon as she turned, facing Jonas as he lounged against the wall, his eyes narrowed on her, his hands shoved into the pockets of his silk slacks.

"I see your disposition hasn't changed," he remarked as Lance came to his feet, moving around the desk and nearing Harmony.

"I can come back later." She tossed Lance a furious look. He could have warned her before she came stomping in here.

"He just arrived." Lance stopped when he was within several feet of her, obviously placing himself to intercede if she decided to confront Jonas.

"Fine. When you're finished with him, let me know. I need a cup of coffee anyway."

"Coffee makes the symptoms of the mating heat worse, Harmony," Jonas announced as she turned for the door. "You wouldn't want that, would you?"

Pasting a smile on her face, she turned back to him as she gave Lance a sultry look.

"Does that mean we'll get to leave early?" she whispered to Lance.

Lance's lips twitched. "Maybe."

"Hmm, maybe I'll have several cups of coffee then. Let me know when you're done."

She would go into caffeine withdrawal before touching another cup of coffee now. She was just managing to get a handle on the needs clawing inside her and wreaking havoc on her control. She wasn't about to make it worse.

"Harmony, you haven't been told you could leave the meeting," Jonas announced as she turned to leave again.

She inhaled slowly, refusing to turn back to him as she gripped the door handle and turned it quickly.

"There was a murder last night in Pinon," Jonas said softly. "A bartender suspected of kidnapping and raping several young women in the area. His throat was slit."

She turned back to him slowly.

"Is that why you showed up here?" Lance snapped before she could say anything.

Harmony looked up at him in surprise. He was furious. His eyes were narrowed on Jonas, his body tense as his fingers wrapped around her wrist to pull her to him.

"It has her M.O." Jonas shrugged, his gaze sharpening on Lance's hold. "He was killed behind the bar after closing and left for his employer to find the next day. If fits her previous kills."

"Suspected kills," she reminded him sweetly. "You have no proof and I denied the charges."

"So you did." He inclined his head mockingly. "But we both know the truth. Where were you last night?"

"With me," Lance snapped. "All night."

"He knows that, Lance," Harmony murmured softly. "He has a tail on me, and I'm betting they're watching the house at night as well."

Amusement gleamed in Jonas's gray eyes. "And we both know how good you are at slipping away." He straightened from the wall, though he kept his hands in his pockets.

Who said Jonas couldn't be smart when the need was there?

"Get the hell out of my office, Jonas," Lance growled then. "You have no proof Harmony wasn't with me last night, and I have all the proof I need that she *was* there. You no longer have any jurisdiction over her."

"Have you been to the crime scene?" she asked Jonas.

Jonas nodded abruptly.

"Was my scent there?"

His lips tightened. She had him there and he knew it. Unfortunately, though, her scent hadn't been at several of her kills in the past, and he was aware of that as well. Death had been amazingly adept in hiding herself.

"No. Your scent wasn't there," he admitted, his voice darkening in anger.

"Then you have no right to accuse me." She smiled back in triumph. "Looks like you need to find your killer elsewhere."

Jonas's gaze slid to Lance then, his eyes mocking as his lips quirked with sardonic amusement.

"She doesn't heel worth shit, does she?" Jonas asked him with an amused indulgence.

"She's not an animal, so I don't expect her to." Lance retained his hold on her as though he worried she would go for the gun strapped to her side. It was tempting, but her self-control was actually better than that.

Jonas grunted before asking, "The mating is going well then?"

Lance's anger spiked immediately. Harmony could smell it, burning like a hot flame with the potential to turn into a conflagration.

"Jonas, your games are getting tiresome," Lance warned him quietly.

Jonas's lips quirked as he watched them closely, looking

for weakness. Harmony could feel him probing at them, searching for a break to exploit.

"As I said earlier, I just stopped by to check on the situation." He shrugged then, as though a brotherly visit should be commonplace. "I'll leave you to your work." His gaze sharpened on Harmony. "I would definitely get the GPS fixed on the Raider if I were you. We wouldn't want any complications to arise from that."

He nodded mockingly before lifting his hands from his pockets and striding to the door. Harmony didn't bother to bid him farewell as he left the room, but she kept her eye on him until the door closed behind his broad back.

"One of these days, I'm going to kick him out of my office," Lance mused as he released her arm. "Now, what's the problem with Davy?"

"We need to go to Pinon." She waved the question about the mechanic away. "I need to see the crime scene."

Lance breathed out roughly. "I've already thought of that. I'll contact Sheriff Grasse and inform her we're heading that way."

"This won't have been a coincidence, Jonas knows that," she finally pointed out. The implications of the murder had hit her the moment Jonas informed them of it. "Someone suspects who I am."

"Then we'll just have to figure out who it is," his voice rasped as it lowered, his drowsy, hungry gaze eating her up. "Go get your report written up while I get hold of Sheriff Grasse and then we'll head to Pinon. I'd like to get back before it gets too late."

◆　　◆　　◆

Sheriff Grasse was a forty-something go-getter with a tough attitude and kind hazel eyes. Crow's-feet crinkled at the corners of her eyes, and laugh lines indented the sides of her lips. But she was all business when Harmony and Lance pulled in behind the small cement building that housed Drink Em Up, a small bar just inside the county line.

She stepped from her dark blue Raider, pulling her glasses from her eyes as she leaned against the door.

"Lance, it's good to see you again." Her smile was friendly as they stepped toward her.

"Katie, how's Ben and the kids?" Lance smiled back, his familiarity with her obvious.

Harmony stood silently as they exchanged pleasantries, maintaining her impatience in the face of social niceties. This was another plus on the side of the assassin. Death had never asked a mark if the kids were doing well.

"Katie, meet Harmony Lancaster, she's on temporary assignment from the Bureau of Breed Affairs." Lance finally introduced them. "Harmony, Katie Grasse, Otero County sheriff."

Harmony nodded coolly. "Can I see the crime scene now?" she asked quietly.

Sheriff Grasse's eyes gleamed in amusement.

"She reminds me of that Wyatt fellow, Lance," she drawled. "All business. Is it a Breed thing?"

"It's a Breed thing," Harmony answered for him. "And Jonas is a pussycat. You just have to know how to handle him."

The other woman blinked at her in surprise before a spurt of laughter left her lips.

"Go on then." She shrugged. "The investigation unit has already been over it. I doubt there's much left."

Harmony moved away from Lance and Sheriff Grasse, following the scent of blood to the dumpster just behind the door.

"Did you bring the pictures of the crime scene?" She knew Lance had requested them.

Bending her knees, she stooped by the bloody stain on

the blacktop, calculating the angle and depth of the wound based on what she saw there.

"Here you go." The file was passed to her with a firm snap.

Opening the manila folder, Harmony stared at the corpse. Plain features, a sharp nose, and his throat had definitely been cut. The angle was wrong for one of her kills though. Something Jonas should have noticed.

"Your killer was taller than the deceased," she murmured. "How tall was the victim?"

"Six feet." The Otero sheriff knelt beside her. "How can you tell?"

"The angle of the cut." She ran her nail over the wound. "According to the height of the killer to the victim, the wounds will be different. The depth of the cut at pressure points is significant. If the bartender was six feet, then your killer was a few inches taller. Perhaps six-three or -four."

"The coroner is still examining the body, but your Bureau director went over it as well. He didn't mention this," Grasse commented.

"He doesn't know knives like I do." Harmony handed the file back to her. "I would guess the weapon was a Special Forces K-bar."

The killer could in fact be a Breed. Or a Council soldier. Special training protocols were developed for the Breeds simply to be able to identify their kills.

Harmony pulled a pair of latex gloves from her pocket and snapped one on before reaching down. She ran her fingers over the bloodstain before lifting them to her nose. The putrid scent of old blood was all she found.

Grimacing, she stood to her feet before narrowing her eyes on the stain.

"Did the crime unit find any evidence?"

"Nothing. Other than the blood and the body, we don't

have jack." The sheriff sighed. "We were hoping having a Breed check it out would give us a lead."

Harmony shook her head. Whoever had made the kill had been careful, and especially careful to use her M.O.

"It's similar to several kills across the States in the past few years," Grasse pointed out then. "Suspected molesters that law enforcement officials hadn't been able to gather proof against. We could have a serial vigilante on our hands."

Or a copycat with an agenda.

Harmony lifted her eyes to Lance then, watching his head tilt, concentrating. What was he thinking? At times she could have sworn he was hearing something no one else could.

"This one is different," she finally answered. "The angle of the cut, the depth and the M.O. It's a copycat."

Grasse's eyes narrowed as Lance shot her a warning look.

"Like I said, I know knives." Harmony shrugged. "And I study the kills made with knives. Trust me, it's different. Your coroner will verify that if he cares to study the other killings closely. I don't know what you have here, but it's not a vigilante killing."

It looked more like a setup.

Grasse breathed out tiredly. "The coroner has already begun going over the other killings at Director Wyatt's request. He was the one who suggested the possibility."

Why would Jonas do that?

Harmony kept her head down, her eyes on the darker stain as she fought to make sense of the sheriff's comment.

"Are those copies of the crime scene pictures, Katie?" Lance asked then. "I'd like to keep them if I could; maybe Harmony can go over them later and spot something."

"Yeah, they're copies." She handed the file over. "I sure hope you find something. Bert Feldon wasn't liked much, but until he was convicted, he had a right to breathe."

If he was innocent, he had a right to breathe, though Har-

mony kept the thought to herself. At this point there was no
way to tell.

"Did you find anything in his home?" she asked the sheriff instead.

Sheriff Grasse shook her head. "It was clean." She
checked her watch then, breathing out roughly. "I have to
head out, but if you need anything else just let me know."

"Thanks again, Katie, and tell Ben I said hi." Lance nodded as she lifted a hand in farewell and turned away.

"I'm ready to go," Harmony said as the sheriff moved to
her vehicle. Harmony refused to look at Lance as she headed
for his Raider.

"Would Jonas try to frame you, Harmony?" The question
Lance posed didn't surprise her.

She opened the door to the Raider and slid into the seat.
She pushed her fingers wearily through her hair.

"The hell if I know what Jonas would do anymore." She
sighed. "But he didn't make that kill." He could, however,
have ordered it.

Harmony remained silent through the ride back to Broken Butte, her head turned, her gaze trained on the scenery
outside the window.

Being trapped inside the Raider with Lance was hell on
the arousal tormenting her, and it made clear thinking next
to impossible.

As Lance pulled the Raider to a stop in front of the house,
Harmony jumped from the vehicle and stalked around it.

"I didn't make that kill," she informed him, the anger beginning to burn inside her. Anger and arousal, frustration
and irritation—they were beginning to build along with the
hunger that ate at her.

"I never imagined you did," he stated as he moved behind
her. The house keys jangled in his hand as they started for
the front door.

"And you came up with that one how?" she snapped, glaring back at him. "You think you're so good that I couldn't slip out of the house without you knowing about it? Trust me, Lance, I'm good enough to do it."

"Yep. You're good enough." He nodded, his expression serious, though if she wasn't mistaken she could see the amusement gleaming in his eyes.

"How would you know?" She snorted as they stepped up on the porch and Lance unlocked the door slowly.

He was too trusting for a sheriff, she thought. He should have been instantly suspicious of her, not instantly defensive.

She stepped into the house cautiously, her gaze going quickly over the entryway, kitchen/dining room and the lower level of the living room as Lance stepped in behind her.

"Security systems can be bypassed, Lance," she reminded him severely.

"But the winds cannot be."

Harmony whirled around as an old man stepped from Lance's room, his bowed legs encased in deerskin pants, a black Metallica shirt covering his upper body. Long gray braids fell across his chest, and his heavily creased face stretched into a smile as Lance caught Harmony's hand on her weapon.

"Settle down, wildcat," he said and sighed. "Meet my grandfather, Joseph Redwolf. Grandfather, this is—"

"The assassin." Black eyes crinkled with a smile as he shuffled forward slowly, his head tilting, his gnarled hands pushing inside the wide pockets of his pants. "She does not look like a killer, Grandson. Perhaps in this case, the winds have not whispered all the secrets to my old ears. What do you think?"

"I think I'm ready for a drink," Lance said and sighed again. "A very long, very stiff drink. Anyone want to join me?"

· CHAPTER 11 ·

"She is a beautiful woman, Grandson. The earth has done well for you," Joseph commented as Lance poured his second drink and wondered when the hell this day was going to end.

"Don't start, Grandfather," he growled.

Joseph chuckled, a rough rasp that reminded him of his grandfather's age. He turned back to the old man, watching him closely. Joseph hadn't been moving around much lately. He'd been spending a lot more time than usual at home.

"Ah, it is good to see you finally settling down." Joseph nodded firmly. "The earth whispers her name with yours, and the music of its pleasure bodes well. The journey you travel together will be one that will challenge you."

Lance snorted at that. He was glad one of them could make sense of the whispers in the wind, because he sure as hell wasn't making any headway.

"But it is one that brings danger." Joseph watched him closely now. "It whispers death but not of blood. There are times the winds are not as giving as others."

It was one of the reasons Lance had fought the messages

carried on the winds. There were never answers, only more questions.

"Do you still fight the secrets it would bring you, Grandson?" Joseph finally asked sadly.

Lance sighed wearily. "I'm trying, Grandfather." He stared back at the old man. "But, like you said, sometimes the winds aren't as giving as others."

Joseph nodded slowly. "But you can hear what is important. You know she is your woman, and that danger follows. Heed them and they will see you through this."

"Or see me dead," Lance muttered before tossing back his drink.

"I hear no cry of your death." Joseph shrugged. "Should you end up dead then it will be at your own ignorance, not the will of the earth."

That was his grandfather, sympathetic to the end.

"It's nice to know something is still left in my hands," Lance growled in frustration. "I was starting to wonder."

His grandfather chuckled at the comment.

"I wished only to stop by and meet your young woman," Joseph said then. "I know now why I heard the cries in the winds though. She is a woman wounded, yes?"

Wounded was a mild word for what he felt inside of Harmony. Sometimes, he could sense her nightmares, sense the pain that drove her and her fear of ever needing anyone.

"Yeah. She is." He smacked the glass to the bar before grimacing tightly. "Jonas brought her here, and I have a feeling he's playing a very dangerous game with her."

"Ah yes, Jonas Wyatt." Joseph sighed. "He is a difficult one, that young Lion. He fights what he is, and what his soul yearns for. When a warrior fights such an elemental part of himself, he is bound to often hurt others. It is his destiny to learn his lessons the hard way."

"At the end of my fist if he keeps this up," Lance

snapped. "I'm growing tired of his games. Especially this game he's playing with Harmony."

"There are many forces I think that would see her taken from you, Grandson. Not just Jonas. The question is, will you allow them to take what is yours alone?" Joseph asked him then. "Understanding is a fine quality in a man. But sometimes a man must show his woman he is indeed a man strong enough to match her. Sometimes, it teaches the woman what she must know when danger comes whispering her name. Perhaps you should think on this."

Lance stared back at his grandfather, once again cursing, albeit silently, the riddles Joseph Redwolf was prone to talk in. He couldn't just come out and tell you anything. Everything had to be a lesson, or a puzzle to figure out.

"How about dinner?" Lance suggested as a way to lighten the mood. As usual, the answers would either come to him, or life would kick his ass with enough force for him to see the point his grandfather had been trying to make.

"Dinner is good, but I promised Megan I would eat with her and her young Breeds after seeing you. She worries for you. Staying away from you at this time is not easy for her, but I understand now why you have asked this of her. The emotions trapped within your young Lioness would overwhelm her."

"Yeah. They would." Hell, they nearly overwhelmed him, and he wasn't empathic. "Give Meg my love, Grandfather. Tell her I'll see her soon."

"I will do this." Joseph nodded as he moved for the front door. "And you keep your young woman close to your side, Lance. Do not give the danger stalking her a chance to strike. She has no true friends other than you. Yet."

And with that final cryptic comment Joseph made his way to the front door and let himself out. Lance poured himself another drink. It was going to be a long evening.

❖   ❖   ❖

There were times when Harmony blessed her animal senses, and there were other times when she cursed them. Walking into the house and realizing she had missed the presence of Lance's grandfather was one of the times she cursed herself.

There were some people who should be avoided at all costs, simply because they were so much a part of nature, of the land around them, that the earth spoke to them. The Lion part of her recognized that in Joseph Redwolf. He was a child of the earth, completely in sync with it and, as such, able to see beyond what others couldn't. Like his grand-daughter, Megan Arness, and yet unlike her.

Harmony hadn't detected the subtle shift of power around her that normally warned her that a psychic was present. But she also knew that there were those who saw things, knew things, without ever tripping her defenses. She had a feeling Lance's grandfather was one of those people. She was beginning to wonder if Lance was, because he kept finding ways beneath her defenses. A look. A touch. A certain tone of voice.

She had a terrible feeling that if she ended up staying there much longer, then walking away was going to kill her. It wasn't her way to form attachments or friends. The potential for heartache only grew. And within a week, the potential was getting seriously out of control here.

As the night deepened, Harmony used the darkness of her room to think. Stretched out on the floor, dripping with sweat from the crunches she worked through, she fought to clear her mind. To concentrate on the burn of her muscles rather than the arousal burning through the rest of her.

She could think through the workouts. Who had killed the bartender? Which enemy did she know would work to frame her rather than shoot her? She was accessible here. There was no way to hide from a sniper's gun, which meant it wasn't a Council-run operation. The Council wanted her, but not dead. She was of no use to them dead. If she was convicted of committing another murder, then as far as they knew, Jonas wouldn't hesitate to kill her.

She had made other enemies, of course. An assassin had a ton of those. But Harmony had been careful. The persona of Death was much different than the one she portrayed as Harmony. Harmony could walk down a city street, shop in the finest stores and have dinner in the best restaurants. Death had to use the cover of night and hide in the shadows.

Wiping the dripping perspiration from her eyes, she collapsed back on the carpet, breathing hard as she fought to catch her breath before beginning another set of the crunches.

Alonzo was in town. He knew of Death, but he didn't know Harmony. He would know there was a Breed on the force, but had he connected the two, he wouldn't be staging an elaborate frame-up. The bastard.

Besides, Alonzo could have no idea that she knew his secrets, his ties to the Council and the operation in France ten years before.

None of this made sense.

She frowned up at the ceiling, fighting to work through something that had no base. There was always a chance the murdered bartender was a freak occurrence, but Harmony didn't deal in coincidences. They didn't exist for her.

Nothing existed for her but Death.

The pain that clenched her chest at the thought of that nearly took her breath. She was twenty-five years old. Twenty of those years had been spent killing.

She lifted her hands from the floor and stared at them, even in the near blackout of the room, she saw the blood. So much blood spilling through her hands, staining her soul and everything she touched.

Everyone she touched.

Oh God, what was she doing here? A half-hysterical laugh nearly passed her lips. What made her think she could do this? That she could ever have the freedom Jonas had offered her.

Six months. He knew she would never last six months. He knew her past would stalk her, find her, and she was terrified that was exactly what had happened.

As she lay there, the sound of the doorknob turning had her jerking her gun from her side and coming to her knees, the safety clicking off as the door swung inward.

"Are you crazy?" she yelled at Lance furiously as she came to her feet in a surge of anger. "Don't ever do that. Never."

He stood framed in the doorway, one hand braced against the jamb as he stared into the room. The light from the hall shadowed him, but she knew it clearly revealed her. Dressed in the snug cotton cami shirt and matching boxers, damp with sweat, no part of her body would be hidden from his gaze.

Her nipples pressed into the cloth and her clit throbbed in anticipation as she stared at him. Shirtless. God, couldn't he even wear a shirt? The only thing saving her from panting in lust was the fact that he was in shadow and she couldn't really see details.

But she could smell. And the smell of him was off-the-charts hot. Desert heat and stormy winds. The combination had the glands at her tongue swelling further and the sweet taste of arousal spilling to her mouth.

Great. Just great, she thought. She had managed to keep this mating heat stuff under control for two days, just to be blindsided by a bare chest and the scent of him.

"Are you just going to stand there?" She stalked over to the nightstand, flipping on the light to at least give herself the advantage of seeing him. Unlike most Breeds, her night vision wasn't exactly exceptional.

Maybe she should have left the lights off.

He shifted as he watched her, hard chest muscles rippling, his abs tightening as the unbuttoned band of his jeans drew her eyes.

"You're soaking wet with sweat," he observed. "Is lying in here working out like a demon better than being in my bed?"

"Yes!" No.

His expression turned chastising as he wagged his finger at her. "Little girls who lie get their butts spanked," he warned her.

That did not turn her on. It didn't.

She crossed her arms over her chest and glared back at him.

"I wouldn't try it if I were you," she grated out.

"What? Spanking you?" The crooked smile that tugged at his lips was one of pure lust. "I promise, baby, you would enjoy it."

She was two seconds from a true growl. And she so hated playing into the stereotype of the Breed.

"Exactly what did you want?" she asked between gritted teeth.

"Exactly?" He arched a brow mockingly. "Are you sure you want me to answer that?"

She glanced at the clock.

"It's half past midnight. Don't you have to work in the morning?"

"Don't you?" he replied, his voice silky dark, stroking over her senses with nearly the same effect of his calloused palms on her flesh.

As he stepped into the bedroom, the air around her pulsed with hunger.

God, what was she going to do about him?

"Lance, please." She stepped back, staring at him desperately now. "Go to bed."

"Come with me, Harmony," he whispered, coming

nearer, the dark teak of his flesh gleaming. "Let me hold you while you sleep again. I'll watch over you, baby."

The temptation of it had a shiver racing over her skin. He had held her while she slept the other night. She had been unable to help it, couldn't hold back. She had meant only to doze, but before she could stop herself she had fallen into the abyss awaiting her. And she had done so dreamlessly.

She shook her head, feeling her hair brush over her shoulders, stroking skin already sensitive, reminding her of his touch.

He came nearer with each second, until he stood only inches from her, the heat of his body surrounding her. She hadn't even known she was chilled until his heat enfolded her.

"You're wet, baby," he whispered, his hand gripping her shirt and pulling it up. "Let me help you out there."

The shirt cleared her head as Harmony blinked up at him in confusion. How did he do this to her?

"Lance." Her hands pressed against his bare chest, then she groaned, realizing defeat was only seconds away as she felt her palms soaking up the heat from his body.

"Yeah, feel that," he crooned. "Let me warm you, baby."

Harmony felt her lips part helplessly, her entire body tensing, preparing for the wild heat of his kiss. Instead, he merely caressed her lips with his mouth.

His hands slid over her waist, calloused palms stroking with fiery pleasure until they cupped the heaving mounds of her breasts. His thumbs stroked her nipples and she felt herself panting.

She was panting for his touch. Her hands gripped his wrists as she felt every nerve ending in her body throbbing, waiting.

She jerked as his thumb and forefinger applied erotic pressure to the hard tip of her nipple, sending a burning surge of pleasure to race through her stomach. Her breath caught at the sensation as her nails pressed into his wrist.

"We can't keep doing this." Her cry was weak, pleading. "Don't do this to me, Lance."

"Do what? Make you admit you need?" His lips moved over her jaw, leaving fire in their wake. "Make you feel what I feel, Harmony? I burn for you baby. Burn for me."

Didn't he know that the flames ate her insides constantly, tearing at her will, her defenses?

"Just feel for me, Harmony," he crooned. "Just for a little while."

When his lips returned to hers, they melted into her, kissing her with a longing and fervor she couldn't deny. Deep, sipping kisses that drugged her mind and sent her senses spinning.

"There, sweetheart." He was breathing hard, rough, as he pulled back, one hand sliding down her torso, over her stomach as she struggled to open her eyes.

A second later his palm slid between her thighs, pressing over the aching center of her body as she felt a dizzying sweep of pleasure tear through her.

She couldn't help clenching her thighs, holding his palm in place. It was cupped snugly over her pussy, the heel of his palm pressing against her clit, grinding against it with devastating results.

Beneath her hands his flesh was heated, beneath her lips the strong column of his neck beckoned. His skin tasted of male arousal and heat, clinging to her tongue and mixing with the hormone spilling from the glands beneath. The intoxicating flavor had her reaching for more, her teeth raking over his skin as her senses came alive.

Her defenses fell away, unable to bear the weight of their combined hunger. The battle to fight the hunger and need surging through her was one that couldn't be fought in his arms.

"There, baby," he whispered against her collarbone, his

head lowering, heading unerringly to the stiff peaks of her nipples as his palm inflamed her clit, pressing the soft cotton of her boxer-style panties against it. He ground his hand against her, tearing a harsh cry from her lips as brilliant flares of pleasure tore through her.

She was lost in him. One touch and she was caving and didn't even care. The past, the present, the danger surrounding her—it all threatened to dissolve around her, and when it did, she knew she would be dead. She couldn't do this. She couldn't let her hunger destroy the only good thing she had ever found in her life.

Loving Lance was a weakness. A weakness that could get him killed.

"No." She tore away from him, not certain where she found the strength to do it.

Stumbling against the bed, she reached down, jerked her shirt from the floor and held it against her breasts as she fought to get away from him.

With the length of the room between them, she turned, staring at his back as he breathed heavily, his head lowered, his hands propped on his hips. He was fighting for control; she could see it in every muscle of his body.

When he turned back to her, she flinched at the brilliance of his blue eyes, the savage cast of his expression.

"How much longer can you run, Harmony?" His voice was a rough rasp. "Can you make it six months, baby?"

"I have to," she cried out, hating the look on his face, the hunger and need, the certainty that she would fall. "Don't you understand, Lance? I can't have this. It doesn't matter what nature wants, or what I want. I can't have this."

She clenched her fists in the hem of her shirt, fighting to hold back the need to return to him, to touch him.

"And why can't you have it?" he barked back. "Because

you're the tough-assed assassin? Poor little Breed who has to fight alone. That's bullshit and you know it."

"No, it's not bullshit," she retorted furiously. "It's the truth, you're just too damned horny to see it."

"Oh, you have the horny right, baby. I'm so damned hard I could fuck you for a week without letting up. And I'll be damned if I'll walk away like this forever. You're my fucking mate. You think you can just walk away from it? That it's just going to go away?"

She flinched as he yelled back at her, the graveled sound of his voice testifying to his growing frustration and anger.

"It's just lust." She swiped her hand through the air, as desperate to believe it as she was for it to be true. "A chemical reaction. It *will* go away."

"And you're only kidding yourself."

Harmony jumped to avoid him as he strode quickly to her, his hand gripping her wrist, jerking her hand to his thighs.

"Feel that, Harmony."

She whimpered as he cupped her fingers over the hard width of his erection beneath his jeans.

"This doesn't go away. I wake up with it and I go to sleep with it. And by God, if you try to tell me you're not just as wet as I am hard, I'll fuck you where you're standing just to prove you're wrong."

"It will go away."

"It's not going to go away," he barked as he jerked back from her just as quickly as he had grabbed her.

"Then I'll have to," she whispered, aching with the needs tearing her apart. "Don't you understand, Lance? Of everyone in my life, you're the only really good thing that has touched it. You're asking me to take a chance on letting what I am destroy you. I can't do that. I can't stay here. I can never stay here. Death is hunted, Lance, by Council soldiers and law enforcement officials alike. And whether you want to admit it or not, I will be found eventually."

He stilled.

"I thought you were a fighter," he said quietly. "The kid who shot her way out of hell and took out the monsters intent on destroying her was a fighter. What she grew into is something else entirely. That kid knew how to live. What happened to her when she grew up, Harmony?"

"She learned that only death matters," she told him sadly. "Because that's where it all ends, Lance. Everything I touch ends in death."

"How could it?" he snapped. "Because you keep running, Harmony. Maybe if you stopped running, just for a little while, you would find something worth fighting for. It takes more guts to stand and fight than it does to hide and kill. Try it out once, baby, you might find it worth your time." His gaze raked over her again. "Or maybe that's your problem. You don't have to fear what you don't have to face. Do you?"

"That's not true." She shook her head wildly.

He wasn't right. He couldn't be right. She wasn't scared of anything, anyone. She was Death.

"It is true, Harmony. Have fun killing yourself with sit-ups while you try to deny it. Personally, I had a much more pleasurable cure in mind. But you just do it your way. For now."

"What do you mean by that?" Her eyes narrowed on him suspiciously as she fought the feeling that Lance's patience was quickly running out.

"Exactly what I said. Try doing push-ups. They seem to help more." His smile was tight as he walked out of the room. The threat lingered behind him though. As did the clawing, heated need.

Dropping to the floor, she started the push-ups.

CHAPTER 12

Lance replaced the decrepit Raider with his own the next evening. Unfortunately, he came with it. To add insult to injury, he changed the schedule as well.

"If I'm going to stay up all damned night long, then I might as well be working," he had snapped that morning when he informed her of the change.

As the call came in on a disturbance and fight at one of the more popular bars, she almost rubbed her hands in glee. She sat forward, straining against the seat belt as Lance raced toward the establishment.

She hadn't had a good fight in months. Unfortunately, as the adrenaline began to race through her veins, the heat building in her body increased. The arousal was almost a narcotic in her blood as her skin sensitized and her nerve endings began to throb.

She was throwing off the seat belt and jerking the door open before the Raider had come to a complete stop. Ignoring Lance as he called out her name, she headed for the bar and the fight inside.

"Oh, no you don't." He caught her arm, pulling her to a surprised stop as she stared up at him in shock.

"What?"

"Take their statements!" He pointed imperiously toward the small crowd outside. "Now."

"But the fight . . ." Oh God, she really needed to expend energy. She could feel the need cramping her stomach, building in her veins.

"Statements," he snarled, the look in his eyes causing her to hesitate. "Now."

She snarled furiously, flashing her canines as the sound rumbled from her throat. Gripping her hand, he slapped his notebook into it.

"Now." That tone was primal, such a completely alpha sound that she was taken aback for a moment. "Right now."

She took the statements, fuming at the injustice of it as he and the other deputies began clearing the bar.

"That was so not fair," she snapped as he strode from the bar an hour later, a bruise forming at his temple as he dragged a raw-boned cowboy by his shirt collar to a waiting patrol car. "I could have helped."

He grunted rudely.

"You wouldn't have a black eye if you had let me help," she retorted, her fist clenched around his mangled notebook. "I can't believe you did this."

She couldn't believe she had blindly obeyed him like some submissive wimp that didn't know how to fight back. She had never ever obeyed a man in her life. Why the hell was she starting now?

"Your attitude is starting to severely suck, Sheriff," she informed him, trying not to look too deeply into the fact that she had figuratively tucked her tail and obeyed.

"Did you get those statements?"

"Every last one," she responded with false sweetness,

glaring back at him as he met her gaze without the first sign of apology. "You should have let me in there."

"Why?" he barked as he turned and led the way to the Raider. "So you could expend some of that energy raging through your body? I don't think so. Get in the Raider."

He jerked her door open as she stalked past him.

"That is just the most idiotic thing I've heard come out of your mouth," she snapped after he had slammed her door closed and was striding around to his own side. "I'm not a pet you can place in the corner and tell to sit."

"That's a dog." He twisted the key in the ignition before pushing the Raider into gear. "Everyone knows cats don't train worth shit."

Indignation snapped inside her.

"I am not a cat," she hissed.

Shit. She hated that sound.

She hated the smirk that crossed his lips as well.

"Do you think this is going to get me in your bed?" She turned on him mockingly, her lip lifting in a sneer. "I don't hardly think so, lover. You'll have to provide a little bit more excitement than taking fucking statements to get me that riled."

Lance merely grunted in response. And she just hated it when he did that.

As Harmony opened her mouth to blast him, Dispatch called in with a domestic disturbance. At once Lance stilled, going icy with fury as he answered the call.

"What is it?" She could feel the anger coursing around him.

"Tommy Mason." He bit the name out. "The last time we were called to the house, he had nearly beaten his wife to death. She swore he hadn't touched her. He's managed to get around every fucking family violence law on the books."

Harmony breathed in slowly.

"Maybe I'm the wrong one to take on this call," she finally said. "I don't do well in these situations, Lance."

Things like this were what had gotten her into her present situation. The injustice of the monsters of the world literally getting away with torture and murder. Seeing the shell-shocked eyes of young victims, or the broken, lifeless bodies of young women. Justice didn't always make the rabid animals of the world pay for their crimes.

"Then you better start." He accelerated the Raider as he pulled out of the bar's parking lot, flipped on the sirens and headed toward the outskirts of town.

"Sheriff, we have shots fired," Dispatch reported as Lance made a quick turn. "Mason fired at the State Police as they pulled in. We now have a hostage situation."

Lance's muttered curse had the hair at the back of her neck standing on end as the Raider careened around a curve and the flashing lights of the State Police cruisers came in sight.

"Stay in the Raider," he ordered her quietly. "I'll take care of this."

"Like hell," she informed him coolly.

"Look, Harmony, Mason's wife has a kid. He's turned this into a hostage situation, and if he's drinking, he's going to be unpredictable."

"You made the decision to bring me here." If there was a child involved, there wasn't a chance in hell she was staying in the Raider.

"And I was wrong," he said quietly, his gaze suddenly softening, turning regretful. "I won't risk you like this. Stay in the Raider."

"Don't worry, Sheriff, I won't embarrass you." Her smile, she hoped, was reassuring. She couldn't prick at him when he was doing something so totally unexpected. Hell, he almost made her feel warm without his touch. "You take care of your end and I'll take care of mine."

The Raider pulled to a stop behind the State Police cruisers. Harmony followed as Lance exited the vehicle, bending to keep low as they moved to the commander.

"He started firing as soon as we pulled in, Lance." His badge tagged him as Commander Steven Noonan.

Several inches shorter than Lance, he was stooped next to the opened door of his car as he stared back at the house.

"He has her in the front bedroom. Every time we try to move in, he fires. He's threatening to kill the woman."

"Is Jaime in there?" Lance asked.

"He hasn't mentioned the kid, but the neighbors say the boy was home." The commander grimaced. "We haven't seen a sign of him though."

With Lance's attention distracted by the commander, Harmony slid slowly back beside the cruiser, heading for the shadowy ditch that ran along the front of the house. Watching the house in full view of the armed man wasn't the wisest course of action as far as she was concerned, and it sure as hell wasn't going to help that kid and his mother.

Harmony had a much better idea, and she wasn't stupid enough to ask for permission.

Keeping low, as she reached the back of the cruiser she slid along the ground, intending to crawl to the ditch that began just on the other side of the vehicle.

"Stop!" A strong hand latched around her ankle.

Rolling to her back, she stared at Lance. "I can get them free without anyone dying. I swear it." She stared back at him calmly. "Why risk lives? You know I can do it, Lance."

"And if the kid is dead?" he growled, keeping his voice low despite the fury throbbing in it. "What will you do then, Harmony?"

She knew what he was asking. If she killed, Jonas would have her. Especially in this situation.

She inhaled sharply. "Then the bastard will live. For

now," she snapped back. "Unless or until your fine justice system decides he might not be guilty. Then we may have to rethink the matter."

Lance's eyes narrowed.

"I'm fast and I'm quiet. He'll never see me coming. He's a two-bit wife beater, Lance. Not a Coyote on the hunt. I can take him."

A shot fired from inside and the sound of a woman's cry had him flinching. Slowly, he released her ankle. Reaching into the small utility bag at the side of his belt, he pulled free a set of personal comm links that fit over the ear, the small mic extending out to lie on the cheek.

"Use this." He handed one to her as he fit the other over his ear. "If I have to use a body bag tonight, I won't be happy, Harmony," he informed her quietly, the sound of his voice coming through the link as she fitted it in place and allowed the wire-thin mic to curve over her cheek.

"No body bags," she promised with a smile, before blowing him a quick kiss.

Rolling to her stomach, she pushed herself into the drainage ditch and began scuttling toward the deeper shadows several feet past the house.

The black material of her uniform blended in with the darkness, giving her the additional camouflage needed when she crawled out of the ditch and into the weeds and brush that grew at the edge of the property.

Keeping to her stomach in the long shadows, she crawled over the rough grass and rock-strewn yard, keeping her eyes on the window that gave a view into that side of the house.

"I'm moving in along the side of the house," she whispered into the mic as she finally moved against the outside of the building. Coming to her feet, she flattened herself against the siding. "Is there a back door?"

"It leads into the kitchen," Lance answered. "There's a

short hallway that then leads to the living room and, beside it, the bedroom where he's holding her."

"I'm on it. Beginning radio silence." She flipped the mic up, leaving only the receiver active as she made her way to the back of the house.

Passing the back door, she moved instead to the window at the far end of the house. It was securely locked, but the small metal lock was easily turned when she slid her knife beneath the frame and began prying upward.

Within minutes she was sliding the window open and moving into the house. She could hear him now. His voice was slurred, enraged as he cursed from the front bedroom.

"Harmony, one of the neighbors who came up has reported that Mason keeps a knife on him. A switchblade." Lance spoke in her ear. "He's a mean gutter fighter, so be careful."

So the bad boy liked to play with knives. Well, so did she.

She slid the window closed before looking around carefully. She had come into the boy's room; his scent was all over it. There were few toys, only a small bed and dresser, a few scattered shirts. Inhaling at the bleakness that attested to what his life must be like, she moved toward the doorway, listening to Tommy Mason scream at his wife.

"You stupid whore. I warned you what would happen if you tried to leave. Didn't I warn you?"

She could hear a woman sobbing, but she couldn't hear the child.

She found the little boy in the living room, huddled into a corner, his hands covering his ears as he rocked himself back and forward. Tears marred his dirt streaked face and his eyes were clenched closed.

Moving in close, she simultaneously laid her hand over his lips and crooned a soft "Easy, sweetie" at his ear.

His eyes flared open.

"Shhh," she whispered again, her touch gentle as she ran it quickly over his fragile, shaking body. "Are you hurt?"

He shook his head no, but his eyes were wild, frantic as his mother cried out his name from the other room.

"I have to yell if anyone comes," his voice trembled as he fought to speak. "He'll hurt her again. I have to scream."

She set her fingers against his lips.

"Trust me."

He shook his head desperately, tears pouring from wild blue eyes as his body jerked with silent sobs.

"Have you ever seen a Breed?"

He almost stilled, his eyes widening. Most children were fascinated by the subject of Breeds. They wrote letters to the Sanctuary, and a few times, Harmony knew, Tanner Reynolds, the Breed liaison, had enchanted children at several schools. They were the newest version of superheroes to the little minds.

Lifting her lip, she showed him the canines, a bit small perhaps, but definitely impressive. He blinked back at her in shock.

"I bet if you stay very, very quiet, I can make sure your momma is fine. And I'll make sure he never comes back. Can you be quiet for just a few more minutes and give me the chance?"

A silent sob rattled his little body. He was obviously malnourished, terrified. "Very good," she crooned at his ear once again. "Now be very, very quiet. Okay?"

He nodded desperately.

Harmony flipped the mic down, activating the link.

"The child is safe. To your left as you enter, huddled into the corner. I'm going for the mother."

"Easy, Harmony," Lance warned, his voice worried. "Keep the link active."

She flipped it up. The wire was a distraction she didn't need.

Pressing her finger to her lips as she gave the boy one last look, she moved back to the doorway. She waited until she was certain the boy wouldn't see her before she slid the K-bar from the sheath at her side and moved back to the hallway. The bedroom door was open, the room lit by the flashing lights from the cruisers outside.

"Sons of bitches. They had no right interfering in my business." The sound of a hand meeting flesh was followed by a woman's broken cry. "This is all your fault, you whiny-assed bitch."

Moving on her stomach, Harmony began to inch her way through the entrance, staying low and silent as Tommy Ma son screamed at his wife. Her feet had cleared the doorway when the wide, hulky excuse of a man pulled a switchblade from his pants and flipped it open.

He gripped his wife's long hair in one hand and lifted the knife with the other. And Harmony knew her time had run out. Rolling quickly, she came to her feet, her knife slicing through the hair he gripped as she slung the woman to the floor.

"What the hell?" He surged back, his gaze first surprised, then narrowing with fury on Harmony. "You're one dead whore."

Harmony sighed dramatically. "So I've heard."

He had to come out of the house alive, she reminded herself as she rammed the flat of her hand against his nose, pulling back just in time to temper her blow. As he flew backward, she caught his wrist, wrenched the knife from his grip then twisted until he fell to his knees. A hard knee to the small of his back and he was on the floor as she snapped the restraints around his wrists.

"It's like this, asshole," she hissed at his ear. "You're under arrest."

Then she gripped his hair, pulled his head back and slammed it into the floor. The first time, he managed to groan and buck furiously. The second time he slumped beneath her, his large body going boneless.

It was almost too easy. The adrenaline surging through her body hadn't been given the fight it needed. It pulsed and hammered through her veins as an icy burn began to build beneath her flesh.

Jumping from the fallen man's back, she shook her hands then rubbed at her thighs. Geez. What the hell was up with this?

"Harmony, dammit, answer me," Lance snapped into the link as she realized she had been hearing his voice for several seconds.

She inhaled slowly, her gaze going around the room before finding the wary form of the young woman stumbling through the door.

"Harmony . . . Now, dammit." His voice was rough, and sent lust coursing through her.

Flipping the mic down, she crooned into the link. "I have a present for you, baby. Want to come collect?"

Yep, it was lust.

CHAPTER 13

The moment her voice crooned over the comm link, Lance felt the response surge through his body. His cock was already painfully erect, but the sexy tone of her voice had it jerking in his jeans, impossibly harder and ready to fuck.

Damn her. She picked a hell of a time to turn into a sex kitten.

"Okay, Steven, let's move in. She has him."

He was aware of Steven's quick, surprised look as they headed into the house, with the paramedics coming in behind them.

Lance waved them to the corner where the mother, Liza, was cradling her young son. She was bloody, beaten, but appeared conscious.

Moving quickly, he and the two State Police officers moved into the bedroom, guns drawn, before pulling up to a quick stop.

Tommy Mason was spewing vulgarity as Harmony sat on her haunches listening to him, her head tilted, a mocking smile on her face as she ran her thumb slowly down the edge of her blade.

"You think you're so smart," Mason spat. "You freak. You're nothing but a nasty damned animal and you'll get yours."

Harmony lifted her head to Lance. "He's just full of information," she drawled. "All kinds of supremacist rhetoric. You have some fine folks in your fair town, Sheriff Jacobs."

She moved aside as the officers gripped Mason's arms and picked him up from the floor. Harmony slid the knife deftly into its sheath and stared back at him expectantly.

"I'm hungry," she stated. "Didn't I see a fast-food joint earlier? Think we could detour before we have to take care of all that nasty paperwork?"

He watched her closely. Her eyes were unnaturally bright, her voice huskier than normal.

"Are you okay?" He moved to her, his gaze going over her carefully. "Did he manage to cut you?"

She gave an unladylike snort. "Please." She waved the question away. "He was such an amateur. People should learn how to use knives before attempting to play with them." She reached behind her and pulled the switchblade, encased in an evidence bag, from her belt. "Here you go. I didn't even get any of my nasty little paw prints on it."

He took the bag carefully, allowing his fingers to brush hers, feeling the unnatural cold of her fingertips.

"Let's go get those statements taken care of," he said and sighed. "Steven and his men will take care of Mason."

"Are they going to lock him up?" She moved ahead of him as they left the bedroom and headed for the front door.

"They'll lock him up. He'll be lucky if he sees the outside of a cell in the next twenty years. Shooting at the State Police is a heavy crime."

Lance had seen the officer carefully lifting a pistol from the bedroom floor and putting it in an evidence bag as his partner read Mason his rights.

"They'll lock him up for shooting at a police officer but not for beating the hell out of his wife?" Harmony shook her head as they moved outside. "The world is a sick, sick place, Lance."

"We do our best, Harmony."

"And when your personal best isn't good enough?" she asked as they reached the Raider.

As she turned to him, Lance saw the shadows that filled her amazing green eyes. They were pure, brilliant, with no specks of darker color. Almost mesmerizing.

"When my personal best hasn't been good enough, I keep fighting," he sighed as he leaned against the door, trapping her between him and the interior of the vehicle. "I come out here every time the neighbors call. I try to help Liza as best I can. Until she lets go of her fear enough to help me put him behind bars, then there's nothing I can do."

"And the little boy?"

"I do my best, Harmony." He knew the question she was asking, the warning behind it. "I uphold the law, baby. I don't make it."

She inhaled slowly. "I'm not cut out for this job. Maybe Lenny will trade places with me."

They both knew that wasn't possible. The papers she had signed had been clearly written. Harmony had to work patrol, not a desk.

"You have to take satisfaction from the good you can accomplish," he whispered, reaching out to touch her pale cheek. "When you see the arrest turn into a conviction, when you know you've done your job well enough to stop the leaks in the system. The good outweighs the bad, Harmony."

"If he gets free again, he'll kill them both," she told him. "He told that boy to scream if anyone came in. And he almost screamed. He'll make that child pay. And when he does, I'll go hunting."

And there was Death. He heard the transformation in her voice, watched as she stared back at him ruthlessly.

"Will you let Jonas win that easily?" he asked. "How many other children could you help by living, Harmony?"

"What will it matter if I've failed one of the few who gave me his trust?" she asked him then. "Don't let that bastard escape your law, Lance, or he may well find Death's justice."

Then she reached up, laying both hands against his chest as a breath shuddered from her. And he felt it then. The heat in his body building, reaching out to her as the winds whispered of pain at his ear.

Reaching up, he covered the backs of her hands with his own, standing silently as she let her head lean forward to rest against his chest as well. Other eyes watched them, and Lance knew it. As the ambulance pulled from the drive, the other officers moved slowly to their vehicles, glancing back at them curiously. And Mason. Lance could feel his gaze boring into his back, stripping through him as hatred pressed against him.

Tommy Mason was going to be a problem. Lance could feel it.

"Sorry." Harmony straightened with an abrupt movement, pulling her hands from his chest and straightening her shoulders as she stared up at him defiantly.

His hands still held hers. Turning them over, he looked down at her reddened skin and knew that the mating heat was taking its toll.

She had touched another man. The hormonal forces inside her didn't differentiate between touches. It was showing her, warning her, that no other male's touch would do.

"I didn't think about this," he whispered as he lifted her hands to his lips and placed a kiss in the center.

She inhaled roughly as Lance felt arousal tearing through him. Dammit, wrong place. Definitely the wrong place for this.

"Let's get those reports written so we can head home."
He released her slowly. "We can check in on Liza and Jaime
at the hospital if you want to, when we're finished."

She shook her head firmly as she ducked away from him
and slid into the Raider.

"It's better if we don't," she finally whispered. "Better for
all of us."

As they drove to the department, Lance kept his window
down a bare inch, allowing the winds to move through the
vehicle, to whisper at his ear. Warnings. Danger. Pain. And
Tommy Mason's name.

He pulled into the parking lot of the Sheriff's Department and sighed wearily before leaving the vehicle, staying
close to Harmony as they moved up the steps toward the entrance.

Inside, a crowd milled within the reception area, which
wasn't that unusual on a Friday night. The State Police cruisers were parked at the curb, which meant Steven and his
partner, Lyle, were booking Mason.

Following Harmony, he stepped into mayhem. With no
warning, no whisper of the wind to guide him, he came face-
to-face with Reverend H. R. Alonzo.

"Sheriff Jacobs, your actions tonight border on the crimi-
nal." Alonzo stood with perhaps half a dozen of his society
members backing him as deputies looked on warily.

Harmony tried to move to the side, to skirt the crowd and
escape the coming confrontation. Until one of the larger men
stepped in front of her, his hand reaching out to grip her arm.

Harmony hissed. A furious feline sound of anger as she
bared her teeth and jerked back from him.

"Alonzo, what the hell are you doing here?" Lance
grabbed Harmony's arm before it could go for her knife, and
pushed her behind him.

"You can't save her." Righteous indignation flushed the

reverend's heavy jowls as his pale blue eyes burned with fanaticism. "We saw what she did to that poor man the State Police just brought in. The brutality of her attack was uncalled for."

Lance stared back at him coldly. Brutality, his ass.

"If you have a complaint to file, come back in the morning," he snapped. "Until then, get the hell out of my way."

"Do you think you can force these animals on God-fearing people." Alonzo's voice rose, the strident question posed in a sermonizing tone that grated on Lance's nerves.

Behind him, he could feel Harmony watching, waiting. The air began to hum with danger then.

"Alonzo, it's too damned late for this," Lance growled as he gripped Harmony's arm and began to move around the crowd. They shifted with him as their voices began to rise in volume.

"Since when do we cater to animals, Sheriff?" one woman's voice rang out. "It's bad enough we have that cousin of yours consorting with those creatures and messing up our town."

He swung his gaze to one of the matrons of the city, a prudish, troublemaking old busybody who protested everything under the sun. He should have known she would be here.

"Take it up with the City Council, Matilda," he snapped. "Not here."

"He's as ensnared by the creature as his cousin is to her own pet," Alonzo cried out. "Abominations are what they are. It's time to cast them out of this God-fearing town . . ."

"David, clear this place out!" Lance snarled at the deputies watching in indecision, as he began to push his way through the crowd, tugging Harmony along with him.

A second later she was torn from him. Turning, Lance watched in fury as a heavyset male attempted to twist her arm, to force her to cower. Deputies were rushing to the confrontation, but before they could push through the crowd, Harmony turned, twisted and within a breath had the much larger man on his back, her gun lodged beneath his chin.

Lance was thanking God it wasn't the knife.

"You have just assaulted an officer of the law." Her smile was smug, despite the edge of pain in her gaze. "It is with great personal pleasure that I inform you that you are under arrest."

"Get these people out of here," Lance yelled to a deputy as he turned to Alonzo's triumphant expression.

"Your society member just assaulted one of my deputies," he informed him furiously. "As the leader of this little get-together, maybe I should arrest you while I'm at it."

Lance could feel the rage building inside him as he forced himself not to plant his fist in the reverend's gloating, overblown face.

"My lawyer will be here in the morning," Alonzo assured him as the rest of the crowd began to move toward the door. "Don't worry, Sheriff, I'll make certain I do God's work, with or without your help."

"God's work?" Harmony was breathing roughly as she came to her feet, turning her attacker over to the deputies as she rushed for the reverend. "Let me show you—"

"Harmony," Lance snapped, turning on her quickly. "You have reports."

She stopped in her tracks, the tone of his voice causing her to hesitate, before her eyes narrowed and her gaze focused over his shoulder.

"Now," he reminded her firmly.

He could see the tension shuddering through her body and knew the pain was beginning to build inside her. Two men in one night that she had been forced to protect herself or others against.

Her lips thinned before the upper curve curled menacingly.

"Reports," she said slowly, her eyes never leaving Alonzo.
"Of course, Sheriff. Just let me get on that. I can play later."
The muttered threat wasn't lost on him or Alonzo.

"Only animals react in such a way . . ."

Before Lance could stop himself his fist was bunched in
the material of the stiff shirt the reverend wore as he lifted
the other man to his tiptoes.

"Get the hell out of my department," he snarled. "And
while you're talking to your lawyers, tell them to expect a
call from the county prosecutor as well."

Lance pushed him toward the door, hating the fury rising
inside him. He had fought for calm all his life, fought to find
that balance inside himself that Harmony had yet to learn.
But there were people, such as Reverend Alonzo, who could
disrupt it every time.

Alonzo jerked back and straightened his shirt with a huff
as his bulbous nose twitched in anger.

"You haven't seen the last of me, Sheriff. It's my duty to
make certain these creatures don't infect us all. And I will
see my duty through. No matter the obstacles. I have sworn
my duty to God—"

"And I'm sure he thinks about as much of it as I do,"
Lance growled. "Now, get the hell out of here."

Turning, he waved Lenny toward the reverend.

"Make sure he finds the door. Fast," he ordered the
deputy as he stalked to his office. "And make certain he
doesn't return."

Lance slammed the door behind him before stalking
across the room to where Harmony was rubbing her hands
together, her expression frantic.

"My hands are freezing." She stared up at him in distress.
"Or burning. I can't make it stop."

Harmony didn't know whether to laugh or to cry. What had been merely uncomfortable, irritating, before was now becoming strident. The cold burn in her hands and along the front of her body felt blistering. Especially between her thighs, where she had been forced to straddle the two men.

As Lance gripped her hands, she expected another of those tender kisses in the centers of her palms. It had helped before. Instead, he pushed her hands beneath the loose tail of his shirt as he gripped her head with his free hand.

And he kissed her.

He devoured her.

His lips plundered her own with deep, drugging kisses as his tongue slipped and slid against hers. Harmony moaned in overwhelming relief and hunger as the heavy, swollen sensation of the glands beneath her tongue began to ease. The sweet taste of it fired her senses further, sensitized her flesh, but nothing could have made her need Lance more than she already did.

Adrenaline pumped through her body; her greatest weakness was that surging excitement. Coming down from it normally filled her with depression, with a need for the human comfort she had always denied herself. She wasn't depressed now though. She was desperate. Hungry.

Her hand tore at the small snaps on his shirt, flipping the edges apart before her arms curled around his neck. The silk of his hair was a comfort against her palms, but the heat of his body was a fire in winter, warming all the cold lonely places inside her.

And she needed more of him. Before she completely understood exactly what she was doing, she was trying to climb his body. Her thighs wrapped around his as she pressed her aching pussy into the wedge of his cock, rubbing against him, moaning in exquisite pleasure as his hands gripped the cheeks of her ass and held her to him as they ate at each other's lips.

The kisses were intoxicating, fiery. Harmony felt the cold burn beneath her flesh retreating as they became deeper, hungrier.

"Goddamned office isn't the place for this." Lance tore his lips from hers as he moved, his voice husky, lusty.

Harmony gasped as he lowered them to the small couch across the room. With her legs wrapped around his hips and his body now coming over hers, the press of his cock against her sensitive flesh was firmer, more heated.

"Oh, I like that." She shifted beneath him, her hips stroking over the hard, jeans-covered erection.

"I bet you do." The half laugh, half grunt had a small smile tugging at her lips. "We're going to keep fucking in my office, I'm going to end up fired."

"I'll protect you." She panted as his head lowered, his lips moving to her neck. "Tell them I held a gun to your head . . . Oh God. Lance . . ." His hands slid beneath her top, cupping her breasts with firm, demanding fingers as his teeth raked over her neck.

"Like that?" He nipped at her neck, then soothed the little pleasure-pain with his tongue.

"Oh, I like," she moaned, arching closer to him, gasping as he gripped her nipples in his thumbs and forefingers and rolled them deliciously. "I like that too."

She was panting, drunk with pleasure. She had held herself back from him despite the demands of her body, and she realized then that it was only making the need grow.

"God, you taste good." He came back to her lips, covering them, taking them both on a mindless journey of pleasure as Harmony writhed beneath him.

"Lance, I need more." She pressed her hips closer as his lips moved back to her neck, then lower to her collarbone. "I need more now."

"In a minute. One taste at a time," he growled as she

arched her back, feeling his lips moving over the upper curves of her breasts that her snug shirt revealed.

"More. Now . . ."

She tossed her head, turning it to the side as her eyes widened in shock. Jonas stepped into the office, closing the door as he stared back at them mockingly.

"This isn't my night," she whispered as Lance paused, his head turning as well. "Do you think we could just ignore him?"

That brought a frown to Jonas's dark face, but a chuckle from Lance.

"He'll get testy," he told her with a sigh before moving to kiss her quickly on the lips.

She caught his head, intending to hold him to her for just a second more. A second lengthened, his moan dulled her senses, and she nearly forgot that they had company of the worst sort.

"Hellion." Lance moved back before she could stop him, though his smile was frankly approving as he gripped her arms and pulled her to her feet. "Go get those reports written. I'll take care of this."

"What's there to take care of?" She straightened her shirt as she stared back at her brother.

"I can see she hasn't changed much," Jonas stated as his lips quirked in amusement. "And from the report I heard from the society members outside, she hasn't gotten any slower."

"Actually I have," she drawled. "A week ago I wouldn't have hesitated to pull the trigger."

"Reports, Harmony." Lance caught her eye, the warning in his gaze determined as he resnapped his shirt.

"Fine. Reports." She straightened her shirt again. "I swear, I never had to write a report when I killed the bastards. Slice their throats and walk away. No paperwork, no

hassle. Unless you have a brother determined to kill you."
She smiled snidely back at Jonas.

He inclined his head in acknowledgment as she walked
from the room. Snarling silently, she made her way to the
desk and plopped into the hard wood seat before finding the
papers she needed. Stupid reports. Assassins didn't file reports. This was ridiculous.

✦   ✦   ✦

"How can I help you, Jonas?" Lance waved him to a chair
before moving behind the desk and taking his own.

His body was humming with lust; the need to push the
Breed out the door and finish what had begun on that sofa
was nearly overwhelming.

Jonas took his seat, his expression as coldly mocking as
ever. There was something about Jonas that both repelled
and drew a person. It was there in those quicksilver eyes—a
ruthlessness, a sense of purpose that you were never quite
certain you could trust.

Lance knew he couldn't be trusted.

"Is she settling in okay?" Jonas leaned back in his chair,
his expression curious.

"She's doing fine." Lance nodded. "But I have a feeling
that's not exactly why you're here at . . ." He looked at the
clock. "One o'clock in the morning."

"I was passing through." Jonas shrugged. "I've been at
Megan and Braden's this evening. Braden told me you had
changed your schedule so I thought I'd drop by."

That was interesting. He had a feeling Jonas was never
curious about anything; he always had an agenda.

"Cut the shit, Jonas," he growled. "Drop your little bomb
and head on out. It doesn't take Harmony that damned long
to write her reports, and I have a feeling that for the time being, you two are better off separated."

Jonas's lips quirked.

"In all seriousness, as I said, I merely stopped by to see how she was doing . . ."

"Or to see if she had conceived yet?" Lance leaned forward as he lowered his voice. "Braden mentioned once that a Breed can smell new life. Were you curious enough to check and see if you had managed to defeat her?"

Jonas stared at him silently.

Lance shook his head wearily as he leaned back in his chair.

"I'm not a stupid man, Jonas. What do you want from her? You always have a reason for everything you do. You knew when you brought her here what would happen. Just as you knew the chances for early conception if she didn't get the hormonal supplement in time. Is she pregnant?"

Jonas's face was devoid of expression by the time Lance finished.

"What do you want from her, Jonas?" he asked him, his voice grating. "What put her in a situation you could almost bet she would fail within if your intent was to save her?"

That bothered him. Jonas was her brother; his main concern should have been in making certain she succeeded, not in making it as hard for her as possible.

"Is she learning how to work within the law for a change?" Jonas asked, rather than answering the question.

"Perfectly," Lance snapped. "Now answer the question. What do you want from her?"

Jonas stared back at him silently.

Lance shook his head. "Forget it. I'll figure it out eventually. And if I find out you're putting her in harm's way, I'll make you pay. Breed or not. You will pay, Jonas."

Jonas had played with Megan and her loyalties the year before, attempting to blame Lance for the leak in the office, to force her into throwing herself into the nightmare of emotions caused by two Breed deaths. Megan's abilities to pick up on their emotions as they died had been important in the investigation to find their murderer. How he had attempted to maneuver her hadn't sat well with Lance, or Megan's then lover, Braden.

"I can see checking up on her is a useless endeavor then." Jonas rose to his feet, his expression forbidding as their gazes clashed. "Keep a leash on her, Lance. I'd hate to have to give her over to Breed Law if she crosses the line again."

Lance came slowly to his feet. "And I'd hate to have to kill you if you tried, Jonas," he answered coldly, tensing at the threat implied in the other man's voice. "Make no mistake, your games will get you killed if they involve Harmony much more. Law or no law, what's mine stays mine."

✦ CHAPTER 14 ✦

Make no mistake, your games will get you killed if they involve Harmony much more. Law or no law, what's mine stays mine.

Lance and Jonas's conversation hadn't been too hard for her to keep up with while she typed out her report. Lance's final warning had shocked her though, and held her in the little office until Jonas left.

His defense of her made no sense to her. He knew what she was. He had read her file. How could he defend her so easily?

"You know, I really did kill all those people in my file," she stated as they entered his home several hours later.

Standing by the closed door, she watched as he toed his boots off, his dark blue eyes staring back into hers calmly.

"I know that, Harmony." He nodded as he straightened, standing before her, the lack of scorn or judgment in his expression confusing her further.

"I killed them in cold blood," she added. "I hunted them. Tracked them. And I felt their blood flow over my fingers. And I don't regret it, Lance."

"I know you don't." His expression was somber.

"How can you just accept it?" she whispered. "You're a sheriff. You deal in the law, you said it yourself. How can you claim me so easily?"

It made no sense. She could barely stand herself.

"A child has no defenses," he said then. "What was done to you as a child was inexcusable. How you've dealt with that as an adult is more than forgivable. But you know as well as I do that the time for it has come to an end. In ways, Jonas is right. To survive, you're going to have to learn how to work within the system."

"A system that lets monsters roam free?" she sneered as her chest tightened painfully. "Do you know what they did to those children, Lance? Do you have any idea . . . ?"

"Do you think you can save them all, Harmony?" He stared back at her remorselessly. "Every life you've taken has taken a piece of your soul. I held you while you slept, after Jonas brought you to the office. I saw the tears you shed and heard the pain you felt. Do you think you're not killing yourself like this?"

She flinched. She had known there was a chance she had dreamed, but he had never mentioned it, never let her guess.

"I'm just one person," she whispered. "A creation, that's all."

"No, dammit, that's not all you are, Harmony," he bit out, his hands gripping her upper arms as he gave her a little shake. "Look at yourself, baby. You don't sleep, you barely eat. You run on nerves and sheer gut stubbornness alone. How much longer can you do that? How much longer before it catches up with you and you mess up? How much longer do you think you can avoid the repercussions of it? You will be caught. You will be arrested. And you will die."

Harmony inhaled roughly, seeing the pain in his eyes, the determination in his face to keep that from happening.

"They are children," she cried out before she could stop herself. "Helpless. Dear God, Lance—"

"Work within the law, Harmony," he ground out. "You're smart, and you're intuitive as hell. Use those abilities to find the proof and bring them to justice. Justice does work, baby. When you use the law to your advantage."

"While children are dying."

"While you're alive to put as many of them as possible behind bars," he yelled back at her. "For God's sake, what good are you going to do a single child if you're dead?"

"I save as many as I can." She shook her head desperately.

"Bullshit!" He released her as quickly as he had grabbed her. "You know yourself that this isn't working, Harmony. It's destroying you."

"I don't know what else to do," she cried out furiously. "I can't stand it, Lance. I can't stand to see the pain in the eyes of children who have been abused. I can't stand knowing I was created and used to kill even one of the people who could have saved them."

She slapped her hand to her mouth, turning away from him as comprehension flooded his expression.

"The kills you made as a child," he said behind her. "You're still trying to make up for them, aren't you?"

Her chest was so tight with pain she could barely breathe. A hard chill wracked her body and she could feel the cold icing in her soul.

"The assassinations I performed as a child, each victim fought for children and their rights," she whispered, shaking her head at the futility of even remembering. "Each one of them. They were exemplary parents, and they fought for the children who had no parents worthy of the name."

"And you think this is how they would want you to repay the fight they took on?" His arms came around her, as though he knew the dark, cold places that tormented her. "If you knew anything of their lives, then you know it's not."

Harmony fought to control her breathing, to control the dampness that flooded her eyes. She was tired, strung out from exhaustion and arousal and emotions that just didn't make sense to her anymore.

"They died for their beliefs," she whispered. "They suspected the Council was creating us. Information had been smuggled from the labs several times and it was brought to their attention. Before they could save any of us, they were killed. I killed them."

She tried to jerk away from him, tried to put distance between herself and the man weakening her from the inside out.

"You were lied to and you were used," he whispered at her ear. "You know that as well as I do. Just as you know that you were killing yourself from the inside out over the blood you were shedding before Jonas caught you. If you hadn't been, he would have never found you."

"That's not true . . ."

"It is true, baby." He held onto her firmly. "That's why you've gone along with this game he's playing. Keeping whatever it is that he wants hidden and trying to atone for the deaths. You know as well as I do, that you'd had enough."

Had she? Had she somehow let Jonas capture her?

"What do you have, Harmony, that Jonas wants? What is making him so desperate that he'll sacrifice you for it?"

Harmony knew exactly what Jonas was after, what she could never let him have: the information she had stolen from the labs the day she escaped. The last remaining proof that as of ten years ago, the first Feline Breed, created nearly a century before, still lived.

"Jonas wants revenge." It was partially the truth. "Revenge for his mother's death."

"Jonas is a smart man." He let her go slowly, allowing her

to turn and face him once again. "And he's smart enough to
know the truth by now. He can read as well as I can, and the
reports from the other labs and scientists on Dr. LaRue were
pretty conclusive. Now, one more time, what does Jonas
want from you?"

She stared around the dimly lit entryway, the shadowed
living room and kitchen as she swallowed tightly.

"I can't tell you," she whispered almost soundlessly.

He sighed deeply as he shook his head. "I'm too tired for
this, Harmony. When you're ready to talk, let me know. But
do us both a favor and do it while I can help you."

It had never been her way to confide to anyone. Even
Dane, the man who had saved her countless times over, and
had been her first lover, didn't know the truth.

Harmony stepped into the shower, adjusted the spray then
leaned her forehead against the shower wall, barely feeling
the heat of the water as it beat over her skin. But she felt her
tears as the silent sobs shook her body with brutal intensity.

Jonas would see her dead before it was over. No matter
what Lance believed, Jonas did blame her for their mother's
death. Madame LaRue had been a monster. Within the papers Harmony had hidden were the orders to kill each Breed
in the labs rather than risk their discovery. It was the reason
she had killed Madame as well as the five scientists under
her, before escaping.

The proof she held would have vindicated her, but the
cost was too high. She couldn't betray others to save herself. If she did, then she was no better than those who had
created her.

The injustice of it had never really slapped her until now.
Something about this mating with Lance had changed her.
Or perhaps awakened her. She wasn't certain which. The
longer she spent with him, the weaker she became, the more
she needed him.

As she wrapped her arms around her chest, fighting to hold back her sobs, she realized that for the first time in her life, there was something she couldn't make herself walk away from, and it was very likely to get them both killed. And that terrified her. Lance deserved more; he deserved better than a woman whose hands were forever stained by the blood of innocent deaths.

"Harmony."

She gasped as Lance's voice washed over her, then his arms surrounded her. She pushed against his hard, naked chest, fighting to pull herself together, to escape long enough to find her strength again.

"You're killing me," he whispered at her ear. "I hear your cries even when you aren't shedding the tears. But the pain that echoes from your tears is breaking my heart."

◆　　◆　　◆

Lance stared into her shocked eyes as she lifted her head. Brilliant neon green, awash with her tears, shadowed with the pain destroying her. Destroying him. The air around him was heavy with her need, physical as well as emotional, and pulled at him as nothing else could.

Clasping her head between his hands, he ran his thumbs over her cheeks.

"I can't stop." She jerked as another sob tore through her. "Oh God, Lance, what's wrong with me? I don't cry. Death doesn't cry."

"Death died ten years ago," he whispered as he lowered his lips to hers. "Don't you know that, baby? She's gone. There's just Harmony now."

He wondered if she even understood why she had chosen the name she had. Harmony. Peace. A blending of what she was and what she needed to be. The part of her that fought to make sense of her world and to fit into it.

"My sweet little kitten," he whispered, brushing his lips over hers as he held her tear-filled gaze. "You keep trying to run from this and you keep hiding. Those scientists may have created your body, but the earth gave you life. A perfect, beautiful soul created for me alone. Just as I was created for you. We're children of this earth, Harmony. You can't escape that, any more than I can. Not any longer."

He knew that running from the gift he had to hear the whispers in the wind wasn't going to work. Her life and her future were going to depend on his ability to protect her. Not so much physically as the protection of her heart, her soul. There was too much coming together inside his mind, too many coincidences adding up and he knew the coming days would mean her life, or her death.

The wind whispered of the danger to her. He heard her name in its sighs, the keening cry of her destruction, and felt the caress of danger at the back of his neck. And the knowledge that her soul had been bonded to his for a reason. She was the other part of him. The heart he had searched for for so many years.

"I'm an abomination," she whispered tearfully. "A killer."

He lifted his head, smoothing his thumb over her lips.

"You're my mate. My soul. Am I a killer, Harmony? Would the earth give me a killer for my mate?"

His lips took hers again, feeling her soften against him, tasting the heat and seductive taste of her hunger.

Her fingers slid slowly into his hair, tangling into the strands until they pulled at his scalp with a burning bite.

Lance bit at her lips in retaliation, only to take her frustrated growl into his mouth as he deepened the kiss and pressed her against the shower wall. His hands slid into the damp strands of her hair, holding her close, tugging at her scalp as she pulled at his. The effect was instantaneous.

A little *rawr* left her lips as she arched close to him, the bare mound of her pussy against his thigh as he slid it between her legs.

She was slick and hot, the juices of her arousal burning hot against his flesh.

"Sweet little kitten," he repeated, pulling back from her kiss and staring into her brilliant eyes.

"Hurry," she whispered, her swollen lips parted as she panted for breath. "I need you."

"I need you. Your touch. Your sweet heat. The taste of you. Let me have you, Harmony. All of you."

Harmony stared back at him, weakening against his touch. It wasn't just the pleasure, it was the emotion in his eyes, in his expression. She felt her own defenses disintegrating. If he took her as he wanted to, then she would never be able to deny him again.

"Trust me, Harmony." His lips touched hers again, firm and heated, parting them, stroking inside with a gentle lap of his tongue.

"I'm frightened, Lance." The words fell unbidden from her lips. "If you take all of me, what will be left when you no longer want me?"

He stared back at her, shock reflected in his dark eyes.

"No longer want you, baby?" he whispered then. "Don't you know I've dreamed of you? Heard your name whispered at my ear by the air that sustains us, and dreamed of your kiss. Sweet Harmony, I would die without you."

His hands ran up her arms, gripping her hands and removing her fingers from his hair.

"I could use the cuffs again," he whispered wickedly, the erotic rasp of his voice sending shivers racing down her spine. "I could dry you slow and easy and take you to my bed, restrain you, leave you helpless against my touch."

And he would use that helplessness. He would play it. He would drive her insane with her own pleasure.

The shower shut down, and moments later she was standing before him as he ran a thick, fluffy towel over her body.

"I don't need the cuffs."

Lance paused as he knelt before her, a second later running the towel over one leg then the next.

"What do you need?" His voice was hoarse as he knelt before her, staring back at her. "Tell me what you need to give yourself to me, Harmony."

Her lips trembled as she felt the tears falling from her eyes once again.

"Hold me," she whispered. "Please, just hold me."

The clash of emotions inside her were destroying her. The cold places in her soul seemed icy, while the heat of Lance's body promised warmth and ease.

She wanted to touch him; she needed to. As Lance laid her back in his big bed, rising over her, his lips taking hers, Harmony was helpless against the need to feel his flesh, his warmth. Her hands moved over his chest, his shoulders. She moaned at the fiery heat of his body and writhed against him, desperate to get closer.

With every drugging kiss, every stroke of his calloused hands over her flesh, Harmony felt another part of her soul surrender to him.

"You go to my head faster than liquor," he groaned as his lips trailed across her jaw, then to her neck. "And have I mentioned how much I love the feel of your skin?"

Harmony jerked in response as he cupped a breast, gripping a tight nipple between his thumb and forefinger as he began to work it gently.

Flames shot from her nipple to her clit—a hard burst of heat that clenched her stomach and threatened to steal her breath.

"Like that, baby?" His lips moved to the tight point. "Let's see how much you like this."

His fingers moved as his mouth replaced them, drawing the elongated bud in as his hand trailed over her stomach.

Her legs parted for his questing fingers as her fingers tightened in his hair, holding his lips to her breast as she arched beneath him. She fought to breathe, to hold on to her senses just a little while longer, to enjoy each touch of his fingers, lips and tongue against her flesh.

She was winning the war until his fingers parted the folds of her pussy and his thumb rasped around the throbbing bud of her clit.

"God yes," she moaned, opening her thighs farther. "Please. Please . . ."

As his thumb tormented her, his fingers moved lower, sliding in the slick juices that had gathered on her bare flesh, until they pressed against the tender opening of her vagina.

Sensation exploded around her; pleasure too close to ecstasy rocked through her being. She was no longer cold, she was burning. Flames licked from her pussy to her clit, clenched her womb and then sped through the rest of her body.

As his teeth tormented her nipple, his fingers played a torturous game of seduction between her thighs. She was panting, her hips arching as ragged cries tore from her throat.

A second later she felt his fingers enter her. Two, pressed closed together, drove into the aching, saturated depths of her pussy.

Harmony screamed out her pleasure as her knees bent and she fought for release.

"Not yet, baby," he growled, his lips moving from her breast to lick a path of fire along her belly. "First, I get to taste that sweet, soft pussy. Have I mentioned how hungry I've been for the taste of you?"

"I can't stand it." She shook her head weakly, fighting to

hold on to him as he gripped her hands and pressed them to the bed.

"Stay there." He nipped at her abdomen. "Let me love you, Harmony. Let me taste every sweet inch of this perfect body."

Harmony watched as Lance moved between her thighs, his hands pressing her knees farther apart as he stared back at her. Brilliant dark blue eyes gleamed with male lust as he licked his lips a second before his head lowered.

Flickering pinpoints of agonizing pleasure rushed through her as his tongue became an erotic whip. It lashed over her violently sensitive flesh, teased, prodded, licked and tasted every swollen inch of her pussy.

His fingers were demons. Inside the gripping depths of her vagina his fingers probed, the tips curling to reach a spot that had her hips arching from the bed and a strangled scream ripping from her throat.

Not that it did her any good. He continued to torment her, devouring her in a sensual feast that soon had her begging, crying for completion.

"I love the taste of you," he crooned as his finger pressed firmly into the spot that seemed to have a direct link to her clit. It sent flares of sensation racing through the little bud as she gasped, fighting to breathe amid the pleasure tearing through her.

"You still taste like honeysuckle," he groaned. "And wild roses."

"Please, God. Lance I can't . . ." She cried out as his fingers moved again, straightening, sliding nearly free then plunging inside her in one hard, fast stroke as his tongue returned to her clit.

Shuddering waves of near orgasm raced through her nervous system, stealing her breath and leaving her hanging on a precipice of such intense sensation that she wondered if she would ever survive.

"You're so sweet and tight," he whispered before licking around her clit once more. "You're gripping my fingers like a fist. Feel how tight you are, baby. Why, it's all I can do to keep from coming when I get my cock inside you."

His fingers retreated, then in one slow, delicious movement slid inside her again. Harmony could feel the sensitive tissue parting for him, milking at him as the sensual impalement left her shaking in her need for release.

"Again?" he whispered.

This time, when his fingers entered her, his lips covered her clit and began to suckle it erotically. Strong, heavy thrusts of his fingers inside her, a twist of his wrist, the rasp of calloused fingertips against nerve endings flaming for his touch, and she erupted.

She screamed his name. She heard herself scream his name as her orgasm exploded inside her with devastating results. Her thighs gripped his head as her pussy gripped his fingers, her internal muscles spasming violently as the final barrier shielding her soul was washed away.

Vulnerable. Defenseless. Yet as Lance began to soothe her, his fingers pulling free of her, his lips pressing gently to her thighs, her stomach, it wasn't the weakness she felt.

For the first time she felt complete.

She watched through drowsy eyes as he came to his knees, staring down at her, his expression heavy with hunger and need, and she realized he was just as defenseless against her. He had opened himself to her from the start, and she hadn't even realized it.

"Beautiful," he whispered as he positioned the thrusting, heavy erection between the folds of her pussy. "My sweet beautiful little kitten."

Harmony arched to him as he began to work his cock inside her. Each stroke drove him deeper into the clenching muscles as his hands moved along her thighs, her waist. Finally, when he was buried to the hilt, he rose over her and allowed her arms to wrap around him.

"I'm warm," she gasped then, realizing that the bone-deep cold she had known for so long was gone.

"Very warm," he whispered at her ear, his voice raspy, almost agonized as his hips began to move. "Sweet baby, so fucking warm we're going to burn the house down."

Harmony undulated against him as he paused then, settling closer against her body as he pressed his lips at her neck. Slowly, the stretching burn in her pussy eased as her muscles adapted to the penetration. She could feel him, every inch of his cock throbbing inside her, stretching her until hidden nerve endings were exposed and deliciously caressed.

"Feel us together, Harmony," he whispered. "Do you really want to escape this?"

He didn't give her time to answer him. Harmony bit back another strangled cry as he began to move. Long, slow strokes of his cock impaled her, burned her as she began to writhe beneath him.

She needed more. He was going too slow, torturing her with a slow, even rhythm that stroked her higher yet never triggered the orgasm burning just out of reach.

"God, you're so tight. So fucking sweet," he groaned at her ear. "You make me fly, Harmony."

He made her cry. She fought back her tears as the pleasure began to spiral. Each stroke inside her, each burrowing impalement of his cock stretching her, pushing her higher, stole another part of her soul.

It wasn't just his touch. It wasn't just his acceptance. It was the air heavy with hunger, ripe with emotion. It was feeling his warmth, the very essence of him wrapping around her.

"You steal my soul," she gasped, her nails biting into his shoulders as he paused, his head lifting as he stared down at her.

His gaze was drowsy, dark with sensual heat.

"Where do I end and you begin?" Her whispered cry shocked her; the realization that he owned so much of her would have terrified her if it didn't feel so damned right.

Lance grimaced, baring his teeth a second before his lips lowered to hers. "We begin together, baby. Together. With no end."

His lips covered hers and reality receded. His hips began to pump hard and fast, the brutal pleasure in each stroke tearing through her.

Her cries filled the night as he whispered erotic, sinful words against her lips.

"Fuck me, baby . . . There, sweetheart, hold me tight right there . . . Fuck, you're hot. So fucking hot."

Lance gripped her hip with one hand, her hair with the other, as his lips parted hers, driving his tongue deep as he began to fuck her desperately. Moving. Stroking. Sending her flying as she exploded.

She flew with him. Brilliant explosions of light and ecstasy tore through her as she felt him jerk against her. Her pussy clenched tight on him, holding him deep, convulsing around the hard length of his spurting cock as she screamed out her pleasure.

There. Ecstasy. Rapture. And a merging. She felt a part of him merge with her, deep inside her very spirit, and in that moment, she knew freedom wouldn't come in leaving Lance. Leaving Lance would destroy her.

"I wanted to save Jonas. She was going to kill him."

Drowsy, immeasurably sad, Harmony spoke into the predawn light that filtered through the crack in the dark curtains of the room.

Lance held her close against his chest, his chin resting against her head, his arms wrapped around her, pressing her back against his chest and abdomen.

"Who was going to kill him, Harmony?"

"Jonas," she whispered after a long pause. "Madame LaRue gave birth to him. She cuddled him as a babe and as a toddler. He was given the best of everything the labs could provide, but he was kind. He would brush my hair when he returned from a mission. LaRue always ordered my tests while he was gone. She didn't want him to know the extent of her cruelty. He believed the other scientists controlled her, forced her to the acts she committed in the name of science."

He would brush her hair. It sounded simple, a small enough gesture, but Lance heard the reverence in her voice when she said it. "When Jonas captured me last month, his scientist Elyiana had to take blood and swabs. I hate that. I hate the needles poking into me. He came to my cell a while later. He still had the brush he used when I was at the labs. And he brushed my hair."

Her voice was thick with emotion, and Lance had to blink to force back the rush of moisture as he let her talk. The tone of her voice, reflective, husky, tore at his soul.

"Madame LaRue was going to kill him." Her hands tightened on his arms. "All but a few of us were ordered to die. The other Breeds in that room, the ones I killed, they had been betraying Jonas for months as he planned an escape for all of us. Even Madame." A small shudder raced through her body. "He was her personal experiment, and he could never see it. I was her child as well, but only Jonas knew peace within those labs. Only he knew gentleness. And I wanted to preserve the kindness I saw in him. The memory of a mother. Such memories are precious, aren't they?"

"You wanted to protect him," he whispered. "Because you loved him."

Her breath caught as a silent sob shook her body.

"Within weeks, his personal guards, two Coyotes known for their viciousness, found me. He had sent them. Their final words to me were the message he sent. Rogues die. The last words he said as I ran from the room where I had killed his mother."

Lance swallowed tightly. God help him, he wanted nothing more than to tear Jonas apart. The bastard had no idea what he had done to the child who had risked her life for him.

"You have proof of what she was," he said then. He knew she did. "Why didn't you give it to him?"

She was silent for long moments. "There was so little that we had to hold onto." She inhaled roughly, her voice rasping on her tears. "We knew we were creations of man, rather than of God. That we were created to kill. But Jonas, he had a mother. He had gentle touches and soft words. He had something to dim the hatred and the pain, the brutality of our lives. And giving him the information wouldn't change anything."

She trembled again, her breathing jerky as she pressed tighter against him, and he felt her hunger for all the things she had mentioned. She had fought to protect Jonas's vision of a mother that was a monster because she had hungered so desperately for the illusion herself.

"I couldn't let her kill him," she whispered raggedly. "He brushed my hair . . ." He had given her the one bit of warmth and gentleness in a dark, horrific world.

Lance pulled her closer to him, tucking her in as tight as possible as he buried his face against her hair.

"And now, there's you," she whispered tearfully. "Honorable. Patient. What do I do, Lance, if you die because of me? If the monsters find you and destroy the life that burns so pure inside you?"

And what would he do without her?

"I'm a child of the earth," he told her softly, feeling her still against him. "The winds call to me, the very air around me whispers the secrets of others at my ear. It warns me of danger and it protects me when others would have seen me fall. It led me to that bar the night I met you. As I sat outside, wondering what the hell I was doing there, it whispered your name."

She turned to him slowly, staring up at him with tortured pale green eyes as he lifted himself on an elbow. He wanted to surround her. He wanted to wrap himself around her in such a way that she would never be alone again.

"You have something Jonas wants," he told her then. "I hear the knowledge of it each time I see Jonas, each time you mention his name. A secret or secrets that go far beyond the mother you share."

Lance watched as her face paled and fear filled her eyes.

"Jonas doesn't want revenge, Harmony. The only reason he's still alive is the fact that there's no true malice in him when he's around you. But he does want whatever you're hiding from him. And he wants it bad enough that he'll use you, or me, to get it."

She shook her head slowly as he watched her expression. It went from fear to confusion, her eyes shadowing as she frowned back at him.

"He can't know what I have," she said. "No one knew but the scientists in that office, and I killed them."

"Knew what, Harmony?"

"That the first Breed created still lives." Her voice lowered until it was no more than a breath of sound.

◆   ◆   ◆

Unknown secrets. What came before and still is. The words whispered at his ear, breathed across his mind.

"There's more." Lance ran his hand comfortingly down her arm as she trembled beneath him again. "But considering it's Jonas, only God knows what he wants."

"And if we can't afford to wait to learn what he's after?"

Lance felt her fear then.

"Alonzo knew me as Death, when I was younger. If he recognizes me now, my cover is blown. If that happens, every Coyote still alive and working with the Council will be after me. The price on my head is very high."

God, could it get much worse?

"What was he doing there? How was he involved?" Lance asked.

"I'm not sure what role he played." She sighed. "But he was very important to Madame LaRue, and I know he provided vast amounts of money toward the Breed project."

"Do you have proof Alonzo was part of the Council?" He would love to see the good reverend taken down.

She shook her head. "I don't have that proof. But he was at the lab several times and met with Madame and my trainer. If he recognizes me, Lance . . ."

"Then we'll have to make certain Alonzo doesn't find out." He could feel that danger intensifying around them then, and heard the whisper of relief at his ear, even as the air warned of the danger Alonzo could represent. He didn't know who Harmony was, and that was all that mattered at this point.

A small smile tipped her lips. "Are you listening to the winds?"

He smoothed her hair back from her cheek. "Finally," he acknowledged ruefully. "Grandfather would be pleased with me."

"The Council searched for women who had gifts such as yours," she said. "They were perceived as the perfect incubators for the implanted Breed embryos. It was believed that the women who carried the creations added an element to the final makeup of the Breed. Psychic power is one of the elements they believed could be transferred in such ways."

Embryos and creations. Never babes or children. God help him, but the rage burning in him against those who had scarred her soul from birth terrified him.

He had known that many psychics and Native American women were taken, held captive until the children they were implanted with were born, then released. The women they used in such ways had come from all over the world, and Jonas knew they had searched heavily for psychics.

"I won't let you leave me," he finally said.

"How do I stay?"

He held himself still, silent, staring down at her as she reached up, running the tips of her fingers down his cheek.

"I've never had anyone," she whispered. "I knew better. I knew they would be used to capture me. They'll take you, they'll torture you, and they'll make certain I know. I would give my life for you, but all it would do is ease the pain you would experience because of me. You would die anyway."

A tear fell from her eyes, creating a silvery track down her cheek as her lips trembled.

Lance felt his chest jerk, felt the emotion that welled within him like a cruel fist, clenching around his heart. "We fight to survive. To love. What the earth wills will be, Harmony. Running won't change that. It won't save either of us."

Her face twisted in agony as she turned from him, huddling on her side, her body trembling as he pulled her close once again.

"You've fought to live," he said gently as he wrapped his body around her, feeling his heat flow to her, his soul easing around her. "Fight for us now, Harmony. You've fought for your life, now help me fight for our love."

Their love.

Harmony stared into the room, watching as pale fingers of dawn peeked from the sides of the dark curtains. Was that what she was feeling? Was that what she had been feeling all along? Was this why she couldn't walk away from him?

It wasn't her way to stay when she knew the danger outweighed the chances of escape. It wasn't her way to allow anyone to breach her inner defenses. But Lance had done just that—with the warmth of his body that flowed into her, the pleasure from his touch, the aching realization that Lance had been created for her.

A mating. And he had accepted that mating, accepted her as though he had known her all her life. Because the winds whispered to him.

"What do they say?" she asked. "The winds. What do they tell you about me?"

"That you're wild and incorrigible." A thread of amusement filled his voice.

Her lips kicked up in a grin as she turned back to him. "I'm serious."

"Seriously." His hand cupped her cheek while his thumb smoothed over her parted lips. "I hear your cries echo around me. I hear a whisper of strength and of need and sorrow. I hear your heart. Each time you've denied me I've heard your soul crying out for me. The wind doesn't speak in words, or in explanations. It speaks in laughter, a cry, a wailing denial or a whisper of strength. And I hear all that as the air flows around us, pulling me to you no matter how many times you've pushed me away."

He kissed her lips gently before rising to stare down at her once again.

"I don't know what to do." Her lips trembled as she fought to find a way to make him understand what she felt. But she didn't understand it herself.

"Just be you." He lay beside her again, pulling her against him and letting his warmth wrap around her. "Just be Harmony."

◆　　◆　　◆

That night patrol was destined to be boring. Lance was stuck at the office with paperwork and she was covering for one of the officers who had taken off for family concerns. The dark surrounded her, cocooned her, and left her with too much time to think.

Just be Harmony. Not for the first time, she wondered who Harmony was.

As she made her way through the quiet streets of the main section of Broken Butte, Harmony frowned at the thought.

She had always known who Death was; there was no question there. Death was vengeance. She was the shadow that slid through the night and brought justice to those the law had somehow missed.

She was dark, wrathful, cold and merciless. She didn't regret and she had no second thoughts. As she came to a stop at a red light, she frowned into the lamplit street. But who was Harmony?

She had taken the name as a lark. Harmony Lancaster. Harmony, because that was what was left in Death's wake. Lancaster was the name of the street where she had taken the last innocent life she had allowed the Council to foist on her.

That night was engraved on her memory, stamped into it with the force of a burning brand.

"Let me help you. I can, I can get you to safety." The woman had watched her with such compassion, such fierce determination that Harmony had almost believed it was true.

But her Trainer had warned her that the operative was a master at deceit. At fourteen, trained as Death, she had known only what the "proof" had given her. And that proof marked this woman as a vindictive peddler of juveniles. A woman who ripped innocent children from their homes and sold them to the highest bidder.

"Let me help you." A trembling hand had reached out to Death. "Let me get you to safety."

Death had struck. She gripped the woman's hand, using it as leverage, and let her knife answer for her. She had followed her Trainer's orders, but as she watched the woman crumple lifelessly to the ground, she knew she had shed innocent blood.

Harmony shook the memory from her mind before it could tear through her soul as it did each time she allowed it free. The woman she had killed had been a CIA agent investigating the shadowy group known as the Genetics Council. She had a husband and a child. She had been one of the good guys, and Death had taken her life.

As the light turned green, Harmony turned up another well-lit street, her gaze searching the shadows as she patrolled the quiet. Lights blazed from within the houses; some residents still sat on their porches enjoying the late evening air. The scent of barbecues drifted in the air, and the laughter of children.

This was what Lance fought for. The peace that echoed here, that drifted through the half-lowered windows and wrapped around her.

This was what the agent had fought for as well.

Shaking her head, she pulled onto Community Street. The full block held the community center, ball courts, a tennis court and a public pool that had closed for the night. The lights within the basketball court were still on though, as were the tennis courts', and both were in use.

She pulled the Raider to a stop as she watched the young men play, laughter and teasing insults drifting to her.

"Hey, man, that was just a sissy throw," one youth laughed as he caught the ball. "Let me show you how it's done."

He fumbled the ball, to the delight of his friends and the one who stole it from his hands.

"Man. That is so wrong." Laughter, happiness.

Death had no place here, but Harmony could feel the peace of it wrapping around her. She leaned against the steering wheel, watching the game, a smile pulling at her lips as the boys postured and groaned, grunted and playfully struggled as all young men do when challenging one another.

It wasn't much different than the young male cubs at the labs, she realized. There had been moments between training sessions when they were allowed to rest beneath the warmth of the sun as a gentle breeze played around them. And they had laughed, teased one another and tested their strength. And sometimes they hadn't been punished for it.

She sighed as she rested her chin against the hands that gripped the steering wheel. She had never played. She had never laughed and tested herself in such a teasing way.

"Unit four, is everything okay?" Lenny, the eagle eye watching the unit displays at the office, came over the communications link in the dash.

"Just watching a game, Lenny," she reported as she straightened in her seat. "The boys are out at the community court."

"They're too young for you, Deputy." Lance's teasing voice replaced Lenny's.

Harmony smiled, though she found she wanted to laugh.

"That's affirmative, Sheriff," she drawled, for once, refusing to fight the warmth rising inside her.

She couldn't fight him. She had known last night that her own personal battle to deny the bonding between them was over.

"I'm heading out," she reported. "So far everything's quiet. Is it ever *not* quiet?"

"Oh, we have the occasional fire, fistfight and rocking family dispute," Lance assured her. "They save most of them for the weekends though."

She shook her head. She had answered a call to an attempted burglary that turned out to be a raccoon, and a dispute between a would-be Lothario and the parents of the young girl he was courting. Not that there hadn't been trouble in other areas, just not in her area. Yet.

"I'm going to finish my round then head in. Reports." She grimaced at the paperwork waiting for her back at the office. "Maybe I should try meter maid tomorrow. I bet they don't fill out paperwork."

"You'd be surprised." Lance chuckled. "See you when you get in. Control out."

"Unit four out." She pulled the Raider back onto the street and completed her area before turning and heading back to the Sheriff's Department.

It had been a reasonably quiet night, so it didn't really

surprise her to see Dane step from the shadows at the side of the building as she moved from the Raider.

He leaned against the corner of the building, uncaring who might see him, his expression thoughtful as he watched her. For a moment she considered ignoring him. She should ignore him, she thought in frustration; she wasn't in the mood for him, or Jonas.

Narrowing her eyes, she stared around the parking lot before moving quickly toward the darker area where he awaited her.

"What are you doing here?" She stepped into the shadows, stilling immediately as she realized he hadn't come alone.

"It's time to pull you out, Harmony." His voice was dark, edged with dominance. "It's time to go."

She jerked back as he reached for her.

"Like hell," she hissed, her hand settling on the butt of her weapon as she kept him and Ryan, his partner, within sight. "I'm not going anywhere with you, Dane. I told you that."

"Even if it means your life?" he bit out. "Listen to me, Harmony, you don't want what's going to come down here. And I don't have time to break you out of a fucking cell again. Now, let's go before that sheriff of yours comes looking for you."

"What's coming down, Dane?" She moved when Ryan shifted as though to get behind her. "Ryan, stay where the hell you are. Don't make me fight you."

Both men stilled then. Ryan wasn't as tall as Dane, but he was muscular and quick. Short, dark brown hair framed his sun-darkened face, and pale blue eyes watched her carefully.

"You've never questioned me before," Dane mused. "When I've come to take you away from trouble, you've always followed me."

"I always understood the trouble you were taking me

away from. I'm not in any trouble yet, Dane." And he had always been there.

"It's coming, Harmony." He sighed. "You know it as well as I do."

"Then maybe you can tell me what to look for," she suggested softly. "And while you're at it, why have you always done it?"

"Done what?" His gaze narrowed on her thoughtfully.

"Why you've always gotten me out of trouble. How you've always known I was in trouble. How do you track me, Dane?"

His lips quirked slowly. "I'm intuitive."

"You're full of shit." She should have thought of it before. "How do you know?"

"Let's just say I have certain contacts." He finally shrugged. "Enough contacts to know that after that killing a few days ago, Alonzo is going to try to pin Death to your name."

"He has no proof."

"Harmony, you're risking your sheriff's life . . ."

"I can't leave him, Dane," she snapped. "You don't understand."

"Do you think I don't know you've mated the son of a bitch?" He snarled then. "For God's sake, Harmony. Why didn't you let me take you out when I tried the first time?"

"It was too late." She shook her head furiously. "And it doesn't matter now. I can't run anymore. I'm tired of running."

He stared at her silently, frustration marking his face as their gazes clashed.

"I don't want to force you to leave, Harmony." He sighed again. "But I will."

She stepped back. "Why?"

He grimaced tightly. "Isn't it enough that I care about

you?" he questioned roughly. "Watching you commit suicide is a pain in the ass."

"Not good enough." Her hand tightened on her weapon.

"Goddammit, it's going to be enough though."

She jumped to the side as he moved, placing herself clearly into the well-lit parking lot as he stilled in the shadows.

"It's not enough. Try to force me and you'll make an enemy of me, Dane. Don't do that. For both our sakes." Turning, she stalked to the entrance, her heart leaping to her throat as Lance stepped from the wide doors, his hand on the weapon at his side, his body tense, prepared.

She could smell the danger surrounding him, the determination as he strode down the steps, gripped her arm without a word and began to move her toward the entrance.

"Lance . . ."

"Lie to me and I'll tan your hide," he snapped. "Get into my office and, by God, explanations are due."

◆　　◆　　◆

Dane ground his teeth together at the sound of the sheriff's voice, before motioning Ryan through the shadows of the adjoining park.

No sooner had they moved from the side of the building than two deputies rounded a corner as overhead lights flared on.

The sheriff was a cautious man, and a damned uncanny one at that. How could he have suspected?

Sliding through the shadows, he and Ryan made their way back to the dark SUV parked on the opposite block.

"What now?" Ryan asked as they closed the doors behind them.

"Hell!" Dane clenched the steering wheel as frustration ate at him. "She's never disobeyed me like this."

She would have left immediately at any other time.

"The mating is strong," Ryan murmured. "You can smell him all over her. It's even changed her scent."

"It's going to get her killed." He started the SUV, slid it into gear and pulled silently into the street before turning the headlights on. "That killing in Pinon was just a warning."

"Should we call the old man?"

Dane growled. "Do that and we'll end up with a war here. He's fond of the girl, Rye, you know that."

"He'll kick your ass if she gets hurt," Ryan pointed out.

That wasn't an understatement.

"Shit. We'll take turns and keep an eye on her." He shook his head in resignation. "I knew I shouldn't have taken her home that time. Big, big mistake."

Unfortunately, it had been take her home or let her die. Letting her die hadn't been an option.

"Why not just ask her for the files and be done with it?" Ryan suggested. "Tell her the truth."

Dane shook his head. "She won't give those files up that easily. Besides, it wouldn't save her life. She has the information in her head as well. And Jonas knows it. What Jonas knows, that fucking spy in Sanctuary knows. I'll drop you off at the hotel and pull duty tonight. Let's just hope we can take care of this fast; otherwise the old man just might decide to check it out himself anyway."

That situation was seriously getting on his nerves. If it weren't for the danger Harmony was in at present, he would clean house there himself. He just might do it anyway once this little job was over. His father was getting riled, and when the old man got worked up, his mother wasn't far behind. And in her condition, that wasn't good for any of them.

One of these days, Dane promised himself, Jonas was going to have quite a bit to answer for.

CHAPTER 16

What the hell was going on?

Harmony allowed Lance to retain his hold on her as they entered his office, turning to face him as the door slammed shut behind him.

"You have reports to finish." His voice was hard, simmering with anger. "Get them done so we can head home."

"Lance . . ."

"Et." The sudden finger he raised, the chastisement of whatever she was going to say had her eyes widening as she stared back at him.

"What . . ."

"Reports." His tone was dark, dominant.

A frown snapped between her brows. She would be damned if she was going to let this attitude continue.

"Argue with me right now, and I promise you, that spanking I keep threatening you with is going to happen." His face was suddenly in hers, his nose almost touching hers. "Until the sheer terror evaporates from my system from whatever the *fuck* was going on out there, then I'd suggest you tread lightly."

"I was going to tell you . . ."

"I heard enough!" He stomped away from her, his shoulders stiff, every line of his body radiating rage. "For God's sake, Harmony." He turned back to her as he raked his fingers through his hair in frustration. "Just do the damned reports."

The words were pushed between clenched teeth as anger sizzled in the air between them. What had he heard? And why was he so furious?

"You know, Lance, the alpha thing is a real turn-on," she pointed out. And it was. She was getting wet, fast. "But to be perfectly honest, you are overreacting. I was going to tell you . . ."

"What?" His voice rasped like dark velvet. "That you were in serious danger of being taken from me?" It was obvious he was holding onto his control by a thread. "That whatever or whoever you decided to secretly meet with was within seconds of hurting you?"

Her eyes widened. "Dane wouldn't hurt me."

"Dane!" His fists were clenched as he leaned them on the desk, staring across it as a thread of jealousy stole into his voice. "Let me guess. The same man who's rescued you for the past ten years? The one who keeps a close enough eye on you that he steals you from beneath Coyotes' noses with an inch of your life to spare?"

Her brows arched. "Yeah, that's the one," she answered mockingly. "Should I also point out he's the one who saved my life, countless times . . ."

"The same one who was within seconds of kidnapping your ass," he snarled.

"I wouldn't let that happen . . ."

"This time, you couldn't have stopped it." His jaw bunched as she watched him forcibly restrain himself from saying more. "Go do the damned reports, Harmony. Now. Please."

She inhaled slowly.

"I'm a big girl, Lance," she said slowly. "I've been taking care of myself for a long time."

"Yes, you have." He nodded shortly as he straightened. "And several times those bastards hunting you have damned near killed you. Until I can get a handle on the sheer terror clenching my balls right now, then I'd suggest you drop this subject."

He was impossible.

"Fine." She waved her hand dismissively as she turned her back on him and headed to her office. "I'll go do the damned reports. But later, I'm going to kick your ass for being so stubborn."

He was stubborn? Lance stared at her retreating back in amazement. She had the nerve to call him stubborn? The woman could have written the book on stubborn.

Breathing in roughly, he sat down in his chair, staring at the closed door in disbelief. She had no idea how close she'd come to being taken. Within seconds. He could still remember the imperative cry that suddenly filled the air, making his knees weak as the sound of danger, of Harmony's absence, began to shriek through his mind.

If she resists, we'll take her . . . The hard voice had drifted past his ears as he came out of his chair. *Knock her out and we'll have her on the heli-jet before she awakens.*

It was the first time in his life that actual words had whispered past his ear as the air called to him. She had no idea the danger she had been in. The man who had rescued her for ten years was now intent on taking her.

Why?

He rose from his chair and paced the office, pausing at the window and staring into the dark landscape of the park beyond.

The side of the department was now well lit, something Lance rarely bothered with unless there was an event in the park itself. The lights from the park illuminated the area enough for safety's sake, but there were still shadows to hide within. Shadows that suddenly seemed ominous.

He braced his hands on the window frame as he stared into them, searching for answers, for movement. He should have let her explain, but he'd be damned if he could handle her confidence in the unknown Dane right now.

She was smart, and she was damned tough. But that bastard had been her savior for too many years. That kind of relationship built a trust that could so easily be used against her.

Jonas. Dane. The killing in Pinon. They were all connected somewhere. Somehow. And Alonzo. He had seen the fanatical hatred in the reverend's eyes and knew they hadn't seen the last of him.

"I'm finished." Harmony stalked into the office and slapped the reports on his desk as he turned to her.

He glanced at the clock. It was close enough to midnight to leave for the night. He had finished the paperwork waiting on him and his second-in-command had shown up early.

"Did you have dinner?" he asked with a frown.

She didn't eat enough, and that bothered him. How she managed to keep going on the amount of food and rest she took in amazed the hell out of him.

"Yes. I ate." She frowned heavily. "What does that have to do with anything?"

"Nothing, because I doubt you ate enough to keep a bird alive. Let's go. You can eat with me before we head to the house."

"I'm not hungry."

"Well, I am, and I hate eating alone." At least she was following him—that surprised him.

"You're getting too bossy to suit me," she informed him, moving to his side as they neared the lobby doors.

"I'm not bossy, ask anyone," he growled. "I'm as easygoing as they come."

"I'm glad I wasn't eating when you made that little statement." She gave a mock cough. "I would have choked."

He threw her a glare as they moved through the night, the summer night surrounding them, the hint of rain bringing a relief from summer's heat.

"Let's go—"

"Sheriff Jacobs?"

Lance turned at the sound of the county prosecutor's voice.

He turned to watch as she moved out of her vehicle and walked toward them.

"Stephanie." He nodded in greeting. "You're out late."

"I had to come into the office late." Her smile was strained as she nodded in Harmony's direction. "Alonzo's lawyer just bailed out Ms. Lancaster's assailant."

"He was slow," Lance grunted. "I expected that earlier."

"He also bailed Tommy Mason." She dropped her bombshell with a grimace. "We just released him from lockup."

"Well, low and behold, the U.S. justice system prevails once again." Harmony's snide comment had Lance mirroring Stephanie's grimace.

"He's only out on bail," she assured Harmony. "The trial will be another matter."

"Good luck there." Harmony leaned against the front of the Raider, watching the prosecutor mockingly. "Personally, my money is on Alonzo. He knows how to hire lawyers, Ms. Atwater, and if Mason is part of his organization, then Alonzo will see to it that he goes free."

"Like hell." Lance turned to her then. "Not here, Harmony. Not in this case. Tommy fired on officers and we have your testimony that he was holding his wife hostage. He won't get out of it."

"Then he'll disappear into Alonzo's organization and you'll be lucky if you ever catch up with him." She shrugged as though it didn't matter. "So much for the promise I made to that kid, huh? I bet he's real safe right now." Lance saw the shadows of pain and rage burning in her eyes when she turned that bright, false smile up at him. "So, did you mention dinner? I'm hungry."

She wasn't hungry, she was brooding. He could see it in her.

"Lance, I'm really sorry about this," Stephanie said softly. "The bail was ridiculously high. We had no idea Alonzo would step in like this."

Lance sighed wearily. "Let's pray he sticks to his routine and spends a few nights drinking and having fun before he goes home. I'll have the deputies keep an eye on him and see if we can't pull him back in."

Stephanie nodded her dark head in agreement, her brown eyes concerned as she stared at Harmony.

"Bring him back in, Lance, and we'll keep him this time."

Harmony snorted at that.

"Thanks again, Stephanie."

She nodded again before turning and moving back to her car. Lance turned to Harmony, taking in her emotionless features, her raging eyes as she watched the other woman leave.

"Have you slept with her?" She turned her gaze to him, arching her brow as though curious.

"Did I ask if you've slept with Dane?" he growled. "And what does that have to do with anything?"

"And if I have slept with Dane?" The question wasn't a comfortable one. "I wasn't a virgin when I came to your bed, Lance."

"This has nothing to do with Mason, Harmony," he snapped.

"Mason is a moot point." She lifted her shoulder negligently.

"And that means?"

"Exactly what I said," she told him coldly. "And since I can tell you have slept with her, I should warn you, I could get very jealous. Are you ready to go now?"

She swung away from him, moving with flowing grace around the Raider before jerking the door open and stepping inside. Lance followed suit, feeling the tension mounting inside him as he heard the wailing moan on the wind. It wasn't one of pain, or one of fear. It was the sound of the dead.

The drive to the house was made in silence. Harmony could feel the fears and the rage growing inside her. She had asked Jaime Mason to trust her. To disobey his father and she would make certain he was gone forever. Only to have Alonzo free him.

Justice. Even Death's justice sucked. She couldn't make a move, either as an officer of the law, or as Death, until Tommy Mason struck out at his child. It was the one boundary she had never crossed. And now she was paying for it.

As they stepped into the house, Harmony turned to Lance, watching as he set the alarm before turning to her.

"We were followed." The look on his face was savage.

"Yes. We were." Harmony loosened the Velcro straps that held her holster to her thigh before removing the belt from her hips and heading toward her bedroom.

She was only a few feet from the doorway before a manacle clamped around her upper arm and she was pushed against the wall.

Surprise and heat sizzled through her at the dominance reflected in his dark expression and tightening his normally sensual, full lips.

"As you said earlier, you're a big girl," he stated, his voice rasping. "Don't do something stupid at this point and let him get the jump on you. He will take you, Harmony. You can't trust him."

"He's trying to protect me . . ."

"Bullshit! He's trying to protect himself for some reason," he snarled. "Just like Jonas, Harmony. There's something Dane wants. There's a reason why he's pulled your ass out every damned time the Council managed to capture you. Haven't you ever asked yourself how he knew where you were, the fact that you were taken? According to you, you have no friends. Why did he do it?"

It was a question that plagued her more and more often.

"There's always a job to do," she retorted, hearing the flimsiness of her excuse. "Something he needs me for."

"A job he couldn't do on his own? He could rescue you from Coyotes, but he couldn't do whatever he sent you out for?"

Harmony shook her head desperately. "There's nothing I have that anyone could know about."

"Do you really believe no one but the scientists you killed in those labs knew about the information you stole?" he growled. "What about the rest of the information you had? You stole a computer hard drive, hard copies of experiments and reports, as well as the information on the first Leo. What other secrets are you hiding, Harmony?"

She stared back at him in confusion. He was destroying her preconceived notions, just as Dane was destroying her trust in him. She had always depended on Dane, she realized then. Had always known that somehow, some way, he had her back.

"I don't know," she finally answered. "The files on the hard drive are encrypted and I couldn't break the code. The only thing I was certain of were that the hard copies of the information on the first Leo were the only proof in existence that he lived. Madame LaRue was too triumphant, too assured of herself to have made a mistake and let the information out."

"And you're protecting him." His hands loosened on her arms, but his body held her firmly in place. "You spend your fucking life killing to protect others. Who protects you, Harmony, that you don't first have to pay a price?"

"There's always a price to be paid." She had accepted that long ago. Even before her escape from the labs, before she had met Dane or learned the ways of the world she lived in. "If the first Leo is alive, then he deserves to live in peace. In what safety he's found." Leo was her forefather, her only connection to a lineage; she couldn't allow him to be destroyed, any more than she could have allowed Jonas to be destroyed.

"The price you're getting ready to pay is unacceptable."

Harmony shivered at the low, raspy tone of his voice and the heavy, aroused dominance that filled his face.

"And, by God, you won't be paying it alone," he continued a second before his head lowered.

Her response was instantaneous. She had never known hunger, never known need until Lance. This hunger, this need, was all consuming, terrifying, and sent her arching to him as her lips opened beneath his.

It wasn't a long, hungry kiss. They were short, desperate kisses as his hands released her to tug at her shirt, to fight to pull the material over her head.

Did she hear material rip?

Hell, she didn't care. He was no less desperate to get her naked than she was to get the clothes from his body.

She wasn't a fool. She knew how very close she had come to being taken from him. But one thing about it, eventually she would have awakened and she would have fought through hell itself to be back here.

Right here in Lance's arms.

"Fucking shirt has to go." He tore his lips from hers, leaning back long enough to finish tearing it down the front. So it had been her shirt ripping.

He pushed the material to the side, baring her swollen, lace-covered breasts as he stared down at them with a drowsy, erotic expression.

"Good Lord, I love your breasts." His hands framed the rapidly rising and falling mounds. "And your sweet, pretty nipples."

His fingers ran beneath the soft lace before lowering it, using the bra to frame her flesh as he revealed it.

"There. Just like that," he crooned.

Her head tipped back as his lips swooped down, taking a hard tip beneath them as he lifted her in his arms and began moving.

"I need you," she panted, feeling the flames building in her womb, shooting to her pussy. "I need you now."

"You'll have me. Now."

Before she could do more than gasp, he had her on her feet, turned, then pressed to the bed.

"Get on your knees."

A shudder shook her at the submissiveness of the position she knew he wanted from her. He pushed her shoulders down as one hand gripped her pants.

Within seconds her lower body was bare and he was moving, kneeling behind her.

For some reason, she had expected foreplay. Except for the one event in his office, Lance was always very big on foreplay.

But there was no foreplay.

She screamed as she felt his cock penetrate the liquid heat of her vagina. Her back arched, the long wail of agonizing pleasure that tore from her would have shocked her if she'd had enough sense to think at the moment.

"You're still so fucking tight you kill me," he snarled as he gripped her hips, his own shifting, stroking her inside, sending shooting fragments of pleasure to torment her nerve endings.

She was so full. He was hot, hard, and he took her breath with the pleasure that suffused her, the emotion that built inside her.

His control was gone. How he had sustained it this long she wasn't certain, but it was shot. She could feel it. Gloried in it.

As he began to move, the heavy length of his cock fucking into her with hard-driving strokes, Harmony could do nothing but brace herself, fight for breath and take him.

She was helpless beneath him. Lost in a world of sudden, irrevocable pleasure with no beginning and no end. There was only Lance and the brilliant heat of his touch, his possession.

"Damn you. Are you going to let them take this from us, Harmony?" He thrust inside her hard and deep, each impalement taking her breath, stealing another part of her ability to think. To reason. "Are you going to let anyone take this from you?"

The orgasm, when it hit, was unexpected. His arm curled beneath her; his fingers found the blistering ache of her clitoris and stroked it with devastating results.

She knew she screamed his name. She felt her muscles tighten then dissolve as excruciating pleasure whipped through her. Stars exploded around her and she was lost in the chaos. The pleasure. Her head thrown back as she let her body, her senses, absorb every pounding thrust that elevated her release.

She was lost and she knew it. The sexual dominance that had lurked just beneath the surface was free. Lance wasn't a man to be crossed; she had known that all along. He wasn't a man who would stand back and hope for the best.

And he wasn't standing back now.

"We're not finished." The rough statement, delivered in a graveled, hungry voice, had her womb clenching and her breath catching.

"Wait . . ." Just a moment. Just long enough for the violent sensitivity to ease within the muscles clenching his thick cock.

"For what?" He leaned over her, holding her still as his thighs flexed, causing the throbbing crest of his erection to stroke her internally. "What am I waiting for, Harmony? For you to think? For you to trust someone who will fucking destroy us?"

His hips jerked against her, driving him deeper as her breath shuddered in her chest and her fists knotted into the blankets beneath her.

"For some bastard to decide you're better off without *me*?"

"No!" The agonizing emotion she heard in his voice tore at her heart as she felt his lips at her neck, his breathing hard, harsh at her ear.

And she felt his pain. His fear. The scent of it wrapped around her, mingling with his determination, his strength.

"Mine." He nipped her ear as she felt the slow retreat of his cock, rasping over burning nerve endings. "Do you hear me, Harmony? You're fucking mine!"

The latter part of the declaration came with a hard, quick thrust that had her bucking beneath him. Oh God, it was so good. The whipping tendrils of pleasure seemed to flare from her sensitized pussy along the rest of her body. Her nipples ached, her clit began to throb in renewed need and her flesh began to sensitize to the point that she could feel the air against it, moving over it. Another caress. Another pleasure that had her crying for more, muted little feline growls leaving her throat.

"You like that, baby?"

"Yes . . ." Whimpers were all she could manage. "Oh

God yes, Lance. I love it." She pressed back, feeling the slower impalement, the rock and shift of his hips, the press of his balls against her swollen clit as he drove in to the hilt.

"Are you going to let them take this from us, Harmony?" His voice turned to a croon.

"No. No. I swear . . ." Her head thrashed as she reached desperately for her building climax. "Please, Lance. Please."

"Always mine, baby." He nipped her ear again, stealing her breath with the animalistic dominance in the act. "Do you hear me? You're fucking mine!"

"Yours." Her cry shocked her. It rose unbidden from her lips, shattering the air around her. "Yours, Lance. Always Yours."

The sound that came from his throat could have been a Breed's rough growl. But her declaration broke the last threads holding his control.

The thrusts inside her were rough, primitive. But that was what she needed, she realized. So hard they shook the bed, shafting inside her as she began to fly. As though he pierced her spirit and set it free with the exquisite pleasure ripping through every nerve ending in her body.

Even the air around them seemed to obey his will. It caressed her exposed flesh, licked at her nipples as she fought to hold herself in place, breathed over her sweat-dampened skin until the pleasure became too much to bear.

"Lance . . ." Her wailing cry was desperate, shocked, as rapture began to flame around her.

"Come for me, Harmony. Give it to me, baby. Give it all to me . . ." His voice was guttural, so rough, so deep it was animalistic as his cock seemed to swell inside her. "Give it to me, baby. And I'll give you . . ."

She couldn't scream. She couldn't cry. Harmony felt every muscle, every bone in her body lock in place as something began to swell inside her womb. This wasn't pleasure.

It went beyond ecstasy. Her vision turned dark and she began to shudder, deep hard tremors shaking her body as she felt her release begin to pulse through her.

The muscles of her cunt tightened, swelled, trapping him inside her. She heard his agonized, shocked groan, then felt her pussy ripple as her orgasm reached its height, milking his flesh, stroking him until she felt the hard, heated pulse of his semen inside her.

He was growling behind her, whispering something as his body jerked and shuddered against her own.

Harmony collapsed beneath him, unable to maintain the strength in her arms. Her cheek pressed into the blankets as she fought the agonizing tightness in her pussy. Her muscles spasmed with each furious spurt of seed Lance released, and each shattered male groan at her ear.

"Baby." He lay against her back, his voice tortured. "Sweet God. Harmony . . ."

She jerked with the hard spasm that tore through her at his voice, then his own dark groan at her ear.

"Easy, sweetheart." His hands caressed her gently, soothingly. "It's okay, baby. I'm right here."

She was crying, whispering his name, and he was kissing the tears from her cheek.

"I'm here. I'll always be here." One hand smoothed her hair back as the other slid down her hip, her thigh. "Always, Harmony."

One last shuddering tremor racked her body before she felt exhaustion swamp her. True exhaustion. Her breath shuddered from her chest, and softly, gently, darkness closed around her.

❖   ❖   ❖

Some time later, when he came to his senses, Lance gathered their clothing together and headed for the bedroom.

The torn articles were tossed in the trash, the others in the hamper in the washroom, as he palmed his cell phone.

Moving back to the kitchen, he flipped the phone open and punched in Braden's number.

"Cuz, you're becoming a distraction," Braden growled as he answered on the fourth ring, his voice heavy with arousal.

Lance grimaced. He really didn't need to know Megan had a sex life.

"Where do your loyalties lie, Braden?"

There was a long silence as he waited for the Breed to answer.

"Fuck. I knew this was going to happen," he finally snarled into the line. "I knew it. Hell, Lance, my loyalty is with my wife. Period. What hurts Megan hurts me, so I guess I'm stuck with your fucking fight."

He didn't sound happy about it, but Lance knew his cousin's husband. Beneath the growling protest was an edge of excitement. He knew a fight was coming, and Braden did love a good fight.

"She's conceived."

Silence filled the line for long moments.

"Well. Hell." Braden finally breathed out roughly. "You're certain?"

"The winds are." He could feel the answer in the air around him, clear to his soul.

"That's good enough for me." Braden sighed. "What now?"

"Jonas wanted her pregnant for a reason," Lance said softly. "He wanted to use it. What would her pregnancy result in?"

"Her death," Braden grunted. "She's the ultimate killer. Pregnancy would weaken her. Make her vulnerable. Easy to overpower."

"And when Death is in trouble, what happens?" The more

he thought about it, the more he knew exactly what would happen.

"She's taken," Braden answered, suspicion heavy in his voice now. "Always by the same team of men. Taken and hidden."

"That team is here in town. They nearly took her last night. We had a tail on the way home and someone is watching the house now. They're getting ready to move in."

"And Jonas has taken a sudden leave," Braden revealed. "He's unavailable at the moment and no one knows where he and his three best enforcers are. Merc, Rule and Lawe."

"They're here, and they're waiting. What the fuck is behind this, Braden? If Jonas wanted to contact the men who have helped her, why not just ask her?"

"She would never trust him." Braden's sigh was heavy. "When she killed the scientists and escaped from the lab, Jonas truly believed his mother, Madame LaRue, was a victim. That she was forced to cooperate with the other scientists to protect him and Harmony. He had no idea the monster she was. Harmony did. When she tried to tell him, he brushed her off, grew angry. It was years after Madame's death before Jonas learned the true scope of her cruelties. By then, Harmony had learned to distrust him. She would never trust him now and Jonas knows it."

"Then why keep me in the dark?" Lance asked. "If I had known . . ."

"Lance, you don't understand Breeds," Braden growled, his voice rough. "Trust, outside of our own small prides, is not a commodity we have. Jonas knows you, he likes you; otherwise, he wouldn't torment the living hell out of you. But he doesn't trust you. Jonas more than any of us, because of his mother, knows the price of trust."

He wiped his hand over his face as he paced to the closed

window, feeling the darkness surround him, the hint of a presence beyond it.

The cell phone was secure; Lance had made certain of that. And he knew Braden's was. The house was being watched, but whatever he said now was safe.

"What do you need?" Braden finally asked. "You're a part of Megan, a part of my family, Lance. My loyalties lie there, as does my trust."

"Her safety," Lance breathed out roughly. "I have to ensure her safety, Braden, or someone, somehow, will take her from me. I can't let that happen."

He could feel the rage boiling inside him, a complete fury directed toward those who would use her.

"I'll be over tomorrow afternoon." He could hear Braden's determination as well. "Megan says to make certain she stays inside until then. Don't let her out of your sight, Lance."

"That one is a given," Lance growled. "I'll shackle her to me if I have to. She's not going anywhere without me."

Harmony wasn't certain what awakened her. But for the first time since she had come to Lance's home, he slept deeply as she rose, showered and dressed. Dawn was high; streaks of pinks, golds and fiery reds lit up the sky as it eased over the horizon and called to her.

She could feel it pulling at her. The morass of emotions that filled her made her skin itch, made her legs long to run. The walls pressed in on her, and the air around her felt as though it were suffocating her.

And she couldn't stop thinking about Jaime Mason.

As she moved silently through the bedroom, dressed in jeans and a tank top, she stared back at Lance on the bed. She didn't want to wake him up. He made her want so many things, made her want to think of herself rather than the mission she had given herself years before. He made her want to hide in that big bed and forget that the world outside the house existed.

Unfortunately, it did exist, and the need to run, to clear her head, was overriding. Pushing in the code to the security system, she opened the window in the bedroom she had first slept in and slid into the shadows that bordered the house.

She was reasonably certain she wasn't being watched. The gun at one thigh and the knife sheathed to the other afforded her a measure of confidence in protecting herself though.

Having reactivated the security system by pressing the device mounted beside the inside frame, Harmony closed the window with plenty of time to spare before the system detected it. She lingered until the metallic lock clicked in place, then began moving.

She knew Dunc and Ryan. They would be watching from the pines above the house that would afford a clear view of the land surrounding it. Slipping past them might not be easy, but she had done it before, and she was confident she could do it again.

And she could smell the Breed watching the house. Despite his attempt to stay upwind, his scent drifted to her.

Smiling triumphantly, she slipped from the area, finally sliding along the ragged hills and shallow arroyos until she reached the open spaces beyond.

She breathed in roughly as the sun peaked further over the horizon, casting the valley and narrow canyon beyond in a multitude of colors.

The land wasn't desert, nor was it really grassland. It was a mix, blending together with pockets of colorful desert flower bursts and shading trees that created a wonderland.

Smiling, she settled her utility belt about her hips. A small water bottle was anchored behind her back, a utility pack on the other side. Her weapons rested comfortably on her body and she was ready to run.

◆   ◆   ◆

Harmony ran until the blood was singing in her veins and her legs had gone from burning and weak at the exertion to powerful and sure-footed. The rough terrain and shallow gullies were a challenge. This was land she didn't know, and running across it wouldn't have always been considered the brightest move. Not the way Harmony ran. Full tilt, the wind whipping over her body, filling her pores and energizing her.

She could feel the sun kissing her. The cool, early morning air still lingered, yet the promise of heat filled the land. And she loved it.

Running was the one pleasure she had always fought to allow herself. Being confined made her nervous, ill. She hated the walls closing in on her, and craved the wide open spaces. And she found that here. Civilization hadn't encroached far enough to take away the sense of aloneness, the merging of spirit and land.

Finally, the exertion took its toll though, and Harmony knew she would have to stop, rest. She wouldn't have much longer before she had to head back. Lance would be furious when he found her gone, despite the note she'd left. But she needed this. She needed to focus, to clear her mind, to accept the unacceptable.

She couldn't kill Mason. Even as Death, that wouldn't have been acceptable. Death didn't strike until first blood had been shed. But Death had never allowed herself to become involved as Harmony had.

Panting, she slowed her run until she was pacing, cooling off and letting the blood settle naturally in her veins. She inhaled deeply, lifting her face to the cooling breeze and feeling the sweat that poured from her body.

The memory of Jonas rose in her mind. How he would come to her the moment he arrived from a mission, as though he knew the pain that wracked her body. He would move her from the thin cot in the cells and take her to the comfortable private room he had been assigned. And there, he would ease her onto the cool, soft sheets. He would brush her hair. Sometimes, she thought, he might have crooned lullabies.

"Fuck this!" She snarled at the memories. Those days were gone. The girl she had been. The brother he had been.

"Such language from such pretty lips. Would you speak in front of a child in such a way?"

Pivoting to a crouch, her weapon clearing its holster, she stared back at the old man watching her from the shade of a cottonwood several feet away.

Great. She was so damned messed up now that old men could creep up on her. Then her eyes narrowed.

"You're Lance's grandfather," she stated, sliding the gun slowly into its holster as she kept a wary eye on him. "Why are you here?"

"Because you are." His smile flashed with an edge of male charm that reminded her of Lance.

"Fine." She shrugged, still watching him closely. "Now what do you want?"

"Perhaps to get to know my new grandchild." He walked toward her slowly, his bowed legs carrying him to an outcropping of boulders that sat beside a grassy knoll.

He waved his hand over the rocks. A hiss, a scurrying in the brush around it, and a second later a disgruntled rattler slithered from the rocks.

Harmony stepped back, watching the serpent make its way to a narrow ditch, then between the rocks farther below in a shallow arroyo.

"Cool trick." She lifted her brow as though impressed.

Joseph Redwolf grunted. "That is nothing. All creatures of the earth have such abilities. They have only to learn how to use them. Come, sit with me." He patted the wide rock with gnarled fingers.

"I don't know, you remind me too much of Lance. That could be dangerous to my mental state." She crossed her arms over her breasts, seeing the pleased smile that creased his weathered face.

"Ahh, you are a charmer." He shook his finger chidingly at her. "And think to turn an old man's head with flattery."

"I have a feeling flattery is the last thing that would turn your head." A reluctant smile edged at her lips. "Did you know I would be here?"

She stepped over, easing down on the rock as she pulled the water bottle from her utility belt. She remembered her first impression of him and knew he was like Lance. Only stronger. This was a man the earth listened to as well as spoke to.

"I knew. The winds whispered your name and led me here. So I came."

She uncapped her water and handed it to him. When he waved it away, she tilted it back and took a long, refreshing drink.

"So, why would the winds lead you to me?"

"Ahh, the winds sometimes keep a few secrets." He sighed. "I merely follow their guidance."

Somehow, she doubted that.

"You are uncertain of my grandson still?" he asked her then.

Harmony braced her elbows on her knees as she stared at the ground.

"I'm not uncertain of him." She shrugged, uncomfortable. She didn't talk to others easily. Lance was an exception. But she couldn't not talk to his grandfather. She had a feeling he wouldn't let her ignore him anyway.

"Perhaps you are uncertain of yourself," he said softly.

She lifted her head, staring into the distance with a frown.

"Perhaps," she finally admitted softly. "No matter how much I want what he offers, Death is still there."

"And Death bears great guilt and much responsibility."

She nodded at the statement, not even bothering to question how he knew the difference between Death and Harmony.

"My grandson, he is a good man," he said. "I have watched him grow, watched a boy's laughter turn to a man's amusement. I have watched him fall to his knees, force himself up again, and watched him walk proud. He is a man more accepting and understanding than most."

"Death soils him," she whispered. "She brings danger and blood. He'll never be safe."

His laughter shouldn't have shocked her. She stared back at him in disbelief as he reached out, waved his hand, and the breeze in front of them began to churn the dust and dirt, growing larger, picking up more and more until it rose more than twelve feet above them and screamed with power.

Just as quickly, it eased, steadily diminishing until the dark cloud settled back to the ground and the dirt scattered at their feet.

"The earth protects those who seek her embrace." His voice deepened with warning. "My grandson and what is his will always know its protection. No matter which land they step upon or which side their enemies think to attack. She will always protect him, and cherish what is his. The earth gave you to his embrace, and only the earth can tear you away from it."

She turned, staring back at him as his words sank inside her mind, her soul.

"Why would it choose me?" she whispered. "Every part of me is stained with blood."

He snorted. "You did the land a favor in the lives you have taken. But the time for that is now at an end. Return to my grandson, and as you do, decide once and for all. Are you Harmony or are you Death? For the two can no longer entwine and survive. Make your choice now, woman, before you destroy not just yourself, but the man who would give you life."

Make her choice. If she chose Lance, then Death would be gone forever and so would vengeance. And so would the safety of the young women and children she protected. It was a choice she feared could end up destroying her.

✦   ✦   ✦

Jonas slipped through the silent house, eyes narrowed, his senses alert as he sought for signs of something other than death.

His eyes narrowed on the figure lying in the center of the bedroom floor. Tommy Mason's throat had been cut, a near perfect imitation of a Death Caress, the signature slice attributed to the serial vigilante who had struck across the United States and Europe over the past ten years.

There were a few slight anomalies to the cut. Depth, the angle of the cut, the width of the blade used. But not enough that anything other than a Breed could identify. Only someone much too familiar with Death's training would notice the anomalies.

"Where's the wife and kid?" he spoke into the comm link quietly.

"Still locked in the basement. They're alive."

He knelt beside the corpse, studying the body. Mason hadn't been dead long. An hour maybe. Jonas glanced at his watch. It was barely eight in the morning.

"I can't smell anything unusual anywhere else in the house," Merc reported over the link. "Nothing but fear and filth."

Jonas rubbed his hand over his jaw. Someone was definitely framing Harmony, and they expected him to tie the noose around her neck.

Sanctuary's spy, he thought, shaking his head. Only a select number of people had known about Death's presence in the cells below the detention building. He was narrowing the suspects down, but he would have preferred to do so in a different way.

"Someone to report she went running, then someone to come in and make the kill," he murmured over the link. "Time of death will coincide with her absence from Lance's home and make the case for her guilt."

"Only one group that would go to that extreme," Rule stated as he stepped into the bedroom. "Alonzo must know who she is."

Jonas's lips thinned. She wasn't the same girl she had been ten years ago. She had filled out, firmed up; her features had evened out. But if someone had known what to look for, they would have seen the resemblance. Alonzo could have only known that Harmony was here if the spy at Sanctuary had warned him. Son of a bitch, when was the bastard spilling their secrets going to mess up enough to get caught?

He should have killed Alonzo himself. If he hadn't attained such popularity, such notice over the past years, then Jonas would have. Unfortunately, his death would have only brought suspicion on the Breed community.

"Courtesy of our friendly Sanctuary spy," Jonas murmured as he straightened. "At least they left the wife and kid alive."

"Death would never hurt them." Rule shrugged. "What do we do now?"

Jonas rubbed at the back of his neck wearily. "We use it."

"Hell, Jonas." Rule's voice was filled with disbelief. "You can't call Breed Law on her over this. She didn't do it."

"Dammit, Rule!" he snapped. "Do you really think I'm going to see my sister dead for someone else's crime? Hell, I wouldn't pull Breed Law for her crimes, why do it over this?"

"You haven't exactly been brotherly," Rule pointed out. "Why didn't you just ask her to cooperate?"

"Because she would never give him up, whether she trusted me or not. Harmony is nothing if not loyal. The only chance I have of catching him is pushing her until one of them makes a mistake."

"You want that shadow of hers damned bad," Rule pointed out.

"Not bad enough to sacrifice the only good thing that ever came out of those fucking labs," he snarled before inhaling roughly and gathering his control in both hands. "He's the first Leo. He and his mate have what we need. The answers to the aging process. We have to figure out what the hell is going on before proof of it hits the press. I want him bad, Rule, but not bad enough to actually endanger her life with Breed Law. He and his scientist mate hold the answers to the mating heat and the aging, and I want those damned answers."

The discovery of the slim evidence they had attained that the first Leo was indeed still alive, nearly a century after his birth, and still in peak physical condition, had been a fluke.

After Harmony had ignored his messages to meet with him years before, Jonas had begun tracking her. Two years ago, he had nearly caught up with her after Council Coyotes had captured her. He had been only hours late. Harmony had already been rescued.

But her rescuer had left something behind. A bloodied scrap of a shirt. Only one Breed carried the specific imprint of the DNA that the blood contained. The first Leo. The very first Breed ever created. In essence, the father of them all.

Nearly a century before, the first Leo had supposedly died in a fiery helicopter crash while escaping with his scientist mate from the South American lab he was created within.

Where the mate was, Jonas couldn't guess. But he knew where Harmony was, Leo wouldn't be far behind. Unfortunately, the spy operating within Sanctuary was aware of Harmony as well, and now he was betting Alonzo knew.

"Let's get the hell out of here." Jonas turned, careful to make certain he left no evidence of his steps. "Make an anonymous call to the Sheriff's Department in an hour or so and report the wife's and the child's cries. Then we'll fly back in."

"Lance will kill you if you try to take Harmony," Rule warned him as they stepped from the room.

"Lance will fight for her." Jonas grimaced. "But he knows the stakes. And so will she. She'll give me her shadow, and no one will ever know Harmony was here. I'll make sure of that myself."

There were a lot of lengths he would go to in ensuring the survival of the Breeds, but he wouldn't sacrifice his sister, or the child she would eventually conceive. She was the last ounce of gentleness left within his life. And he would make certain it stayed that way.

The phone was ringing as Harmony slipped back into the house. She heard Lance answer it. A few seconds later she heard a vicious curse, a second before he called out her name imperatively.

She moved through the hallway to the doorway, leaning against the frame casually as he jerked sweatpants over his long, muscular legs.

"What's up?"

His head jerked around, his eyes narrowing on her clothes, the weapons, her damp hair.

"Where have you been?" The angry question had her brow lifting.

"I've been running. Why?"

"Running?" he snapped. "After nearly being taken last night you just went off running?"

"I wasn't in any danger," she drawled slowly. "What's the big deal?"

"What time did you leave?" He stalked over to her, stepping directly in front of her before reaching down and sliding her knife from its sheath.

"About dawn."

Harmony watched as his gaze went over the blade, his fingers sliding over it, testing its edge before his gaze lifted and went carefully over her.

His jaw flexed, the muscle jumping beneath the flesh as he watched her.

"What's wrong, Lance?" She straightened slowly. She could see an edge of suspicion in his gaze, a flame of anger burning behind it.

"Did you go to Tommy Mason's house?" he finally asked, his voice dark, warning.

"Mason's?" A frown furrowed her brow as she watched him. "Why would I go to Mason's? He hasn't done anything yet."

"Don't joke about this, dammit!" His hand clenched on the hilt of the dagger. "Did you go there?"

"No, Lance, I didn't go there." She shook her head slowly. "Why?"

"Get cleaned up. Mason's been murdered. His wife and son were locked in the basement and his throat was slit just after dawn. We're heading straight there."

Harmony stiffened in shock at the information.

"And you think I did it?" she asked him carefully. "I told you I wasn't there, Lance. Isn't that enough?"

If it wasn't, then she would be damned if she'd tell him who she was with. Fuck it. She should have known better than to believe in complete trust, she thought painfully. Love. Bullshit. "It's enough for me," he snapped, but she could tell it really wasn't. "It won't be for Jonas. Now get cleaned up." He handed her the knife as he repeated the order. "We have a crime scene to investigate."

She took the K-bar and sheathed it slowly, her eyes never leaving him. It was enough for him, but he didn't really believe her.

The smile that pulled at her lips had nothing to do with amusement.

"Yeah, sure, Lance. I'll get ready." She stepped back from him, lifting her chin as she pushed back the disillusionment, the pain. "I'll even hurry."

✦   ✦   ✦

Lance watched her leave, his chest clenching painfully as he searched for the answers he needed in the air around him. It was strangely quiet. There were no echoes of cries or of innocence, as though the winds had deserted him. She wouldn't lie to him, but that wouldn't stop Jonas. And now, when he needed the whispers in the air, they were gone.

God, didn't that just figure. Not that he believed she had actually committed the crime. Once she denied it, he knew she hadn't. But someone had, and they were damned determined to frame Harmony for it. His teeth ground together as he forced himself to the shower rather than follow Harmony.

What the hell was he supposed to do now? He had to ask her, he had to know if she had done it. Not that he would have blamed her if she had. He knew her, knew the demons that rode her, and he knew how hard this had to be on her.

Jaime Mason was a tiny little kid for his age. He was always dirty, and always terrified. Liza, his mother, wasn't much better. Both were too young to know how the hell to handle the fear Tommy Mason could mete out. And that was something he knew haunted Harmony. That weakness and fear. The knowledge that monsters used it so easily.

Biting back his curse, he rushed through his shower, forcing himself to wake up, to think. This was going to turn into a nightmare if he wasn't damned careful. He could feel it. Jonas wouldn't be able to keep from using this against her.

Harmony was waiting for him half an hour later when he strode through the hallway. Leaning against the kitchen doorway, her thumbs braced in the wide, leather belt strapped across her hips.

"Let's go," he said. "I want to get there before the scene gets too cold."

She followed behind him silently.

"Did you see anyone when you left the house?" he asked as the doors to the Raider closed.

"I didn't see anyone. I could smell Jonas's man Lawe from the front of the house, but I doubt he saw me. I didn't want to be followed."

"Sometimes, you're a little too independent," he growled. "Why didn't you wake me up?"

"Oh, because I'm a big girl." She waved her hand mockingly. "And I didn't want to argue over a simple run."

"A simple run that could have ended in your kidnapping?"

"Maybe. It was a chance I took. I won't accept a cage. Not of any sort. Not even for you."

His hands clenched on the steering wheel. "Even if it means your safety?"

"My safety wasn't involved," she said softly. "If it had been, you would have been warned. The winds speak to you. You would have awakened before I slipped from the house."

He turned to her slowly. She was staring straight ahead, her features perfectly composed, but he could feel the pain radiating from her.

"Someone saw you leave the house," he said softly. "They used your need to run to frame you for a murder that's going to bring Jonas down on your ass. You're not alone anymore, Harmony. It's not you against the world. It's both of us. And maybe it's time you start considering that."

She was going to drive him to a stroke if this happened on a regular basis. Deliberately placing her life in danger, knowing the odds were stacked against her, and pitting herself against them anyway.

He wasn't experienced enough in the messages the wind brought him; he had yet to take his grandfather up on the training that would aid him in calling the wind to him. Until he knew he could protect her, knew the winds would call to him if she was away from him, in enough time to save her, then he couldn't relax.

As he turned the Raider onto the main road, he glanced at her silent profile. She was so fucking used to being alone, to answering to no one. This would be hard on her, and once she learned she had conceived, it would be even harder on both of them.

Restraining the need to return home, to reassure her, Lance pressed his foot to the gas pedal instead and sped to the Mason home. The evidence against her could be too easily used. And Lance knew Jonas; he would use it. Whatever he wanted from Harmony, this would play right into his plans.

✦   ✦   ✦

The wound was consistent with the bartender's. Harmony hunched down and tilted her head, staring at where the cut began. From left to right, beginning just under the left ear and ending in an upward angle just below the right ear. The murderer was strong, strong enough to hold Tommy Mason still by his head while he made the cut.

From the angle, she could tell Mason's head had been tilted back against something.

Harmony braced her forearms on her knees and narrowed her eyes as she tracked the wound. It was very neatly made, precise. The blade was most definitely a K-bar, but it hadn't been specially modified. Her blade held an edge that even the Special Forces members who carried them didn't attain.

Someone hadn't done their homework. But it didn't surprise her that she was being framed. Someone knew she was here, which meant Jonas hadn't found his little spy at Sanctuary.

"You know, that position is just wrong on so many levels, Harmony."

Harmony lifted her gaze to Lance as he stepped into the bedroom, eyeing her as she straddled Mason's body.

"The lighting is better," she murmured. "Someone isn't taking proper care of their blade. Come here."

He stepped over to the body.

Harmony used the pencil she had borrowed from a deputy earlier and pointed close to the jagged tear of the otherwise neat upper slice.

"There's a knick in his blade. A pretty good one. If you noticed earlier . . ."

"I noticed . . ." His voice overcut her words.

She gave him a quizzical look, meeting the narrowing of his gaze. She nodded slowly. Was the room bugged? She stared around the bare bedroom. There was a double bed; the sheets were filthy, the blankets torn. In a corner was a small dresser, other than that, the room was empty.

"Dave said Tommy Mason's stats show him as exactly . . ." She checked her notebook. "Five feet, eleven inches. Your killer is six-four. Based on the angle of the bartender's wound, as well as this one, there won't be more than an inch plus or minus margin there."

She stared down closely at Tommy Mason once again.

"There are no defensive wounds on his hands, so he didn't have time to fight. The attack came from the back, definitely. The angle is different if you attack from the front. And there's a very faint earthy scent on his body. It's not natural to his particular stink. I'm guessing your killer spent some time lying in damp ground before he came in."

"Liza said Tommy hustled them into the basement so he

could meet with someone. Someone he didn't want them to see. She said he was prone to do that though."

"No witnesses." She nodded. "It saved her life."

She rose to her feet slowly.

"Is the killer a Breed?" Lance asked as she stepped clear.

"Doubtful. Breeds can't cover their natural scent if they touch anything. Whoever killed him was holding him real close and personal for several seconds. The scent would still be on his clothes."

"I have a report of a Breed who can hide that scent." He posed the idea carefully. "When needed."

Harmony shrugged. "There's a few cases where scent was able to be temporarily disguised by a Breed. But not like this." She waved her hand to the body. "To hide all traces the Breed would have had to attack from the front. This was a sneak attack. And he held his victim for a second or two, savored the kill."

Lance glanced back at the body. "The blood on the front of his clothes," he said. "If the killer had dropped him immediately, it would have run in a different pattern."

"Yep." She stuck the pencil the deputy had given her behind her ear before brushing her hands off and staring around the room again. "Whoever it was is careful though." She pointed to the open window. "All the windows have been opened just enough to allow the air to circulate well, diffusing scents. He was going to make certain he couldn't be detected by me."

There were ways to hide from another Breed, tricks she had learned over the years in her battle to stay at least one step ahead of the Coyotes.

"We have a footprint beneath the window you went through the other night, but nothing else. He's careful, Harmony. Too damned careful."

The window could be coincidence, but hell, she just

didn't believe in coincidences. Someone besides her friendly neighborhood Bureau Lion Breed was watching her.

"He knew I was out of the house this morning," she mused, keeping her voice low as Lance leaned in closer to her. "How many of these assholes are watching me anyway? It's a wonder they aren't tripping over each other. There's no way the killer could have been watching and then set up a meeting. No time. He would have needed a partner."

"No doubt. Liza said Tommy hadn't expected the meeting," Lance said before asking, "Are you finished here?"

She breathed out silently. "I can't find anything, Lance. Whoever did this is being damned careful so far. He knows the tricks."

And something about that tugged at her memory. It was like a subtle itch just between her shoulder blades. An awareness, a familiarity she wasn't certain of.

She had perfect recall; her memory was a tool in and of itself. It wasn't a photographic memory, but Harmony did not forget details. Until now.

"Let's get to the office then and get the report filed. David has the investigation, and until something else breaks, you're off patrol."

"But Jonas . . ."

"Fuck Jonas," Lance snarled as they left the house, his hand lying against her lower back, as his big body seemed to hover over her. "I'll deal with him."

"I hear he's a wham-bam man; you wouldn't enjoy the experience I don't believe." She turned her hand over, checked her nails, then preceded him to the Raider.

"A wham-bam man," he repeated slowly. "God, I didn't need that thought in my head." He seemed to shudder as she opened the vehicle door and jumped inside.

As Harmony moved to close the door, Lance stepped between it and the seat, bending to stare back at her. She met his gaze evenly, wondering if the anger simmering inside her showed in her eyes.

Perhaps she shouldn't be angry. If he wanted to accept Death and Harmony together, who was she to complain?

"Out with it before we get to the office," he ordered, his voice deepening into that alpha tone that seemed to click in her brain and her pussy at the same time.

"Out with what?" Harmony glared back at him. "I don't know what you're talking about."

"That's why you're on the edge of hissing?" he grunted. "Don't bother lying to me, Harmony."

"Why, because the wind is going to tell you the truth?"

"Oh baby, I don't need the damned wind to whisper that one." He pushed his face closer to hers, anger simmering in his gaze. "I can look at your face and tell when you're lying to me."

She pressed her lips together stubbornly. The way he'd acted this morning, that was hard to believe.

"Now would be a good time to start speaking," he snapped. "Because that look just makes me hard, and it makes me just determined enough to consider fucking the answer out of you."

She almost moaned at the thought of the pleasure. Between one breath and the next her body heated, and searing arousal began to pound through her blood.

Praying he couldn't see the response in her face, she continued to stare back at him silently. Thankfully, she was able to hold back her hiss.

She wouldn't forget that he hadn't believed her when she denied killing Mason. She had seen the suspicion in his eyes, and heard it in his response. No matter what he said now, he hadn't believed her then.

It's enough for me. As though it wouldn't be enough in the face of the evidence for anyone else.

"Harmony . . ." He drew her name out warningly.

"Hadn't we better head to the office?" she asked, keeping her voice cold. "As you said, Jonas will be arriving soon and I have a report to write."

Frustration filled his expression as his hand tightened on the door frame. A muscle jumped in his jaw before he stepped back and slammed the door closed, then stalked around the Raider. Arrogant male. She didn't lie—well, except to Jonas, maybe. And sometimes Dane.

She pursed her lips. Okay, she wasn't above lying if it served her purpose. But not to Lance and not about this. For the first time in her life someone had wanted to be something with her, rather than just wanting something from her. She wouldn't betray that, no matter what he thought.

Dammit, she was making herself crazy over something she shouldn't even be worried with. After all, he was stuck with her, right? It wasn't like he could mate someone else, could he? If one followed the example in nature, lions only mated once.

Maybe it was something she needed to find out about. Braden would know; she could ask him about it.

"Harmony, that look on your face . . ."

"Have you ever gone parking?" She was starting to burn with arousal. Not the mating heat arousal, but a need vastly different. This was more natural, freer. She could deny it, if she wanted to. The problem was, she didn't want to.

"Parking?" His expression was a bit confused.

"Yeah. Taking a woman out in the desert and parking and actually doing it in the Raider?"

He wiped his hand over his face.

"You're mad at me because I haven't taken you parking?" he asked carefully.

"No. I'm angry over something much more important."

She waved the question aside. "I'm curious about the parking."

"Curious how?" he asked as he pulled the Raider out onto the main road.

"Well, I've never gone parking." She turned to him, crossing her legs as she stretched her arm between the seats and rested her hand at his nape. Her nails raked over the tough, weather-roughened flesh.

He shivered.

Harmony licked her lips at the response.

"One of these days," he sighed, "I swear, I'm going to spank you."

She let her fingers rake through the lower layer of his long hair.

"Would I like that?"

"Why are you angry at me, Harmony?" He glanced over at her, the gentleness in his eyes, the flush of arousal in his face, weakening her. "You're not curious about the parking or the spanking. Yet. You're hurt. How did I hurt you?"

The knowledge that he had seen so easily into her ruse to distract him with his sexuality had her chest clenching in emotion.

"You didn't believe in me," she whispered, breathing in deeply as she fought back the hurt. "I needed you to believe in me."

"Harmony . . ."

"Sheriff Jacobs, we have a situation here." Lenny's voice came through the radio as Lance spoke her name. "Mr. Wyatt has just landed with three of his enforcers, demanding to see Deputy Lancaster, and Alonzo has a crowd gathered outside the entrance. You better get here fast."

Lance's lip curled in fury as he activated the link on the steering wheel. "We're headed in. We'll pull to the back and use the entrance there. Escort the Bureau boys to my office and check for a protest permit on Alonzo's group. If they don't have one, arrest them."

"Arrest them?" Lenny sounded less than certain that he had heard right.

"Arrest every damned one of them," Lance barked. "I'll deal with them when I get to them. Jacobs out."

"Let the fun begin," Harmony murmured, turning back to face the front of the vehicle as Lance shot her a dark look.

"Son of a bitch!" he cursed under his breath. "I knew I shouldn't have answered the phone this morning."

⋄ CHAPTER 19 ⋄

The back entrance to the Sheriff's Department swung open the minute Lance pulled the Raider to a hard stop in the parking slot, no more than ten feet from the door.

Protestors and journalists were surging around the side of the building as Harmony followed him and moved quickly into the building.

"They have a permit, Sheriff." Lenny was sweating as frustration lined his rounded face. "Somehow they got the mayor to sign it."

"Weasel," Lance snarled as he placed his hand at Harmony's back and led her to his office. "Keep them out of the damned department. Are Wyatt and his crew here?"

"In your office. With their lawyer." Lenny nodded.

Harmony tensed, her hand falling to her weapon. The fact that Jonas had brought his lawyer couldn't mean anything good. Jess Warden was a barracuda; Harmony had seen that when Jonas held her in the cells at Sanctuary. She knew Breed Law like the back of her hand and had become well acquainted in working it.

"Let's get this the hell over with," Lance snapped as they moved to the door.

At the last second, he pushed her behind him and threw the door open.

Jonas was waiting for them. Merc, Rule and Lawe carried their short automatic rifles with casual readiness. They were dressed in the black enforcer mission uniforms, their expressions hard, emotionless. Harmony's hand tightened on her weapon as she stepped into the office behind Lance.

This was it. Jonas had found what he needed. It wouldn't matter that he knew she hadn't made those kills. He could use them. That would be enough for him.

"I need your weapons, Harmony." Jonas's voice was a warning rumble as Lance closed the door behind them. "We need you at Sanctuary for questioning in the death of Tommy Mason."

"Jonas, you don't want to do this," Lance warned him as Harmony felt tension rising in the room. "You know I'm not going to let you take her."

Harmony snorted. "The alpha stuff is really cute," she drawled. "And this standoff is so testosterone-laden I'm about to have overload. Could we get past it, please?"

She loosened her body, consciously relaxing her muscles as she considered her options. The door was next to her; getting free wouldn't be a hardship. Running would be a tad more difficult.

The lawyer, Jess Warden, was possibly the only one to give her words much notice. Jess's lips tilted in amused agreement as she lounged against the front of Lance's desk.

"Harmony, remember when I warned you that Jonas wanted something?" Lance reminded her quietly.

"Yeah? So?" Of course he wanted something. Everyone wanted something from her.

"Ask him what he wants."

She watched as Jonas lifted a brow, his gaze reflecting admiration.

"Your sheriff is quick," he murmured as he inhaled deeply. "In more ways than one."

"Jonas!" Lance's voice was a commanding whip. "Don't burn your bridges here, man."

Jonas's lips tilted in mocking amusement.

"Fine, we'll see if we can make this easy." He shrugged in unconcern. "I want your shadow. You'll follow the mission plan we've put together and help us capture the team that repeatedly rescues you. I want them both."

Dane? He wanted Dane and Ryan? Not the information she had stolen from the labs? She stared back at him in confusion.

"Why?"

"That doesn't concern you, Harmony," he said. "Give me what I want, and your little indiscretions here will be ignored. You'll receive clear status and freedom. Freedom to stay with Lance."

"And if I don't?"

"If you don't, I'm taking you with me, and Breed Law will be enforced. You're a wanted assassin, not just by the Bureau but by regular law enforcement channels as well. As Death, you have a hefty price on your head in several countries. Give me what I want, and I'll ensure, personally, that everyone believes Death is dead. Harmony can live her life in peace."

"This isn't going to happen, Jonas." Lance's voice surprised her. What surprised her more was how easily his hand dropped to the weapon at his side. "Harmony has upheld her end of the deal. I will personally attest to it."

"Can you save Death as easily?" Jonas asked, his voice soft, almost gentle. "She's a wanted killer."

Harmony gauged her chances of making the door. Dane and Ryan would find her; all she had to do was get out of there. She felt agony well deep inside her at the thought of leaving Lance. The warmth, the pleasure of his touch.

"Breed Law will do that for me." She stilled at Lance's voice. "Breed Law cancels when a child is involved. The moment she conceived she was exonerated until and unless she kills again. And she has conceived. You can't take her, Jonas."

Harmony almost smiled. Lance surely knew this wouldn't work. Jonas would know better.

Instead, Jonas nodded. "I scented that the moment she walked in the door. But think about this, Lance. Will she ever be safe with you?"

"I'm not pregnant." The rest of the conversation dissolved as her world narrowed to that single piece of information. "That's not possible."

Her gaze swept around the room, taking in the compassion, sympathy and knowledge in the expressions staring back at her.

"It's not possible," she repeated.

"Harmony, you are pregnant," Jonas stated softly "You and I both know that once your shadow learns of this, he'll take you. He will take you himself, because his single most important goal is protecting you. And that child will weaken you."

"No one captures me unless I want to be captured," she hissed back at him. "You managed it, because fool that I was, I still called you brother." The knowledge of that tore through her soul. "I couldn't harm your men, I couldn't get free without killing them, so I let them take me."

She couldn't breathe. Pulling air into her lungs hurt; the implication of what they were saying was destroying her. How could she have not realized she was pregnant? It was her body, her child. Surely she would know.

For a moment, Jonas's expression seemed to gentle.

"Breed females can rarely scent their own conception. But it's there, Harmony. I can smell it, and the winds have whispered it to Lance. You can't run from it. You're here. And you're pregnant. The man protecting you won't let you stay. Help me capture him before he takes you from Lance anyway."

"Stop it, Jonas," Lance warned, his voice hard.

"He won't take me, because I won't let him." She was pregnant. Lance's child rested inside her. She could feel herself weakening, options she'd thought she had dissolving beneath the knowledge.

"You're weak now, Harmony. And you know he will take you. You're important to him because of the information you stole from those labs. He won't allow anyone else to possess that information. There was no chance of you sharing what you had. Mated, pregnant, you're weak and therefore a threat. He won't allow that. He won't allow you to turn that evidence over to anyone else."

"How do you know?"

"Because he's the first Leo. The first created, Harmony. His genetic typing is the blueprint for every Breed that came after him. And Madame LaRue possessed the last evidence of his existence in the papers and files you stole. You are his weakness."

◆　　◆　　◆

Shock raced through her. Shock that he knew the information the files contained—but that first Leo couldn't be Dane.

She shook her head slowly. "He's too young. There's no scent of a Breed . . ."

"There's no scent at all. You forget, he mated one of the Genetic Council's foremost experts on Breed genetics at the time. If he found a way to cover his scent, then the Breed community can use that knowledge as well."

"He's too young."

"Aging halts between a Breed and his mate once mating heat occurs," he answered. "We have no idea how long mates can live. We need that knowledge."

"Then why hasn't he taken the information?" she snarled. "If this were true, then he would have told me. He would have demanded what I had and I would have easily turned it over to him. This makes no sense, Jonas. You're lying."

"I don't know why he hasn't tried to secure the information himself," he said. "And this was why I brought you here, knowing you would mate with Lance, knowing you would conceive and that the need to protect your mate and your child would supersede your friendship with this man. Harmony, listen to me." His voice roughened as he stared back at her, his quicksilver eyes softer than before. "You are my sister. I know what LaRue was. But I knew you would never believe me, never trust me so easily. We have to have the answers on the mating that the first Leo and his mate hold."

"I'll give him a message . . . ," she argued

"Do you think I didn't try that?" Jonas asked. "Do you think I haven't tried everything before involving you in this way?"

She stepped closer to the door, aware of Lance shielding her despite the sudden readiness of Jonas's enforcers.

"Don't try to run, Harmony. I have men outside the department. Don't make me do this to you."

"You son of a bitch!" Lance's voice echoed with violence. "Do you think I'm going to let you get away with this, Jonas? Do you really think I'll let you use her like this?"

"You can't stop him," she whispered. "Look at him; he knows you can't stop him."

"Like hell I can't." He gripped her wrist before she could run, before she could move the precious inches to the door.

"Harmony." Jonas's voice had gentled further, reminding

her of the brother who had once brushed her hair, of the young man who fought to find an escape for those he led. "We've made every attempt to convince the first Leo to contact us. To help us. We're within months, perhaps a year, of the world learning the truth about the mating heat. You're smart, sweetheart. You know what will happen when that news breaks. Compulsive sexual heat, forced bonding. We'll be exterminated."

Sweetheart. That voice. The edge of aching warmth in his tone. Tears filled her eyes as she blinked furiously and swallowed at the tight ball of emotion lodging in her throat.

She shook her head, feeling the darkness that edged at her mind, the sense of betrayal that tore through her.

"You used me," she whispered painfully, staring back at him as daggers of knowledge ripped through her. "You weren't trying to help me. You were using me."

"I was trying to do both, dammit." He grimaced. "You were going to get caught or killed. You couldn't go on the way you were."

"How did you know I was her mate?" Lance asked, his voice sharp.

"It doesn't matter how I knew," Jonas snapped. "Nothing else matters except what we face right now. She's pregnant. That's your child she's carrying, Lance. A child of the earth. Will you let that be taken from you? Either by me or by the man who protects her?"

"If he could help you, he would have," Harmony cried out.

She knew Dane. He was ruthless, yes. He could be stubborn and often too hard. But he would never turn away his own people in such a way if he were a Breed.

"The very fact that he's alive would answer many of our questions, Harmony," Jonas growled. "He's not your savior. He's protected you for a reason."

"He was there when you weren't," she snarled, trying to

push past Lance as he held her in place. "You sent your fucking Coyotes after me while you were still in the labs. You told them how to catch me. You wanted me dead!"

"I never wanted you dead. I wanted you safe."

"You fucking liar!" The scream that left her throat tore through her chest.

"Enough!" Lance snapped between them. "Stick with the program here, Harmony."

"What program?" she sneered as she turned to stare at Jonas once again. "He has your program all mapped out for you, Lance. Yours, mine and our child's. What an interesting tale I'll have for him when I reveal his safety was purchased with the blood of the only fucking person willing to risk his life to save me, besides you."

"If he cared so much for you, he would help your people, as well as his," Jonas growled.

"I wouldn't spit on you if you were on fire," she hissed. "No wonder he refuses to answer what is undoubtedly one of your infamous commands."

Lance would have laughed at Jonas's expression if the situation weren't so dire. Harmony was so close to running. He could feel it in the air around him, hear her cry for freedom echoing in his head.

"Enough!" His voice rose as Jonas opened his lips to speak. "He's a fucking asshole and we all know it, Harmony. But we can't kill him. We deal with him."

"I'll be certain to extend my thank-yous later," Jonas murmured.

"Stuff them," Lance barked, wrapping his fingers around Harmony's wrist to hold her in place. Her gun hand. Her fingers were twitching too close to her weapon.

Merc, Lawe and Rule were watching closely. Lance knew their entire focus was on Harmony and the attempt they believed she would make to run.

"I'll give you the files I have on him," Harmony said, bargaining then, surprising Lance. "I can get them quickly. You'll have them."

"They won't have what we need, Harmony." He shook his head firmly. "We need the Leo. And we need him now."

Jonas was pushing her and Lance knew it. He was trying to make her run. He wanted her to run. It was one of the reasons Lance had stayed largely quiet to this point. There was information in what wasn't said, in the emotions that whispered through the air.

"Sit." He pushed Harmony into his seat as she stared back at him in surprise.

Leaning close, he stared into her oddly colored, furious eyes. "Silence," he said softly, commandingly. "Now."

Her lips pressed together as fire lit her gaze.

"I won't—"

"Now!" Something snapped inside him. He would be damned if he would let her endanger her life. Not now. Not when she was close to freedom.

She jerked back in the seat, staring at him warily.

"Thank you." He touched her cheek gently, running his fingertips down her jaw before straightening and turning back to Jonas.

The other man watched the exchange warily.

"Are you willing to burn this bridge?" Lance placed his hands on his desktop. "I hear Megan has become very close to your pride leader's wife. She's also not your best fan."

Jonas crossed his arms over his chest. "I'm aware of that."

"Do you really want to make enemies of my entire family, Jonas?" he asked him carefully. "Did you consider that when you were having your little science project conducted in whether Harmony and I would match as mates? That you would not only gain my hatred, but also that of my families?"

Jonas's silver eyes narrowed, burning in his dark face.

"I will do whatever is necessary to save the Breeds, Lance," he growled. "I will fight whoever or whatever I have to. She wouldn't trust me; that is evident. And until the mating and conception had occurred, I couldn't trust you. Now it's up to you and Harmony. Do you help me capture Leo, or do you risk the world learning about mating heat, and possibly destroying your wife, child and your cousin Megan in the process?"

"And if she doesn't do it, then you won't lift your hand to help her?" Lance prodded.

Jonas stared back at Harmony for long, silent moments.

"I would die for my sister. But once the truth about mating heat becomes known, if we're not prepared for it, if we don't have the answers we need to give the public, then I won't be able to save anyone. Not myself, my people or my sister."

✦   ✦   ✦

Dane chewed on the end of his cigar as he watched H. R. Alonzo move among the protestors in front of the Sheriff's Department. It was really hard to imagine the man as a distant uncle. The heavy jowls, short stature and beady little eyes didn't lend much to the Vanderale name. He wasn't a Vanderale though, he was the son of a Vanderale daughter, and it was apparent the genetics hadn't made a successful crossover. Too bad actually. A true Vanderale, though mercenary at heart and too determined to have his way, did have a small measure of decency. It was obvious that the genetics Henry Richard Alonzo had been given were missing that component.

He was an uncle, though. He was the grandson of the man whose sperm had created the first Leo. Elijah Vanderale Demarcy and his wife had given birth to a daughter, then Elijah had turned his attention to the Genetics Council and creating his vision of the perfect son. After all, his wife had refused to bear more children, and as old Vanderale Demarcy had told Leo, a son meant everything. Elijah had been determined to sire a son unlike any other. No matter what it took.

His arrogance and sense of superiority had never been in question. His determination to have a son stronger, more intelligent and unique than any other, could have defined him as mad.

Elijah's seed, genetically altered though it had been, had begun the process. Then he had set about creating an empire for his son. Vanderale Enterprises. A conglomerate of corporations headed by a supposed distant relative. His vision had been remarkably insightful toward the future. Electronics, weapons and specialized vehicles.

Dane shook his head at the old man's vision. He had died not long after Leo's escape from the labs, but he had died knowing he'd given his son freedom and that his son would always know security.

That had been more than sixty years before. Vanderale Enterprises was a thriving, worldwide force now, though the man behind it had always been careful to stay hidden.

Unfortunately, somehow the Alonzos had learned of old Elijah's contribution to the Genetics Council, and his kinship to the Breeds. Poor gents, they were rather upset over it all.

"Leo is getting antsy," Ryan murmured as he moved into the café booth across from him. "He wants an update on her. Now."

Great. The old man wanted an update. That usually meant he was roaring from one end of the estate to the other and threatening to head to Broken Butte himself.

This was his fault, Dane admitted. The first time he had found Harmony, wounded, nearly broken, out of her mind with fever, he had taken her to his mother. Hell, he was no doctor. His mother had at one time been the foremost authority on Breed genetics and ailments. She had been the perfect answer.

Except, as Harmony lay in a fevered haze and cried as the child she was, it had been Leo who sat with her. Who cried with her. Now the old man thought of her as his own. And no one threatened what belonged to Leo Vanderale. If such a person lived, it was only so he could regret it.

He stared back at Ryan silently, narrowing his eyes chastisingly as he read the guilt on his friend's face. Amusement lurked in Rye's dark eyes as he pushed darker hair back from his forehead.

Ryan was considered quite attractive by the females. His features were well sculpted and slightly rough-hewn. His lips were a bit full, his blue eyes most often filled with laughter. And he had a horrible crush on the Leo's fair mate, Dane's mother.

Dane's mother had called earlier, and rather than facing her inquisition, he had given Rye the phone to offer explanations instead. Bad choice. Ryan was so infatuated with the woman that it was all he could do not to stutter when he talked to her. He was always spilling their plans to the deceptively gentle, soft-spoken mate to the first Leo.

Dane turned his head and stared back out the window at the protestors in front of the Sheriff's Department. Leo would never countenance taking Harmony from her mate. It was a good idea, and a workable one, but Dane knew his father. The old man would rupture a blood vessel.

Old man. He almost snorted at the thought. At ninety, Leo was still in his prime, as was his wife. And there was the crux of this little nightmare.

"Jonas has made his move," Dane murmured. "He'll try to bargain with her now. He may well accept the information she has if she refuses what he truly wants."

He should have forced her to give it to him years ago, Dane thought. But protecting it, the thought of what would happen to the first Leo if the Council found him, had kept Harmony fighting to live. Her survival depended on her believing she was the only one who knew of Leo's existence. Dane trusted her—even more, he knew her, as no one but her mate knew her. She had fought like a wildcat to hide and preserve what she had stolen from those labs. She had fought to live, and he had wanted to help. He had needed Harmony to live.

"He wants you," Ryan reminded him.

Ahh yes. Elyiana's report that Jonas was after the shadow that kept saving Harmony's life. The old boy was biting off more than he could chew there. If by chance Jonas managed to capture Dane, he wouldn't keep him long. If Leo was possessive over Harmony, then his feelings were downright obsessive where his only son was concerned.

Not that Dane intended to let himself get caught.

"He's going to accuse her of the killings. He'll pull Breed Law on her and pull her out any minute. Leo's going to have a cow," Rye reminded him.

Dane shook his head. "He'll have an aneurysm. Not a cow."

Ryan's lips quirked.

As a partner, Ryan DeSalvo was the best a Breed could ask for. Especially a hybrid breed with the secrets Dane had. Admitting he was well over fifty years old would have shocked most people. Rye had taken it in stride.

"What's the plan?" Ryan asked as Dane watched the protestors absently.

"Must we have a plan?" Dane leaned back in his seat and placed the smoking cigar between his teeth as he smiled slowly. "Let's wing this one, my friend. I'm interested to see how far Jonas will take this little plan of his. Let's see what he's made of."

HARMONY'S WAY

235

Ryan stared at him in slack-faced amazement. "You're kidding."

Dane grinned. "Not hardly. I think it's time I learned what my little half brother is made of, don't you? The seed the Council preserved from the old man created Jonas. Let's see if he has the same steely determination."

Harmony was a product of another patriarchal Breed line, thankfully. Otherwise, the feelings he had for her would have gotten him killed years before. Leo wasn't very understanding about breaking certain rules. That was one of them. If Dane fucked a Breed female, then he better damned well be one hundred percent certain what her patriarchal line was. Which meant his mother did a thorough genetic typing. Not exactly conducive to a good sex life for a man when his mother was vetting the prospective lover.

It had been bad enough when Leo learned Dane had taken Harmony to his bed. The old man had raged for months, furious that Dane had dared to take her without a mating.

"And the information she has?"

"Unfortunately, we have to secure the files she stole. We can no longer allow her to keep them." Dane removed the cigar from his lips and blew a stream of smoke past his lips as his gaze wandered to the little waitress working across the room. A delectable little thing she was, and he had a need to relieve the tension growing inside him.

As she glanced over at him, he winked slowly and watched her pretty little blush.

"And how do you intend to do that?" Ryan asked suspiciously.

"I won't." He shrugged. "Harmony will. We'll just follow along and relieve her of her bounty. And of course, Jonas will follow to protect her, and possibly apprehend myself. The latter we'll just have to disappoint him in."

"God, you've lost your mind." Rye sat back in his seat slowly. "The old man is going to blow a gasket if he learns of this, Dane. He doesn't like these games you keep playing with the Council and Jonas."

"Who says we have to tell him?" Dane grinned as he replaced his slim cigar between his teeth. "Ryan, I'm going to have to keep you away from my mother. That crush you have on her is going to get you killed, besides the fact it makes you too eager to spill all our secrets."

Ryan grinned. "She's a fine-looking woman, Dane."

"She's my mother." The warning glare didn't help much.

A sigh, one filled with regret, left Ryan. "There are days I wonder about that one . . ."

CHAPTER 20

She was pregnant. Being pregnant wasn't something that an assassin should take lightly, Harmony was certain. It was something that frankly terrified her. And she hadn't been terrified in a very long time.

As Jonas and his crew, lawyer included, left the office and flitted away in their spiffy little black heli-jet, Harmony moved to the couch across the room and sat down wearily.

Strangely, she didn't feel any different. Shouldn't she feel pregnant or something? Shouldn't the world look different or her body feel different?

As Lance stalked to his desk and threw himself into his chair, Harmony leaned her head back against the cushions and contemplated. She didn't like contemplating. She didn't like being stuck between a rock and a hard place, but that was where she was. Thanks to Jonas.

Brother. She gritted her teeth at the thought of their kinship. Then ground them as the logical part of her brain agreed with him. She would have done the same thing. Protecting the Breeds was a precarious job at the moment, and if this mating heat/aging crap got out, then they were all screwed. Hell, it freaked her out, when she wasn't one huge raging hormone intent on getting up close and personal with Lance. Not that she had really allowed herself to think about it to this point. Though dammit, she really should have thought about it by now.

She was so screwed. And not necessarily in a good way.

She was pregnant. She had another life to protect. A child. Lance's child. How was she going to protect herself, her child and Lance? As long as Death was alive, then danger would be drawn to her.

And yet she couldn't countenance betraying Dane either. It didn't matter why he might or might not have been there to rescue her through the past ten years. The fact was that he had. He had cared for her, nursed her through potentially fatal wounds and given her a place to hide when she needed to heal.

He had cared about her. For whatever his reasons, whatever he might want from her, he did care for her. She might be madder than hell at him right now, but she knew that much.

God, could things get any worse? Alonzo was protesting outside the doors, Jonas was determined to capture the only friend she had ever known, and she was mated to a man determined not to let her go. And there wasn't a doubt in her mind that Lance would tie her up and lock her in one of his damned cells if that was what it took to keep her there.

Pregnant.

She laid her hand carefully over her abdomen, frowning as she tried to make sense of that. Evidently the hormonal therapies weren't worth taking. They hadn't stopped the heat and they hadn't stopped conception. All they had done was keep her from running. And she would have run, wouldn't she?

Okay, so she wouldn't have run. She felt like kicking something. From the first night she met Lance she had been hooked and she knew it. Mating heat be damned, the man knew how to touch, how to hold, and how to make a woman addicted without her stupid hormones adding to it.

There had to be a way out of this. A way to give Jonas what he wanted without betraying Dane, and a way to ensure that Dane stayed safe. It wasn't possible that he was the first Leo, no matter what Jonas claimed.

Most of the electronic files were encrypted, but the information on the first Leo had been hard copy. Pages and pages of genetic reports and training profiles. Unless there was more on those hard drives, within the files she had never been able to crack.

She wasn't exactly a hacker. Electronics, unless they ran a security system or a weapon, weren't her thing. Computers were a pain in the ass, and the handheld models just made her crazy. And cell phones were for people with a death wish. They could be hacked, traced and bugged, as she often tried to tell Dane. Therefore, she didn't even have a cell phone to call him on. And she really needed to talk to him now. Because she wanted to know just what the fucking hell he was planning. Maybe she could slide into the connecting office and make a quick call . . .

"Not on your life."

Harmony lifted her head and stared back at her mate. That alpha tone just made a girl's nerve endings stand up and take notice, but really, this was no time for it.

"Stupid wind thing," she half snarled. "That is so wrong, Lance. That's worse than mind reading."

"Get used to it."

She lowered her brows at the grump that had taken the place of her normally indulgent lover. He sat, forearms braced on the desk as he went through a file. A thick file. Her eyes narrowed as he turned a page and she caught a name. Was that her file?

"What are you doing?"

"Trying to figure out how to de-fang that bastard brother of yours," he growled.

Harmony shrugged. "Dane. But he's not the first Leo."

"No shit!" Lance snarled, glaring back at her. "How do you know?"

Harmony rolled her eyes as she surged to her feet.

"For one thing, Dane isn't mated. The first Leo is mated."

"And you know this how?"

She tucked her hands in the back pocket of her jeans as she considered her options in the face of that question.

"Harmony?" There was that damned alpha tone again.

"Well, according to what you've said, once you've mated you don't have sex with anyone else. Right?"

"Yes." He snapped the word off.

"Well." She shifted her shoulders, suddenly uncomfortable. "If Dane is the first Leo, then he broke that little rule."

"Not possible," he growled. "Braden says the males can't even get 'interested' in other women. Now explain how Dane broke that little rule."

She pursed her lips. "Well. Because." She cleared her throat. This was damned uncomfortable. "I've slept with him."

"Goddammit, I fucking knew it!" he snarled as he slammed the file closed. "And why didn't you give this piece of information earlier? When it would have defused Jonas?"

"Because, maybe, it's none of his business," she snarled back, revealing her canines. Okay, now he was just going to piss her off.

"And you think it wouldn't have helped if he knew Dane wasn't the first Leo?"

"Well, I don't know that for sure." She frowned. "What happens if a mate dies? Though really, I don't think he's mated." She was babbling. Harmony Lancaster, aka Death, was turning into a twit. She snapped her mouth closed.

"Look, Jonas isn't going to just stand down," she informed him as he glowered back at her. "Once he gets something into that knot head of his, it stays there. He was like that in the labs and he hasn't changed since."

"And calling your precious Dane will help this how?"

Harmony licked her lips. "Well. I could tell him what's going on."

"And this would help us how?" His voice had roughened, grown angrier.

"He could hide us both. Just until we figure this out . . ."

Lance dropped his head.

"He would do it, Lance," she whispered. "Just until the baby . . ." She swallowed past a rush of tears. "Until it's safe."

She felt her hands trembling, felt emotion swamping her. Oh God, she couldn't stand this.

He lifted his head long seconds later. The fury she expected was absent, but his expression wasn't exactly encouraging.

"Lance, listen to me. He knows how to do it. He's hidden me plenty of times . . ."

"If we run now, we'll never stop running, Harmony." His voice was gentler, but no less authoritative. "I won't have that for us or our child."

Harmony hunched her shoulders as she turned away from him then. What other answer was there?

"We need the files you stole," he announced then.

Harmony swung around. "How will the files help? With the spy in Sanctuary, we can't even do anything with them. There's no way the Leo will be safe if his existence is revealed."

"Jonas was right, Harmony," he warned her. "The existence of the mating heat is a time bomb just waiting to explode. When it does, the Breeds will never know safety."

"What do you suggest then?" She waved her hand mockingly. "Let's just turn him right over to the Council while we're at it. Because the Coyotes will beat the Breed Enforcers to him. There's no way to keep him safe if knowledge of this reaches Sanctuary."

"We get the information and go from there" he said. "With any luck, something about the mating heat will be contained in that hard drive or discs you found."

His voice vibrated with the knowledge. God, this wind stuff was really going to drive her crazy.

She wiped her hands over her face, pressing the heels of her hands against her eyes as she fought with her need not just to protect and find the first Leo but to protect her own reality as well.

"If he's so good at hiding people, then perhaps this Dane is hiding the Leo as well," Lance suggested then. "We could go through the information ourselves . . ."

"Most of it is encrypted." She shook her head. "I can't break the code." She dropped her hands and stared back at him in despair.

Lance smiled as he rose from his desk.

"I have a cousin-in-law who just happens to excel at breaking Council encrypted files," he said. "You can trust Braden, Harmony. We can trust him. We keep what you want to stay hidden and we bargain with Jonas on the rest. That will buy us the time we need to find your Leo."

"We're playing with the identity of the first Leo," she whispered. "And his safety."

"If he's still alive, then he's well experienced in protecting himself. Let's see what you have, then we'll decide. First we weigh our options, then we go from there."

"Getting away from Dane and Jonas won't be easy," she murmured worriedly. "Not to mention whoever our friendly neighborhood copycat assassin is. They could be waiting on this. I still think we should tell Dane."

Lance watched her silently, his gaze thoughtful.

"Oh, they definitely are." He finally moved around the desk and stalked toward her. "But we have an ace up our sleeve, baby. We have the winds. And I have it on the highest authority that there's this badass assassin who knows well how to avoid pesky little tails. Between the two, I think we'll have them beat. As for telling Dane anything, have you considered that maybe he doesn't know about the Leo? If he doesn't, then you don't want to reveal that infor mation. And he'll never leave without an explanation."

"They'll be waiting on me to go for the information. They're going to expect this, Lance." She stayed well clear of the area where she had hidden the leather satchel of information she had stolen. She had kept the hard drive for a while, until she gave up on figuring out how to open the encrypted files. She had packed it protectively then included it with the rest of the stash. That had been years ago.

"Harmony, we don't have a choice." His voice as well as his expression hardened. "I won't let Jonas continue to jerk you around like this. And I'll be damned if I'm going to let that son of a bitch Dane attempt to kidnap you and my child. This stops here!"

Harmony almost shivered at that tone of voice. She did cream. She could feel the juices gathering, heating between her thighs, preparing her. Who knew she could be so female? She sure hadn't. She hadn't been before Lance.

Drawing in a deep breath, she restrained herself from jumping his bones. She couldn't even blame it on the mating heat. The heat flowing through her now was different, but it was also hotter. Brighter. And it was more destructive to her peace of mind than the mating heat had ever been.

Was there a part of her selectively programmed to submission? Or was this natural? Was this love?

"Harmony." His voice was a warning growl as she realized she was still staring up at him with a frown.

"Fine. We get the information." She shoved her hands into her pockets before turning away from him and pacing across the room to stand by the window.

The shade had been drawn, blocking the sight of the playground outside. It didn't matter; she wouldn't have seen the day reflected there anyway.

This was too unfamiliar. What the hell was she supposed to do now? A mate was one thing. She was getting used to the mate stuff. She was handling that, right?

Her hand dropped to her stomach again.

"I'm frightened," she whispered as she lifted her hand and stared back at Lance.

Bitter amusement sliced through her. "I don't think I've ever been frightened before, Lance."

She had shot her way out of the labs, and not once had she known fear. She had gone against serial rapists, killers, crime figures and Coyotes, and she had never batted an eye at the danger she faced. But the thought of a child was terrifying her.

She fought back her tears as she glimpsed his expression. Anger lurked in his gaze, but overriding it was concern and dark determination.

Lance strode quickly across the room and folded her against his body, tucking her head against his chest as his arms held her close. God, how would he survive without her? From first sight she had begun worming her way into his heart and taking over his soul. She breathed life into his world, and he had no intention of allowing anyone to take that from him. Not Jonas, not the unknown Dane and sure as hell not the Genetics Council.

He felt her arms grip his back and the shudder that raced through her body as he pressed his face against her hair.

"Our child is going to be fine," he whispered. "We'll teach him how to play baseball and how to hunt. We'll learn how to bake brownies for him, and how to make him laugh. And we'll protect him, Harmony. I promise you."

She trembled against him again, trying to duck her head as he leaned back to stare down at her.

"Trust me," he whispered.

Her face lifted, her eyes, those beautiful pale green cat's eyes, swimming with tears as she stared back at him.

"Being a woman sucks," she whispered. "I never had this problem until you."

He frowned in confusion. What the hell was she talking about?

"What problem?"

"Needing someone else," she whispered. "Needing him more than I need freedom or need to run. Needing him more than I need what I've fought for, for so long."

He smoothed her hair back from her face, feeling his chest tighten further as she broke his heart all over again. What other women took for granted—the love of a man, needing him, being close to him—his woman saw with an edge of wonder.

"I've always needed you," he told her softly. "I've dreamed of you. Heard your cries whispering to me and felt a hint of your touch in the breeze that caressed me. I always knew, baby."

A tear fell from her eye. "I know how to take life, Lance. I don't know how to create life."

She was going to rip the heart from his chest. Lance lowered his hand to her abdomen, feeling the warmth of her flesh, the tremor of response to his touch.

"You've already created life," he whispered as he lowered his lips to her. "Beautiful sweet life, baby."

Her lips opened for his as a little whimper escaped her throat. A sound filled with vulnerable need and aching hunger. A hunger he knew she felt solely for him. This was his woman, his mate. And by God, he would keep her safe.

But he had to taste her now. Her lips opened for him, taking his kiss as he felt her melt against him. Melt into him.

✦   ✦   ✦

She was lost in Lance's touch. Her hands pressed against his chest, once again drawing in his warmth, feeling the heated passion of his body and more. She could feel his protectiveness, the dominant inclination to shelter her, to ease her as his arms wrapped around her and pleasure began to build inside her.

One of his large, calloused palms slid into her hair, tugging at the strands as heated arcs of electric sensation began to whip through her nerve endings.

Oh, she liked this. This was pleasure. This was more pleasure than any one person should have to fear for, a pleasure she knew she would never again be able to live without.

"I want to take you home," he whispered against her lips again. "I want to be inside you, Harmony. I want to feel you hot and wet, gripping me as you scream beneath me."

Harmony felt her pussy clench in response.

"We could lock the office door." She tried to capture his lips once again, to submerge herself in the pleasure and emotions that she only felt with Lance.

He chuckled as he pulled back farther. "No more office sex," he growled. "I won't be able to walk when we're finished, let alone drive if that wicked little pussy of yours clamps down on me again like it did last night. You left me a wasted shell of a man, baby."

She ran her hands over his chest, then to the powerful muscles of his arms.

"You don't feel like a shell," she whispered. "You feel hard and ready for me. But if you insist, I'll drive for you."

She almost laughed at the indecision on his face for a fleeting second. Then his expression creased into a smile as he shook his head slowly.

"We go home." He gave his head a quick, hard shake as he stepped back from her. "Dave is qualified to replace me on a temporary basis. I completed the paperwork while you were staring at the ceiling growling."

"I was not growling." She frowned back at him fiercely.

"Sorry, baby, you were growling." He pointed his finger back at her as he moved to his desk. "Cutest little sounds I think I've ever heard in my life, but they were definitely little growls."

She did not remember any little growls.

"You're hearing things." She propped her hands on her hips, her frown turning to a glare as he collected a sheaf of papers from his desk and headed back toward her.

"Dream on, kitten." He patted her butt as he moved past her. "Let's go home. We have plans to make."

✦   ✦   ✦

Henry Richard Alonzo watched from the safety of a storefront as the Raider pulled from the back parking lot of the Sheriff's Department and headed up the street. They were both in there. The sheriff and his harlot Breed female. The bitch flaunted her Breed status with that uniform she usually wore and with her sneer toward the world. She was a killer, just as all the females of those species were; he just had to prove it.

He had hoped the two killings he had sanctioned would throw enough suspicion on her to have her targeted by her own laws. She was young enough; similar enough to the Breed suspected in several vigilante killings. He had even received reports from his spy within Sanctuary that Death had been there, beneath Jonas's supervision.

Had she been Death, he wouldn't have had to have his man make the killings though. She would have struck quickly, without mercy.

He rubbed at his jaw and ground his teeth as the Raider disappeared from sight. That stupid sheriff was ruining everything. No doubt he was sleeping with her. Men could not resist the sexuality of the Feline females.

"Reverend." Acker McQuire stepped up to him slowly, his tall, lanky frame moving into the doorway of the store-front. "What now, sir?"

Tall. Blond. A killer as merciless as the one called Death. He had been a Trainer in the labs; he had even spent several months at the French lab, though it had been after Death's escape.

"We watch them," he growled. "Jonas is up to something."

"There was a report from Sanctuary. She could be Death. The heli-jet was tracked from Sanctuary to Carlsbad the night she left. The next day, Harmony Lancaster showed up here and within the Breed database."

Could she be Death?

Henry Richard tucked his hands into the loose pockets of his slacks and stared in the direction the Raider had taken. She was about the right age and build. And there was a re-semblance to the photos he had attained, though it was so slight he couldn't countenance that she was Death.

But it was possible.

"Is there any information on how Jonas captured her, or why he has allowed her to live?"

Even the Breeds had placed a price on Death's head.

"Just that she has something he wants." Acker shook his head, the white-blond strands of his hair lifting in the breeze.

"Then it must be her," he mused. "He would want the information she stole when she escaped."

Jonas Wyatt wasn't the only one who wanted that information. His men had managed to track her to a certain area, but no further. The information she had stolen from the labs the day she had killed the scientists working there had been so sensitive, so important, that millions had been spent trying to locate it.

"We could take her."

Henry shook his head slowly. "We follow her. Jonas will overlook the murders he believes she committed in exchange for the information she has. It could explain why he left without her."

"I duplicated her killings exactly." Acker's assurances didn't matter. All that mattered was the results.

Henry nodded again. "Yes. This would explain everything. They definitely suspect her of the killings, so she may well be Death. Watch her. If they head out of town, then we know we have Death."

Satisfaction raged through him. He was so very close to destroying the Breeds. He could feel it. If this was indeed Death, and Acker had committed the crimes in a manner similar enough to her M.O., then framing her would be that much easier. And satisfying. He would show her how unpredictable the Breeds were, how close to the merciless animals they had been created to be.

He would let nothing steal this chance from him. Enough had been stolen from him because of his grandfather's perfidy in aiding in the creation of these monsters, these abominations against the All Mighty God.

How he wished his grandfather still lived. Henry Vanderal Demarcy had been a fool.

The daughter, H.R.'s mother, hadn't been enough for her father. Vanderale Demarcy had wanted a son, rather than the grandson that would be born later. He had created his son. Allowed his seed to be tainted by Breed coding, so he could betray the daughter he had been given.

Henry Richard Vanderale Demarcy. The bastard. He was H.R.'s grandfather, H.R. had even been named after him, though he refused to use the name Henry Richard, or any part of it. He wanted no part of his patriarchal kin. If he were still alive, H.R. would have killed his grandfather himself. He had helped create these monsters so he would have his perfect son, had stolen most of his vast fortune to give to that son. In doing so, he had left H.R.'s grandmother with barely enough money to hold on to the estate she had been left. And her Vanderale kin in South Africa had certainly held no interest in helping her at the time.

Vanderale Industries was now one of the largest conglomerates in the world, and even they, bastards that they were, supported the Breeds. Though he should have expected no less. Evidently, Vanderale genetics carried a trace of insanity.

He would forgive them no more than he had forgiven his grandfather.

H.R. bared his teeth in fury. The first Leo. The first ever created, the first to escape. And in escaping, he had gained the fortune H.R.'s grandfather had secretly stolen from beneath his wife's nose, then vanished without a trace.

The bastard. H.R.'s family had suffered. They had fought and scraped after his death, until H.R.'s mother had married into the powerful Alonzo family.

His grandfather had betrayed them for his animal son.

Henry swore again, as he had for decades, that each Breed would pay. That he would personally see to it that they were wiped from the face of the earth. They were abominations. Creatures. They had no right to life, and he would make certain they returned to the hell from which they had been spawned. They could join ole Henry Vanderale Demarcy within the fires of everlasting judgment. And he would be the one to send them there.

Wicked, erotic sensuality wrapped around Lance's senses as he leaned against the wall, just inside the door of his home, and stared down in pleasure.

Harmony wasn't a woman to be denied when she decided she wanted something. She'd had his jeans loose before they reached the house, her wicked nails torturing his cock as he fought for breath.

He had no more than managed to get them into the house, than the door slammed behind them and she was on her knees. She was on her knees now, and his were threatening to collapse.

He couldn't take his eyes off her. The sight of her face, her eyes closed, her expression sensual and flushed as he filled her mouth with his cock.

Slick, heated, her tongue licked over the bulging crest before she sucked it noisily to her throat and drove him crazy with the little rumbling growls that vibrated against it.

Clenching his hands in her hair, he braced his back against the wall and fought for control. Control nothing—

hell, he needed strength to stay on his feet. The little wanton was sucking it out of him one moist inch at a time as he panted from the pleasure.

"I'm definitely going to have to spank you." As soon as he could catch his breath. "God, baby . . . yeah. Your mouth is so fucking good."

It was beyond good. It was the second most wondrous place on the earth. The first was wet and hot and waited between her luscious thighs.

Another hard, rumbling purr vibrated in her throat. He swore he felt it clear to his balls. Kneading her hair, he clenched his teeth and fought past the dizzying sensations threatening to swamp him. Hell, he didn't want to come yet. Not yet. Not when it felt so fucking good. When the passion and arousal that transformed Harmony's face held him spellbound.

"Fuck!" His lips pulled back from his teeth as her eyes opened slowly, the engorged head popping free of her lips so her tongue could lick.

She licked like she held a favored treat, curling her hot little tongue beneath the swollen crest before covering it once more with her mouth.

"Witch," he panted. "That hot little mouth is going to get you spanked."

He could see her bare bottom turned up to him now, blushing from his hand as the soft, silken folds below it glistened with her cream.

She hummed heatedly.

"Like that thought?" He fought to breathe as her hand stroked the length of flesh her mouth couldn't consume. Lower, her other hand cupped and massaged his balls, her nails scraping at the flesh with such destructive pleasure he swore he was going to come any second.

She stole his sanity. She was wrapped so firmly around his soul that each touch, each look from her was heaven. This surpassed pleasure though.

Sweat gathered on his forehead, on his chest where his unbuttoned shirt clung to his skin. A ragged moan tore from his lips as her mouth tightened then released him. Her tongue was just killing him.

"I'm not going to be able to hold on, baby." He blinked the sweat from his eyes, his hands tightening in her hair as he tried to pull her from him.

Her teeth scraped warningly. That should have hurt. He didn't like teeth against his cock. But the barest edge raked against him, sending a sunburst exploding before his vision with the pleasure. At the same time, her strokes deepened, the suckling of her mouth intensified, and he was lost. Lance heard his own shout, hoarse with tortured pleasure, as he erupted in her mouth. His cock jerked, throbbed, then his seed spilled to her waiting tongue in hard, heavy spurts. Each eruption had his body jerking as she continued to suckle him gently. His breath wheezed from his chest, his knees nearly buckled, and he leaned forward to counter the weakness.

"God, yeah . . . ," he groaned. "Sweet heaven. Sweet baby."

He was racked by ecstasy and helpless in the grip of it as a final, desperate stream of semen filled her mouth.

She pulled back then, the feel of her lips raking over his cock sending hard tremors of pleasure racing through his nerve endings, as he yanked her quickly to her feet.

He was not going to make it to the bed. It just wasn't possible. Lifting her into his arms, he ignored her frantic objection as he stepped to the living room. There was no time to undress her. If he didn't get inside her, he was going to go crazy with the need.

Stepping before the deep, heavily pillowed chair that just

happened to be the first item of furniture he came to, Lance placed her quickly on her feet.

"Turn." He turned her around as his hands went to the clasp and zipper of her pants.

"There's a couch . . ."

"Fuck it."

"Floor." She was breathing just as hard as he was, her hands fumbling with his pants as he released hers.

"Bend over."

Her pants cleared her rear. The pale, soft, golden globes made him pause as he pushed at her shoulder blades, arching her over until she rested against the back pillow.

"Oh hell yes," he whispered as one hand moved over the soft satin flesh. "Beautiful. Just fucking beautiful, baby."

"You have a thing about butts, Lance." Her words were part moan as his other hand joined the exploration of the creamy cheeks.

"Oh, baby, you just have no idea. And this pretty butt has to be the finest work of art I've ever seen."

There wasn't so much as a blemish to mar the soft gold sheen of skin. Her ass was just plump enough for a man to hold on to, and just curved enough to make watching her walk a hobby in and of itself. He did love watching her walk.

"Lance." She jerked as his fingers slid over the tempting mounds until the tips met soft, delicious, damp heat.

"You're wet, Harmony." He stepped closer, gripping the shaft of his cock and sliding it through the slick glaze.

"Stop teasing me . . ."

"But teasing you makes you that much wetter." He let the head of his cock slide along the sweet folds until it glanced off her swollen clitoris.

Harmony shuddered.

"So warm and wet." He couldn't help but praise her. Hell,

he was damned near drooling for her, and still, just the feel of her was enough to hold him spellbound.

"Lance. I need you." Her voice throbbed; aching arousal and need turned her normally vibrant tone to a rich, husky purr.

And she needed him.

Lance lifted his head blindly as his cock found the sweet, tight entrance to her pussy. Her muscles gripped him, sucking him in slowly as he rose over her. His hands braced the back of the chair as his lips touched her ear.

"I love you," he whispered gently.

◆   ◆   ◆

Harmony's cry shocked her. As he whispered those last three words, he thrust inside her, hard and heavy, pushing through sensitive tissue and gripping muscles and sending fire racing through her body.

Her back arched as she tried to straighten, only to find herself held in place by the hard hands that covered hers and the heavy chest against her back.

"You're tight, baby," he crooned at her ear as his hips flexed, caressing her internally as she tried to breathe. She needed to breathe. But every time she tried, he moved again, sending torturous pleasure to tear through her senses.

As she tipped her head back, rumbling cries came from her throat, as his lips caressed her jaw, his teeth raking against it and sending scalding friction to sizzle along her nerve endings.

"I need you . . ." She could barely speak as she tried to move her hips, fought to work herself on the length of iron impaling her.

God, his cock was so thick it burned as it spread her internal muscles apart.

"You have me, baby." He nipped at her chin before his lips moved back to her ear. "Every bit of me."

He began to move then, with strokes that were in no way easy or gentle. Hunger tore through both of them, sharpening the edge of arousal to desperation.

She had never felt the intensity that she felt with Lance, the need for more—more pleasure, more of the emotions swirling through her chest and tightening her throat. She had never realized until this man that she needed anything beyond vengeance.

What she felt now though she knew she would never be able to live without. The connection, the bonding to another person. The warmth that filled her soul with his every touch.

"There, baby . . ."

She whimpered as his thrusts began to increase, her fingers clenching in the fabric of the chair. One hand left hers to grip her hip, holding her steady as his cock tunneled inside her with hard, heated thrusts.

The tingling, tormenting sensations racing from her vagina through the rest of her body had her begging for release. It was so close. She could feel it burning in her womb, in her clit, and yet he held her back, easing his thrusts, then increasing the pace, only to ease back once again.

She was growling. Strained little sounds of animalistic pleasure were coming from her throat as her back arched and she fought to tighten around him, to hold his shuttling cock in place each time he retreated.

"Bad girl." The sharp, stinging little caress to her ass had her stilling, pausing at the additional sensation. Was it painful or pleasurable?

She pushed back against him again.

"Like that, baby?" His hand landed again, on the opposite cheek of her rear. "How pretty your little ass blushes."

The next stinging little slap was harder, the sensations

flaring deeper inside her as a starburst ruptured behind her closed eyes. She tightened around him again, gasping at the extremity of the sensations racing through her.

"I told you I was going to spank you, baby."

Another slap, a hard thrust. Retreat, smack, thrust. Her senses where whipping, nerve endings screaming in need as she felt the fire building in her womb. She was close. Oh God, so close.

Then he gripped her hips with both hands and began thrusting inside her furiously. The hard length of his cock separated and pulled at her muscles, caressing, inflaming sensitive nerve endings as a long, muted wail left her throat.

Her orgasm didn't just explode through her. She felt herself imploding, every cell and muscle in her body gathering, reaching then flaming through her with shocking results. Lance's cry was a distant sound at her ear. The feel of his body, covering her, holding her, shielding her as racking shudders raced through her, added to the overwhelming pleasure.

"Sweet baby," he whispered at her ear as she fought to hold him inside her, her vagina rippling along his cock as he spurted into her a final time.

◆   ◆   ◆

Harmony was a weak-willed mess when Lance moved, sliding from her and adjusting his pants before lifting her in his arms. Her head fell to his shoulder, her eyes closing as she fought to get a handle on her emotions.

She decided she hated emotion.

He strode to the shower, quickly undressed them both and pushed her beneath the warmth of the water. She watched him as he bathed her, his hands gentle, his expression a mix of rueful lust and gentle amusement as she frowned back at him.

He didn't speak, and she didn't have the energy to make

enough sense of what she felt, what she could feel growing inside her soul, to discuss it. So she watched him instead, wondering at the man who knelt so easily before her to finish washing her before he turned her to the spray and began on her backside.

"There, all clean," he whispered, turning quickly to the spray and washing his hair before taking a clean washrag and cleaning himself briskly. He was much rougher on his own body.

The washrag spread a stream of bubbles over his face first, then his neck, shoulders and powerful chest. Moving lower, he quickly cleaned his still half-erect cock and the heavy sac below before washing his legs. He was quick, efficient and didn't waste time. He applied the same force toward washing his body as he did toward his life. Except for her.

Harmony watched from the opposite side of the water stream as he rinsed, realizing that with her, Lance broke his own rules in some way.

Unwritten rules. She understood that. He was a man who took life as it came and fixed what was in his power to fix. And he did so without waste. He wasn't a man to posture or to make excuses if he failed. He saw all the different shades of the world, and he did his part and more if the opportunity arose, to make the world a better place.

"You deserve better," she said sadly as he turned the shower off and grabbed two thick, fluffy towels.

"Better than what?" He began drying her. Slow, gentle movements, as though he relished touching her.

"Better than a killer with an ugly past and even uglier disposition." She stared back at him as he tossed her towel aside and began drying himself.

He didn't speak. At first she thought he intended to ignore her statement. Once he'd dried himself and tossed the towel aside, though, he leveled a long, assessing look at her.

"I would die for you, Harmony." He said the words simply, easily. "I love you. And I've never said that to another woman outside my own family, in my life. All I am belongs to you. Ugly past and all. And no man could ask for more than what you are." His hands clasped her face as she felt tears welling in your eyes. "Beautiful, strong. Capable. I have more than I ever deserved, in you. And don't forget it." His eyes sparkled wickedly. "Or I might have to spank you again. Now, get ready. We have plans to make."

He patted her rear, an affectionate reminder of the spanking she would receive. Unfortunately, she had liked that spanking way more than she should have.

✦   ✦   ✦

"Where's the information hidden?" An hour later Lance cleared the dinner dishes from the table and refilled their coffee cups before returning.

Harmony leaned back in her chair and watched him. She could feel the change in him. This was what made Lance such a powerful force in the county. He solved problems, and he was ready to solve this one. Now.

She breathed out roughly, leaning forward as she gripped the coffee cup between her hands. "Boulder, Colorado," she said softly. "I have them hidden in the mountains."

"Why not a safe-deposit box or storage area?"

She shook her head. "Video cameras. There's no way to hide completely from them, and some of the Trainers the Council possessed could have picked me up easily, no matter my disguises when I was younger."

He nodded at that. "Do you have a cabin . . . ?"

"It's not that simple, Lance." She wished it were. "The hike is a long one. It's hidden someplace where I knew it would be protected, no matter what. Getting it won't be easy."

"I'm not heading out of here blind," he snapped. "There are no bugs in the house, and no one listening from outside. We're safe here, Harmony. Now, where is it?"

Her lips twitched. The hard male force that lay dormant beneath the easygoing sheriff was in full force now. She leaned back in her chair and watched him closely.

"It's in a small cave occupied year-round by one cougar lioness or another. Though for the past few years, the same one has managed to hold onto it. The satchel itself is sealed into a protective, lined box with a coded lock. Any attempts to move it or break into it without the code destroy the interior."

His brow lifted as she basked in the approval she saw in his gaze.

"Smart," he murmured.

"I thought so."

"You're going to have to give the Breed Cabinet the information . . ."

She shook her head furiously. "There's a spy in Sanctuary. Leo would be murdered or captured before the Enforcers could ever figure out where he was hidden. That is not a workable solution."

He sat back in his chair, pushing his hands through his hair as he stared up at the ceiling for long moments.

"What about Braden? He's aware of the spy. He and Megan could work on this."

"It could endanger their work with the Breeds they've already taken under their wing." She shook her head at that one too. "I don't know, Lance."

"It's our only choice," he told her roughly. "He'll know someone to contact outside Sanctuary if nothing else. The Breeds are a cohesive unit, but like everything else, certain branches work under the radar from the others. It's our only answer, because after this, you're no longer in the game."

There was that dominant tone again. It sent shivers up her spine even as she leveled him a hard look.

"You can't take the killer out of the Breed," she told him quietly.

"No, but I can take my Breed out of the killing arena." He leaned forward, his gaze hardening as he watched her. "And never doubt, baby, that you're being taken out."

And why did that send a strange little thrill racing through her body?

"We can discuss this later," she said, rather than arguing over something so pointless. Hell, she wanted out, she realized. She wanted to sleep in Lance's arms every night and feel their child grow inside her.

"We're not far from Boulder," he mused then. "But there's too many damned eyes watching us. I'll call Braden and have him put together what we need and meet us tonight on the other side of the courthouse. There's an underground tunnel that leads over there from the days that the downstairs cells were used regularly. We can sneak over to the courthouse and slip away from there."

That could work. Harmony straightened in her chair as she let the plan roll through her mind. "We could hit Boulder by daybreak." She nodded. "We'll take a room until dark. It's the only way to slip into the mountains unnoticed if we're being followed."

"We won't be followed. But we'll go in after dark anyway, just to be safe. Get me a list of what you need and I'll put Braden on it."

Her brows lifted. "You mean I get to contribute?" she asked sweetly.

Lance grunted, his gaze heating up at her sarcasm.

"If I could lock you up and keep you, I would," he growled, though she had a feeling they both knew better. "You scare the hell out of me, Harmony, but this is your world. You know a damned sight more about it than I do. This time, I'll follow you."

She was going to go into shock. She stared back at him in disbelief, knowing that following was not a word this man usually played with.

"I didn't say I would like it," he growled. "I said I'd do it. There's a hell of a difference. And I'll spank you for it later."

Damn, there was that purr again. She blinked at the little rumble that came from her chest.

"Minx." His eyes were like dark blue flames as he stared back at her. "Keep that up and I'll just tie you up in the bed until this is over. That sound makes me harder than hell."

"The mating heat is going away," she pointed out.

"Tell that to my dick." He rose from his chair, and sure enough, the bulge in his jeans was there. Thick. Heavy. Her mouth watered. "And stop looking at me like that. Get your list together and we'll head out."

Bossy, that's what he was. Harmony watched as he moved from the table, all business despite the hard-on straining beneath his jeans. But he was also willing to work with her. She liked that. She hadn't expected it, but she liked it. Her eyes followed him, lingering on his hard back as he turned away from her, feeling the further softening in her chest.

She loved him.

That fact hit her like a two-by-four against the head. For a moment, she even swore she saw stars.

She loved him.

It was quite possibly the most weakening and yet the most strengthening emotion she had ever known in her life. This was why she hadn't been able to leave him. Even knowing the danger she represented to his life, the heartache she had feared was coming, she hadn't been able to leave because she had fallen in love with him that first night.

When he had touched her as though she were something beautiful, something fragile and to be cherished; when he had whispered his naughty demands at her ear and made her feel like the woman she had never been, she had fallen in love with him.

"Harmony, that look on your face is going to get you fucked and we're already eating daylight here. Get the list together and let's get moving. I want this taken care of."

"A quickie . . ."

"You've had your quickie," he growled, the dark demand in his voice making her insides melt. "I want all night. Hell. I want fucking forever. Now let's take care of it."

CHAPTER 22

The sniper rifle surprised her.

Harmony had known that Lance had been on the SWAT team in Chicago; she had even been aware that he was a sharpshooter. Yet when he pulled the specially designed sniper rifle from its case and began to put it together, she could only watch him.

He handled the weapon like an extension of himself—confidently, certain of each move he made as the different parts of the weapon were cleaned, then put in place.

With each added part, he checked the weapon for any flaws, any weakness.

She studied his expression as he worked at the small table in the hotel room they had finally settled on. His face was set, composed, relaxed. There was no frown marring his strong brow, no sense of anger tightening his mouth.

As she cleaned and checked her own weapons on the extra bed in the room, she realized that perhaps there were parts of Lance that she didn't know as well as she should. Parts of him that perhaps she was frightened to know.

He was a man of many layers, of many depths, and infinite patience. She had never met a male as patient, and yet with such a sense of inner strength as Lance held. Unlike Breed males, Lance didn't push his dominance, his power. He used it when he had to, when it became apparent that cool logic or patience wouldn't achieve the results he was searching for. But he didn't feel the need to impress that dominance on anyone.

Unlike Jonas, Lance didn't play games, he didn't manipulate or threaten. Like the wind, what he couldn't go through, he went around or chipped at, layer by layer. But this was the first time she had seen the warrior she had only caught glimpses of before. In his face, in the prepared readiness of his muscles and the cool, objective look in his blue eyes as he studied his weapon, she saw a man who had no qualms in taking that final step to do what he felt was necessary.

It sent a strange tingle of arousal through her body. The certainty that in ways, many ways perhaps, he was stronger than she was, stronger than the Breeds she had known. He was a man who understood and believed in the laws of the land. In justice. But he was also a man who understood that even those laws had a limit.

Tonight, his laws and his justice wouldn't exist. And she regretted that. Dragging him into her world wasn't what she had wanted to do.

Tearing her eyes from him, she lowered her head and concentrated on cleaning her own weapon, on preparing for the night they would awaken to later. It was barely daylight now; the ride from Broken Butte to Estes Park had been made ahead of schedule. Of course, the fact that the wind seemed to push at their vehicle had helped. Lance had broken speed limits and driven with a calm efficiency that she admitted had made her nervous.

He had spoken little. His gaze had been fierce, his expression set. They had eaten breakfast before checking in, and the minute the door locked behind them, he had picked up the metal case he had carried in with his duffel bag and begun assembling the rifle.

Harmony had followed his example, beginning her own pre-battle rituals. But it was different now. As she searched inside her for that core of ice, for the shadow called Death, she realized it wasn't there anymore. Rather than feeling the vengeance clawing inside her, she could only feel regret.

Emotions rose, twisting, churning inside her chest until she wondered at the fact that she could breathe for them. As though something inside her had changed with this mating, some intrinsic, important part of her that had once enabled her to kill so easily. It felt . . . missing.

She shook her head unconsciously, frowning as she tried to make sense of herself. Had the potential to love always been inside her? She had never felt it before, had never known the need to love, until Lance.

Laying the ammunition clips aside, she laid her hand on her abdomen, her fingers rubbing at the area imperceptibly. A baby. What was she supposed to do with a baby?

But her arms ached to hold it, and as she closed her eyes, she saw tiny features framed by Lance's thick black hair, seeing the world through his midnight blue eyes. A little boy perhaps, one who could know laughter.

A cold shudder raced over her body as her eyes jerked open and she moved from the bed. It wasn't that innocent picture she saw, it was the labs, the babies whose ragged cries echoed through the cold stone walls as they wailed for attention. Their cries piercing as they screamed for warmth.

Little faces flushed with rage, eyes staring out at the world in wounded fury as nothing but the cries of others answered their demands.

"Are you normally this jittery before a job?" Lance's voice broke through the nightmarish memory as she swung around to face him. "We need to leave."

Fear and anger knotted her insides as she paced to the closed curtains, her hands rubbing at the chill bumps that had risen on her arms. "And go where?" Harmony's gaze flickered to him as he carefully broke the gun apart again and laid the pieces in the foam padding of the metal case. "My first idea was better." She breathed in a shallow, quick gasp. "Dane will hide us until the child is born. We'll be safe. The baby will be safe."

Lance clipped the case closed before lifting it from the table and setting it on the floor. Watching her closely, he leaned back in the chair, bracing his arms on the sides, and watched her with grim determination. "If we start running now, we'll never stop. And neither will our child." Lance's voice was firm, final.

This was a side of Lance that, she admitted, made her pause. The dominance was like a fire in those blue eyes and in the chiseled planes of his face. A part of her responded to the sheer force she glimpsed in him then. It made her want to submit to him, made her want to give him whatever he was demanding. But he was demanding her soul now.

"I can't let you do this." She lifted her chin, meeting his gaze head-on. "There's too much at stake and too many dangers that could have followed us here."

"Of course we were followed." His smile was tight, controlled. "We lost them in Boulder, but I'm sure they'll catch up to us soon enough."

Shock vibrated through her system.

"You knew we were followed?" she whispered.

She had suspected it when he drove through Boulder rather than the more direct route around the outside of the city, but she hadn't been certain. Her own radar, the prickle at the back of her neck, hadn't been present, so she hadn't been certain.

Jonas shrugged. "I thought I glimpsed the heli-jet in the distance in the rearview mirror, but I wasn't certain. It could have been a plane, hell, it could have been a shadow. But we were followed."

She wrapped her arms across her chest then, breathing in deeply. God, she hated all these emotions churning chaotically inside her. As though once she had begun feeling, it wouldn't stop. It wouldn't ease or give her peace.

"That's all the more reason to contact Dane." She breathed in deeply. "He'll know where to hide us . . ."

"I don't need one of your ex-lovers to protect my woman or my child," he stated grimly. "Don't push this, Harmony, because you're going to lose."

"Is that what this is over?" She stood there, blank, amazed. "You won't accept his help because I slept with him?"

"I am perfectly capable of protecting my woman and my child," he informed her, his voice deepening. He retained his patience, though his gaze hardened. "We retrieve the information you have and get it back to Braden. From there, we'll know how to handle Jonas."

Men! She stared back at Lance in bemusement.

"Lance, I don't doubt you would protect us. The point is that if we found a place to have the baby in safety, then we could fight the rest later."

"If running or hiding would assure your life and our child's, then I would be perfectly capable of hiding us. Son of a bitch, Harmony. I understand your history with the bastard, but we do this my way, not his."

"I'm not doubting you . . ."

"Well, excuse me if it sounds like it," he snapped.

"You're bargaining with other people's lives," she whispered desperately. "We can't do that, Lance."

"I'd bargain with the devil himself for your fucking safety." An edge of impatience colored his voice. "If the first Leo exists, then his location is not going to be in those files. If the Council ever had a hint of where he was, they would have struck. A few power-hungry Council scientists would not have sat on that information before using it."

He sat there so calmly, commanding, determined that this was going to go his way, period. For a moment, Harmony almost gave in. She almost agreed.

Then the faces of those babies in the labs flashed before her mind again. Screaming for attention, for warmth. They hadn't known warmth, had never known love or a gentle touch. That was the fate that awaited her child if the Council took her—that, or death.

Straightening her shoulders, she let her own determined gaze meet his.

"Then I'll leave alone. I know how to contact Dane . . ."

She didn't expect his response, though she should have. His patience evaporated as her eyes widened. A hint of fear flew through her a second before he reached her, his hands gripping her upper arms firmly.

"Like fucking hell!" His features were contorted with fury, his eyes burning with it. "Attempt it, Harmony, just fucking attempt it and I swear to God I'll slap you in cuffs so fast it will make your head spin."

Her lips parted as she stared back at him, shocked at the burning heat that flowed from his hands into her arms.

"Let me go." She jerked against his hold.

"Do you think I'm going to let you keep running?" His gaze bored into hers. "That I'm incapable of protecting you and our child?"

"That's not what I meant." She shook her head desperately. "You don't understand . . ."

"I understand that Jonas, Dane and these fucking files

have haunted you for ten years, and it's coming to an end here."

His head lowered, his lips drawing back from his teeth in a primitive snarl.

"It ends here. Right here, by God."

"Even if it means our lives?" she cried out, fighting to hold back her fears, her tears. "They've followed us, Lance. We can't even be certain who it is that followed, or who's waiting. Don't ask me to take this chance. Please."

He dropped a hand to her abdomen, his palm covering it, his eyes darkening to a near black.

"If it meant your life, I'd know it," he snapped. "I would feel it and the winds would scream that knowledge to me. This is the only way."

"No." She jerked at his hold again.

"Yes."

He didn't give her time to argue. As her lips opened to curse him, his were there, covering them as his arms pulled her against his chest.

Arousal should have been the last thing in her mind, the last thing she responded to. They were in the middle of a war zone and it was about to get worse, she could feel it. But his lips on hers were a sensual, erotic act of mastery. He didn't ask for her kiss, nor was he tentative. He demanded. He controlled. And ultimately, Harmony found herself submitting to the wicked, erotic nips at her lips by sharp teeth and the hungry growl that came from her own throat.

That dominance was her undoing. Female Breeds must have been programmed to submit to the males, though until Lance, that genetic coding had never made an impression on her. With Lance, she couldn't deny it. She couldn't deny her need, or her hunger, any more than she could deny the fears that, for the moment, dissolved beneath his passion.

His hands trailed down her arms, broad, calloused hands

that stroked her flesh with sensual roughness and replaced the chill of foreboding with heated, wicked lashes of pleasure.

She was lost in him. As impossible as it should have been, as furious as she was with him, he still managed to consume her, to build the hunger simmering within her to a full, raging blaze.

She tore at his clothes, nothing so important now as feeling his flesh against hers, the warmth of his body stroking over her.

Her shirt fell beneath his hands, just as her jeans parted seconds later. Gasping, panting for air, they groped and ripped at clothing, socks, shoes, until Lance was tumbling her to the bed, his large, harder body coming over her as his lips tore from hers.

"Mine!" He reasserted his claim as he parted her thighs, his cock pressing into the slick, heated depths of her vagina. "Tell me, damn you! Tell me you're mine."

"Yours." She could barely breathe, but she couldn't stop the word being torn from her lips as she stared back at him, shocked by the intensity of his eyes.

They blazed in his dark face, deep blue flames of determination, dominance and powerful male force, glowing with an otherworldly light.

"No one will take you from me," he snapped, one hand tangling in her hair as his cock surged inside her, fierce, hot, stretching her to her limits as she arched into the thrust.

She would have closed her eyes, but she couldn't break his gaze. He held her trapped, staring into her eyes, breaching her soul even as his erection breached the aching depths of her pussy.

She would have closed herself from him if she could. The distracting pleasure washing through her broke her concentration, fractured her ability to hold that inner part of herself aloof.

"Don't . . ." She begged him to release her, not with his body, but with that inner link she could feel forging inside her soul.

He rose above her, the width of his shoulders gleaming, damp with sweat. She could feel the power flowing through him, the strength that was so much a part of him wrapping around her, sheltering her. Protecting her.

"I won't let you run." His voice throbbed with furious determination. "I won't lose you. Or this."

He moved then, his hips drawing back, stroking exposed nerve endings, sending her senses reeling with pleasure as she arched against him to hold him inside her.

"Can you run from this, Harmony?" His hips twisted as he penetrated her again, a fierce, hard thrust that sent him tunneling to the depths of her as she gasped at the heat exploding through her. "Tell me, baby. Tell me you can walk away from this."

If it had just been the pleasure, she could have walked away. But it was more. As he fucked her with hard gliding strokes, he infused her soul as well. Heat moved from his body to hers, chasing away the cold determination she had fought to rebuild inside her heart.

One hand gripped her hair, kneading, pulling at the strands and adding another level of sensation. The other hand cupped her breast, lifting it, until his mouth covered her nipple, his tongue flaying it with whiplashing pleasure.

He broke through every defense she could muster and left it lying, crumpled at her feet, as her hands gripped his hair and held him to her breast.

His hips pumped against hers, churning, thrusting, stroking inside her as his pelvis rasped against her swollen clit. The sensual stroke and slide, retreat and entrance were driving her insane. The pleasure built, layer upon layer, until nothing existed inside her but the need, the hunger clawing at her womb and in her soul.

"Feel it!" He lifted his head, staring down at her, his expression strained as the spiraling intensity of pleasure began to build. "You won't run. Do you hear me?"

She shook her head, fighting to breathe, to think.

"Say it, Harmony." His voice was a dominant, commanding baritone that rippled through her senses.

He wanted surrender. She shook her head, fighting against it, fighting the need to give it.

"Say it, damn you!" One hand gripped her hip to hold her still as he slammed inside her, his legs widening, pushing her thighs apart as he shifted and touched her deeper.

"Don't do this." Baring her teeth, Harmony fought to hold on to herself. "No."

"Say it. You're mine, damn you. Fucking mine. You will follow me. Say it."

His hand gripped her wrist as her nails dug into his shoulder and he slammed her hands to the bed. Her punishment came in a slow, torturous withdrawal of his cock from her inner grip. A sensual, heated slide of powerful flesh over desperate nerve endings.

Transferring her wrists to one hand, he clamped her firmly to the bed as he gripped her hip once again and held her still beneath him. With the strength of his body he controlled her, just as he was fighting to control her with his will as well.

"I won't," she moaned, fighting against fear and hunger and the overriding need to do as he demanded.

"You will, Harmony."

Before she could struggle, he moved, sliding free of her before turning her to her stomach and trapping her against the bed.

"Damn you, Lance." She fought as he lifted her hips, shoving a pillow beneath them before thrusting inside her aching pussy again.

"Stay still." His hand tapped the side of her ass in a warning little slap. "Give me what I want, baby, and you'll get what you want."

"I can't do this." Her fingers clenched in the blankets. "I won't . . ."

"You will, Harmony. Say the words. Tell me you'll follow me. I won't let you run."

Pressing her forehead into the blankets, she shook her head furiously.

"Oh, I think you will, sweetheart." The soft, warning croon should have prepared her, but it didn't.

She jerked as she felt him lean back, felt his cock throb inside her with a hard pulse before his hands separated the smooth cheeks of her rear.

"You're so wet." His fingers moved to where her pussy stretched around him. "So sweet and slick, all over." He smoothed the rush of liquid from where it seeped past her vagina, back, back.

"Oh God!" Her eyes flew open as she stared into the room with dazed shock.

His finger pressed against the small, hidden entrance of her rear. His thumb massaged, pressed. It wasn't the touch so much as it was the impression of dominant control, of her own submission, that threw her mind into a frenzy or confusion.

She felt him leaning over her then, his arm reaching to the night table where his shaving kit rested. As he moved, his cock stroked into her, taking her breath, leaving her little oxygen to gasp as she watched him remove the small tube of lubrication he carried.

Harmony shuddered beneath him then.

"There, sweetheart." His hand caressed over her rear as

he straightened behind her again, the movement causing her to shudder in pleasure beneath him.

"Lance . . ."

"It's okay, baby." She felt the cooling lubrication against her rear entrance. "It's all okay."

"Oh God . . . Damn you, Lance."

His finger slid inside that back entrance, sending thrilling flames across nerve endings never stroked in such a way before.

"Never had this before, baby?" His finger shuttled in and out for several strokes. "What about this?"

A second joined the first, stretching her as tremors of ecstasy wracked her body and perspiration began to dampen her flesh.

"Do you know, little cat . . ." His voice was a soft croon. "My strong little kitten. You haven't had this because you refuse to submit to any man. To anyone's dominance over you. You didn't belong, Harmony. Let's see if you belong now." Another finger pierced her.

She was crying, whimpering little sounds of pleasure and pain that stoked the hunger higher and left her mindless with the need for release.

"Give me what I want, Harmony." His voice was strained as his fingers fucked her with the same slow rhythm he was setting with his cock. The dual penetration was mind numbing, dragging her sensibilities beneath the wake of the pleasure.

"Lance . . ."

"That's not what I want to hear." He wasn't heeding her whimpering pleas. "Tell me, Harmony. Tell me who you belong to. Who you follow."

The fierce need, the raging lust echoed in his voice with the demand for surrender. Total surrender.

She shook her head again, unable to voice the denial when everything inside her screamed that she give in to him.

"No. Lance, please . . ." She found the strength to whisper, to beg as she felt the thick length of his erection leaving her empty, unsatisfied.

"Easy, sweetheart."

Her breath caught in her throat as the head of his cock tucked at her rear instead.

"Lance?" The feminine thrill of sensual fear that echoed in her voice might shock her later, but for now, the fear of the unknown held her in its grip.

Emotions clashed inside her, the press of his cock against her ultra-tight entrance sending more than the thrill of the forbidden racing through her. This was the ultimate dominance, the impression of sensual, wicked control gripping her mind as he began to stretch her.

She couldn't take him. She had never before been able to take such a touch.

"Trust," he whispered then. "See how well you trust me, baby." His voice was a guttural growl as she tried to scream against the heavy invasion.

He was taking her, slowly; inch by inch her body was accepting him, the anal penetration scouring her mind as her body relaxed, even against her will, and she felt the length of him invade her in a slow, measured thrust.

"Mine." His voice was primal now, throbbing with the demand. "Mine."

He rose over her, his body covering hers as he began to move, thrusting inside her with a diabolical rhythm as one hand moved beneath the front of her hips and his fingers speared inside her pussy.

"Tell me. Now!"

"Yes." With her hoarse scream she felt the last of her inhibitions, the final shield of her defenses, collapse. "Yours. I'm yours."

Sobs of need fell from her lips as tears washed from her eyes. The pleasure was overwhelming; the strength and purpose of the man filling her, stimulating her, stealing her mind and her soul, rocked her with a shocking sense of belonging.

"Will you follow me?" He was gasping at her ear, his body heaving against hers, his fingers and his cock fucking her with a ruthless determination to secure every part of her.

"I'll follow . . ." She shuddered as something inside her clawed for release. "I'll follow . . ." And she knew she had no other choice, she never had.

As the final submission, the final vow to give someone else control filtered through her mind, she felt her body dissolve.

The orgasm that exploded inside her was a white-hot cataclysm that burned through her soul. The past was obliterated beneath the pleasure; the future contained nothing but Lance—his touch, his heavy moans, his teeth at her shoulder as he bit her with shocking strength seconds before she felt his explosion.

The furious blast of his semen filling her rear as his fingers filled her spasming pussy was too much. Another blinding release tore through her, ripping over nerve endings, throwing her higher and leaving her to trust Lance to catch her.

Trust. As the final shudders rippled through her body and she collapsed beneath him, exhaustion pulling her beneath its black velvet surface, that thought flitted across her mind. Yes, she trusted Lance, but did she trust herself?

CHAPTER 23

Harmony had lived within these mountains for months at a time throughout the past ten years. She had camped there, used it as a base and made herself known to the elements of the land that possessed it. She knew each tree, each stone outcropping and the denizens of the forest that moved within a rhythm of time unchanged.

The owls that watched them didn't hoot in curiosity at their passage, the opossum that watched from beneath a boulder didn't send out a warning and the raccoon searching for food beneath a fallen log took no notice of them.

Lance shared her scent, therefore he was accepted, and Harmony was one of their own—neither predator nor prey, a part of the land that they had been born within, the scent of the mountain infused into her being.

Crouching next to a fallen, centuries-old log, Harmony used the special night-vision goggles Lance had brought with him to survey the forest. Her night vision wasn't nearly as good as it should have been, but her hearing had always made up for it.

She could hear nothing unusual as they approached the

cougar's den, she could smell nothing unusual, but her neck itched.

"Do you feel it?" The sound of her question carried no further than the large man kneeling next to her.

"You're safe." The confidence in his voice did little to ease the fears driving her.

She would have turned back miles before had he not pushed her further. He was unrelenting; the dominance she had only glimpsed in Broken Butte was showing itself in full force now. It should have grated at her sense of independence, her own strength; instead it bolstered it. If only she could rid herself of that itch at her neck. That primal awareness that something was off, something not entirely right about the whole venture. And she couldn't shake the feeling that Lance was hiding something from her. The man who had assured her in Broken Butte that this was her world, and that he could follow, had changed the rules.

Not that, in a way, he wasn't following her. He was. Sort of. He was covering her back, letting her lead them deeper into the forest despite every instinct inside her that urged her to turn back.

Scanning the area once again, she could detect no signs of life other than that of nature. Breathing in deeply, she rose, straightening as she began to move deeper into the boulder-strewn mountainside, heading for the shallow cave where the box of information and files had been hidden.

The night blended in shades of the mechanical green, reds and violets of the night-vision goggles as they picked up the landscape and the teaming wildlife within it. The night was never still. Crouched in the shadows, a wolf watched as they passed by, his amber eyes narrowed in suspicion, though he let them pass easily.

Harmony was aware of Lance at her back, the powerful automatic rifle he carried loaded and ready. He had slipped the safety off as they began to move again, hoping, she knew, that she wouldn't hear the almost silent slide of metal against metal. But she had.

He wasn't as comfortable with this as he assured her he was. He could feel the vibrations of danger, and she was certain the soft breeze rushing past them was bringing him much more information than he had shared with her.

Half an hour later they eased along the rough ground, sidestepping a scurrying mouse before moving past the small, scattered boulders and brush that hid the entrance of the cave beyond.

She lifted her hand to announce her intention to stop before moving into the small clearing. Gazing up, she scanned the trees, the mountain pines, aspens and white spruce that grew to towering heights.

"Get it done, Harmony." Lance's voice was a low, confident murmur. "I'll cover you from here."

She bit her lip in indecision.

"Are you sure?"

"The winds are sure, baby." He breathed softly behind her. "This is your freedom. Now go."

Go. The final word was a command, the force behind it goading her into action. Crouching, she worked her way around the perimeter, her shoulder blades tight with tension as she kept to the shadows. Not that shadows would do her much good if Coyotes watched, or even humans with goggles similar to hers. The night was no longer as safe as it had once been for the creatures within it.

Bending low, she entered the cave slowly, purring softly as she heard the mother cougar issue a warning hiss. She moved into the cave, her gaze softening at the lioness curled in the back. Two cubs stared back at Harmony inquisitively as the mother's amber eyes narrowed and she drew in Harmony's scent slowly.

A rumbling growl of welcome left the big cat's throat. Harmony's scent was a part of the cave, and this cat was the same that had held onto the area for the past five years. She had raised her cubs here, hunted here.

"Yes, we're old friends, aren't we?" Harmony murmured, the words nearly lost beneath the small purring growls that she used to speak to the cougar. "I came for what's mine. That's all."

Moving to her knees to further reassure the mother, Harmony crawled to the fissure that opened within a deep shadow at the side. The case was still there, cool to the touch and layered by years of dust.

As she pulled it free and prepared to turn, she found herself faced with two playful cubs, their little paws batting at her ear as kittenish growls left their throats.

The mother had risen but watched with patient caution several feet away. Timidly, Harmony reached out, her fingers tickling the little male beneath his belly as he caught at her gloved wrist.

A smile tugged at her lips as the sister growled and tumbled her brother in jealousy. With the babes distracted by each other, Harmony began her withdrawal. Her eyes connected with the mother as the lioness's head jerked up, her eyes going to the entrance and narrowing.

"I know," Harmony whispered painfully. "They're waiting on me, aren't they?"

Tears flooded her eyes as she pressed her free hand to her abdomen protectively and the cougar stared back at her.

"Stay here. No matter what," she whispered. "Keep your babes safe. For me."

She jerked as the first shot fired, her head turning to the

entrance as fear surged through her heart. Lance was out there alone.

Turning, Harmony tore quickly to the entrance, her weapon clearing her holster as she used the leather strap on the metal case to anchor it to her back and leave her hands free.

"Lance." She rolled from the entrance, feeling dirt and debris pepper around her as she found the safety of a boulder beyond.

The sons of bitches had managed to come in upwind, which explained why she hadn't smelled them, why she had only felt them. God, she should have heeded her own instincts rather than Lance's.

"Stay down. They're at twelve and three," he barked into the link she had flipped down at the side of her ear. "We have at least a half a dozen out there gunning for us."

He had moved. He was no longer at her back, but in front of her. Scuttling between boulders and fallen logs, Harmony fired at the flashes of fire in the night that indicated their positions.

There might have been more than half a dozen. She peppered the night with gunfire, knowing their best chance was to head down the mountain and get the hell out of there. Standing and fighting wasn't going to work. They were outmanned, and possibly outgunned.

She heard an enraged canine scream as her lips tightened in satisfaction and she turned to the flash of gunfire to her right. The night had erupted with violence.

"We have to head down the mountain," she snapped into the link. "This is no place to make a stand. There's more cover in town and less chance of being trapped."

"Get out of here," Lance snapped in reply. "I'll be behind you."

She heard it in his voice then, smelled it in the air. He was lying to her. He wasn't just being evasive, which was harder to detect. He wasn't going to follow her.

"What have you done?" she cried into the link, terror racing through her blood. "You go, I'll cover your six. Don't fuck with me here, Lance."

She heard his curse then.

"Harmony. Go." Hard demand filled his voice. As did resignation. He wasn't going to come out of that forest alive.

Harmony felt terror race over her flesh, weakening her, nearly collapsing her lungs with her need to scream. They were surrounded, firing was automatic, and she knew the chances of escape were growing slimmer.

Eyes narrowed, she surveyed the flashes of gunfire through the goggles she wore, firing back, hitting what didn't move fast enough, only to have another replace what she hit. She should have known it was a trap. Dammit, she should have never disregarded her own instincts.

"I'm not going without you, Lance. Get a move on it. We head out now."

"I said go." His voice was firm, demanding at her ear. She could almost feel his strength, his warmth. She couldn't live without feeling it again.

"We don't have much time." She heard the tears in her voice, the ragged plea she would have never voiced before. "Get your ass out of here. I'll cover—"

"I love you, Harmony."

"No! You fucking bastard, don't you do this to me!"

Harmony felt as though she were moving in slow motion. There were too many around them; they were closing in, gaining ground despite the shots she fired and the marks she hit. If they didn't go, if they didn't go now, then they were going to die.

Lance was picking off his own targets, but he was stationary, keeping their only line of escape open.

"Lance, we can both get out of this," she screamed into the link. "I won't go alone."

"Go. Now." His voice was a fierce, commanding lash. "Get your ass back to Estes Park. Dane will find you . . ."

"No." She was forced to retreat, searching for a break as she rapidly reloaded and began firing again.

He was too far away from her. She would have to get to him. God, he couldn't do this. He couldn't leave her alone, not now. She couldn't be alone now.

Chills raced over her flesh as she gauged the distance between them. There were fewer assailants now. There was a slim chance that, together, they could shoot their way out of this.

It was a long shot. The path between them was less than twenty-five feet. There was little cover, but enough. Maybe just enough.

"Go on, baby. Get the hell out of here." Lance's voice was steady, patient. "I'll keep them off your ass."

"Get ready, I'm coming to you . . ."

"No!"

"Damn you. We live together or we die together. Take your choice."

✦   ✦   ✦

Lance inhaled roughly. He had known it would happen this way. He had known what would happen. He had heard his own death in the wind, heard its price for surrender, its demand for payment. He would miss Harmony. Even in death, he would miss her.

He lifted his head, his eyes narrowing behind the night-vision goggles as he timed what he knew was coming. He hadn't questioned the knowledge when it came to him during the long drive to Colorado. He hadn't debated it or attempted to find a way to change it. Nothing came without a price. The life and happiness of his woman and child was worth more to him than his own life ever would be.

Covering Harmony, he slid from the protection of the boulders he had placed himself behind, giving the shooters the target they were looking for. The price of her freedom was his blood. She would be safe. The winds had made their promise, and his blood would seal it.

Her precious Dane would hide her and the child Lance had created with her. They would be protected, and that was all that mattered. He might not understand the price the winds claimed for her freedom, for her life, but he wouldn't deny it.

He could hear the wind howling through the mountain-side, its demand for his blood a banshee cry he couldn't ig-nore. And in that moment he saw why. As she moved to save him, a tall blond-haired soldier stepped from the shadows, a maniacal smile twisting his lips. The bastard stepped from cover, his gun aiming for her, his expression twisted into a snarl of fury as he fired at her.

Lance threw himself in front of Harmony, knowing the moment the bullet left the barrel that it would strike flesh. Better his chest than hers. Better his heart than the one who had never known freedom, never known love. The winds had whispered its promise for his sacrifice. His child's laughter, his woman's freedom. They would survive.

    ❖ ❖ ❖

Harmony felt the impact of Lance's body against hers as they went down. She knew. Her eyes went to his chest as her howl rent the air. An enraged feline scream that echoed with a cougar's cry.

"Motherfucker!" Her gun came up, her finger depressing the trigger as the rounds slammed into the figure. "You dis-eased fucking bastard!"

She saw his eyes widen in shock, as though he believed he couldn't die. As though he had the right to live, to destroy what belonged to her.

She knew him, one of the fanatical bastards who had joined Alonzo. Alonzo would pay as well. So help her God, if Lance died on her, then they would all pay.

She threw her gun as she came to her knees, before tossing the satchel that contained the information she had thought was so important to preserve. She had no idea where it fell; she didn't give a damn.

Her hands hovered over Lance's chest; she didn't care who fired at her now. It didn't matter. Death was preferable to the horrible, aching agony twisting through her mind now.

No pain could come close to this. No horror could ever compare to staring into Lance's dark eyes as she pushed the goggles from his face, and seeing the knowledge in his eyes.

"No . . ." Her moan joined the distant cry of the wind, the sound of explosions around her, a loud hum throbbing in the air.

None of it mattered.

"Shhh." Lance's expression twisted with pain as she tried to stop the blood flowing from his chest. It fell over her fingers, a silky, heated fall of life that blistered her hands.

"No. No. No. Oh God. Don't leave me. Don't leave me." She was crying. She could feel the tears running down her cheeks as she watched a single droplet slide from his eye.

"It had to be," he whispered sluggishly. "I knew it had to be."

Screams echoed around them. Gunfire. The sound of a motor. She didn't know what was going on, she didn't care.

"Don't leave me." She gagged at the thought of being without him now. Of being alone. "Please, God. Lance. Please."

His face twisted with pain as she felt her stomach cramping with the cold, horrible knowledge that this was her fault.

She had killed him after all.

"I'll follow you," she cried. "Just as I swore, I'll follow you."

"No . . . Live free . . ." His expression twisted in pain.

"I'll follow you," she screamed. "You made me care. You made me feel, damn you. I won't do it without you. I can't do it without you."

As she moved to touch his face, hard hands jerked at her shoulders, attempting to drag her from him. Enraged, feral, she fought back, seeing the shadows merging around them. Death was taking him, jerking her from his side to tear his soul from his body. Her payment. This was her payment for taking innocent lives as a child. Life was being taken from her now.

"Take me," she screamed, fighting the clawlike hands pulling at her, fighting to hold back her blows. "Take me. Kill me. Don't take him. Please . . . please . . ."

The sharp blow to her face barely registered, but the voice screaming at her ear did.

"Harmony, goddammit, let us help him."

Jonas!

Shadows cleared, and suddenly the brilliance of the heli-jet's lights struck his tormented expression.

"He's prepped. Let's fly."

She swung her head around. Rule, Merc and Lawe were standing protectively around Elyiana and the two Breeds lifting the stretcher they had strapped Lance onto.

She jerked from Jonas's hold.

"Move!" Grabbing her arm again, he forced her to the heli-jet. "We have more of those bastards that attacked you coming up the mountain."

She jerked, staring behind them as the others moved

ahead, some sixth sense warning her. Dane stepped from another shadow, his face streaked with dirt and grime, his expression furious. Concerned.

Lance was being taken from her because of this. Because of a past that wouldn't die, and a future that had never been meant for her. Because she was weak, because she had cared more for others than she had cared for his safety. As she watched, Dane moved through the shadows before stopping and retrieving the satchel she had tossed aside.

Keeping step with Jonas, she turned her back on him, she let the last tie she had to her past free. Jonas wanted Dane, and he had to know Dane was there. But he was saving Lance. Lance was all that mattered.

"Go. Go." Jonas all but threw her into the heli-jet as she turned back, stumbling, scrambling to get to Lance.

"Hold onto him, Harmony," Elyiana barked, grabbing her hands and placing them at his head as she stared into her eyes fiercely. "Don't let him go. Talk to him. It's bad. Real bad. Fight for him now, Harmony."

His eyes were open, but dazed, shocked. She held his head and as she cried, whispered the only thing she knew that mattered.

"I love you. Please, Lance, don't leave me. You don't want me to follow you, you really don't. Please, please don't leave me."

He had to live. He had to live for her, for their child, because Harmony knew that without him, there was no life, no love, there was no freedom.

CHAPTER 24

The flight to Boulder took only minutes. Harmony cradled Lance's head as Elyiana worked at the wound on his chest, attempting to halt the flow of blood, barking reports over the link at her ear, to the hospital surgeons awaiting them.

"I love you. Don't leave me . . ." Harmony whispered the words over and over again as she held his glazed gaze with her own.

She smoothed his hair, still feeling the power in his incredible body, the force of the man that he was. God, why had he done something so insane?

"We're landing, Ely," Jonas snapped as the heli-jet began to bank. "Surgeons are awaiting to assist and they have a room ready. Let's get ready to haul ass."

"Don't leave me," she whispered again, shaking, feeling the horror of the night as it echoed through her veins. "Don't leave me, Lance."

He stared back at her, his eyes clearing for a second, just a second.

"I love you . . . Harmony."

Her tears rolled faster at his words. She hadn't truly believed, not wholly. So much blood had stained her soul that she hadn't believed he could really love her. That she could love.

"Move." The doors whipped open as hands reached for the stretcher and she was torn from him once again.

"Let's go." Jonas was there, helping her from the heli-jet as she stumbled again, fighting to keep up with Lance, and yet unable to.

"They're taking him straight to surgery," Jonas growled in her ear. "The best surgeons in the city were called in the minute we landed in the forest. We have three of the nation's best trauma surgeons here plus Ely."

His arm was wrapped around her shoulders, his other hand holding her arm as he practically carried her into the entrance from the heli-pad.

She was shaking. Harmony could feel the shudders tearing through her, could hear the ragged growls at the back of her throat, and she couldn't stop them.

"He wouldn't run," she whispered. "I begged him to run . . ."

"You would have run into a trap," he snapped. "There were men coming up the mountain behind you. Alonzo was more than prepared for this, Harmony. Do you actually believe no one knew what you took from those labs? Why do you think those fucking Council soldiers and Coyotes were always after you?"

Lance would have known there were more men coming up the mountain. The winds would have warned him. Why had he done this? It made no sense. They could have run, sent Dane or even, God forbid, Jonas after the information if he had warned her of what awaited them. There had been many other ways to go rather than this one.

"I told him not to go." She trembled as they raced to the elevator. "I wanted to call Dane. He should have called Dane."

"Yeah, running would have been a good idea," he snarled, furious. "Goddammit, I try to fucking save your hide and you keep running."

"Save me?" She jerked back. "You call bargaining for a friend's life saving me?"

"He's the first fucking Leo, you stubborn woman." His canines flashed at the side of his mouth. "I have to find him, I have no choice. And you're so friggin' hardheaded you would have never bargained with me."

She jerked as though he had slapped her.

"I gave you my life," she sobbed then. What did pride matter at this point? None of it mattered. "I stole that information, I killed those scientists and Breeds to save your life."

Before she realized what she was doing, her palm flew out, slapping at his shocked, bewildered face.

"She ordered your death," she screamed. "Ordered it and they were going to carry out her demands. They lied to you. They betrayed you. I killed them to save you, you bastard."

Jonas jerked back.

"They would have found a way to warn me."

Her laughter was cruel, hard. God, how she hated him at that moment. Hated every moment she had run, every bullet she had taken and every cold night she had ever spent, alone, because she had loved her brother. "The Breeds plotting to escape with you told her about your plans for escape," she snarled. "The bold idea you hatched to use them to hold the scientists hostage while you connected the communications to an outside line and told the world about us. They used you. Just as Madame LaRue used you."

His eyes narrowed then, his expression turning stony.

"I saved you." Her lips twisted mockingly. "And you never fucking cared, did you, Jonas? You never suspected."

"I cared once I knew the truth," he said, his voice quiet as his quicksilver eyes darkened. "All I needed was the truth, Harmony, and you had it hid. Why, little sister, didn't you come to me after the rescues instead of running from me?"

Her lips twisted painfully. "Because you should have trusted me. What use do I have for someone who always requires proof? When does the trust begin, Jonas?"

The elevator doors slid open as Harmony's head began to pound with the years that stretched behind her. She had wanted to save him for what?

Flinching back from his touch, she stepped from the elevator, wiping at the tears that stained her face, giving no thought to the blood that marred her hands and now streaked her pale expression. She moved woodenly, her concentration on the operating room that lay just beyond the waiting room Jonas led her to.

She could hear Ely's voice, the murmur of the supporting team of surgeons and nurses, the beep of life support. What was said around her didn't matter. She wrapped her arms around her chest and leaned against the wall just outside the operating room and fought to hold onto the only link she had left to Lance.

He was her soul. How had she not realized that he had become her soul in such a short time? That all the barriers she had believed she held in place had dissolved beneath his touch? How had she missed it?

She lowered her head, feeling the loss of the hard, cold core of resolve she had once used to get her through each day. There had been no dreams before Lance. No hopes and no fears. There had been a daily fight to survive, to do what she had set out to do so long ago. She had saved Jonas, and she had been biding her time.

What then?

Harmony realized she had no plans after that. For ten years she had survived on that final goal, had fought mercilessly for it. Alone.

Nights spent killing, days spent trying to sleep through the nightmares that haunted her, and through it all, she knew, she had no plans after that end goal had been achieved. She would have died. Eventually. It wouldn't have taken long for her enemies to tire of attempting to capture her. Eventually, they would have killed her.

And perhaps that would have been best. If she had died before now, Lance would have never felt this need to sacrifice himself.

What had she done? Silent sobs shook her body as she fought to brace herself against the pain.

"We're not going to make it."

Harmony felt her heart stop as she heard Ely speak from the operating room.

"The wound is too severe . . ."

"The bleeding is growing worse . . ."

"BP is falling . . ."

"We can't repair the damage fast enough . . ."

"BP is critical . . ."

The hard signal of the heart monitor began to flatline as Harmony's agonized, feral scream tore from her throat.

◆　　◆　　◆

Lance felt the winds. They whispered over his body as he stood beneath the hot desert sun, his arms widespread, his head lifted to the gentle caress. It reminded him of Harmony. Her scent was in the air, honeysuckle and roses; he could almost taste the soft, delicate treat of her kiss.

He was dying. He could feel the chill racing through his body, competing with the warmth of the sun, and the sorrow that filled him was like a fiery ache.

*Then he heard his son's laughter and Harmony's gentle
voice calling him in. There was no fear in the tone; there was
amused indulgence, a comforting, maternal sound he had always loved hearing from his own mother.*

*Harmony was safe. There could be no regret in her safety;
his regret was that his arms weren't there to hold her. He
would never taste her laughter, never cradle his child against
his chest. He would never know his woman's happiness.*

*"The price was paid. Blood was shed. Your life for hers,"
a voice whispered then, gentle, soothing. "Your return depends only upon your own will."*

*His eyes opened. The winds blew before him, shimmering,
iridescent, glittering beneath the brilliant rays of the sun.
The force of it was nearly blinding, filled with heat and whispering promises that shook him to the core of his being.*

*"Are you strong enough to return, child of the wind?" the
voice whispered. "Strong enough to hold onto all you died
for? You have held your end. A life for a life, blood for blood."*

"I can return?"

*"A life for a life. Blood for blood. The bargain was met.
Your return depends only upon your desire to be."*

*He heard the scream then, feral, agonized, a sound filled
with such misery, such bleak, resounding sorrow that at first
he wondered if it were his own.*

*Through the shimmering waves of heat and air, he saw
her then. She was fighting someone. Jonas. He was holding her to the floor as Megan and Braden attempted to help
hold her still. Her hands were clawing at a door, her head
tilted back, blood and dirt and tears streaking her face as
she wailed his name.*

*"Harmony." He whispered her name, reaching out to her.
His hands sank into the shimmering waves of life, reaching
for her, not even minding the hard, brutal jerk of his body.*

Then darkness filled his vision and his own cry echoed

inside his mind as he fought to find her once again. He had to get to Harmony.

"Rest, child of the wind," the voice whispered as his body became leaden, his soul aching for the sound of Harmony's voice. "Rest for now . . ."

◆   ◆   ◆

It didn't matter that the empath held her in her arms or that Braden and Jonas were arguing quietly in a corner. Through gritty eyes, Harmony stared at the clock on the waiting room wall and counted the time, second by second.

She could hear the muted beep of the heart monitor in the operating room, the proof that Lance had come back, and so far, he was still alive. The sounds of the surgeons' voices had drifted away for the most part. She didn't want to know what they said; she couldn't live with the knowledge of what had happened to his insides.

How many times had she killed with a single gunshot to the heart? The knife was her preferred method of killing, not her only one.

She was aware of Megan's hand petting through her hair gently as Harmony's head lay in her lap. The other woman treated her as a child, and for the moment, Harmony didn't have the will to resist. Lance's parents were on their way to Boulder, via the Breeds' heli-jet. They would arrive soon. And she was supposed to be there. She was supposed to face them, the woman who had nearly killed their son.

Cousins, aunts and uncles were said to be rushing to the hospital. Harmony had no idea how she was going to face them all.

"They'll love you." It took a moment for Megan's soft voice to penetrate. "Lance loves you. You carry his baby and he chose to risk his life for you. You didn't force him to do it, Harmony. He did what he knew he had to."

"He didn't have to," she whispered. "He should have let me die."

"And he would have followed you," Megan sighed. "At least this way, he's fighting to live. Whether he does or not, you are still a part of our family. Just as your child is."

If he didn't live, she would follow him. Megan and Braden would raise the baby with all the love Harmony had no idea how to give. She would follow Lance. Just as she had sworn she would.

"Harmony . . ." Megan protested. "That wasn't what Lance wanted."

Harmony knew the empath was reading her emotions, perhaps even her thoughts. It no longer mattered.

"I told him," she whispered. "I warned him, the choice is his. Life or death. I'll follow wherever he goes."

She wouldn't live without him, and she knew it. She was aware of Jonas and Braden watching her worriedly, of the silence that filled the waiting room.

"He died so you would live." Megan's voice was tearful. "You'll let him sacrifice himself for nothing?"

Not for nothing. The child they had created had to live, she knew that. But Harmony knew she couldn't go on alone. The ghost of all she could have had would haunt her forever.

"His child will live." Tears Harmony didn't know she could still shed bled from her eyes. "I can't fight anymore, Megan." She swallowed tightly. "There's no fight left in me."

Even though Megan argued with her, she knew there would be no changing Harmony's mind. It was no more than she would do if anything ever happened to Braden. He was her world. Her light. He was all her hopes and her dreams, and her greatest desire. It would be no different for Lance and Harmony.

She had stayed away from the couple, not because of Lance's fears for her, but because Megan had sensed Har-

mony's battles and she knew there would have been no way
to disguise her sorrow, her compassion. Harmony hadn't
needed that. Not then. She needed it now.

Megan lifted her eyes to Jonas, aware of her own tears.
The solid core of determination inside the young woman
she held was unbreakable. It wasn't grief or sorrow talking.
This was the woman who had fought, had sacrificed and
who had lived with nightmares every day of her life. Megan
knew that if they lost Lance, they would lose Harmony as
well.

Jonas's emotions, though well guarded, were easy enough
for her to read. His heart was breaking. Right there inside
that stone wall of a chest, beyond the mocking sarcasm and
the manipulating games, he was breaking apart.

Megan had kept her silence on Jonas. She rarely agreed
with him and she let him maintain his facade of vengeful,
righteous Breed fury. It wouldn't pay to ever let him know
that she saw deeper than that, that she saw his nightmares.
That she saw his pain.

"Fight for Lance then." She turned her attention back to
Harmony as she felt the fragile, weak force of Lance's emotions searching around her.

He was alive. So fiercely alive and determined to protect
Harmony, even now. Megan could feel it. He had sensed his
mate's pain, her agony, and nothing short of death, perhaps
not even death, would keep Lance's spirit from seeking her
out, attempting to comfort her. It was the first sign Megan
had seen that they hadn't lost him. Until now, she hadn't
been certain herself that he would live.

Relief poured through her. She had been waiting for him.
She knew her cousin.

"Harmony, let me take you to Lance." The girl jerked as
though to get up. "Just stay still. There's only one way to do

it, and it might not work. You can help him fight. Help him fight, Harmony."

He was so weak. She had never felt his life force so weak, and it terrified her. As she settled her hands over Harmony's head, she let herself reach out to him. She called his name, met the searching tendrils of psychic warmth, and then she let Harmony do the rest.

She was shocked by the sudden pouring of heat from Harmony's body, through her own, and toward Lance's searching mind. As though Harmony had been waiting for him, preparing for him.

How the woman managed the will to send such energy through a channel so fragile, Megan had no idea. But she swore, as she closed her eyes and maintained the bridge between reality and spirituality, that she felt them embrace.

◆ ◆ ◆

Was she asleep? Had she finally lost the will to even stay conscious? Harmony felt Lance reaching for her, his arms holding her, and though he would have given her the heat he always tried to instill in her, she gave her own instead.

Joy exploded inside her as she felt the unraveling in her soul. As though the tattered remains of past demons and nightmares were burned away, and in their place, something new was being born. She could feel Lance. He was alive. He was there, holding her, his lips pressed to her forehead, his voice murmuring, comforting. Forgiving.

Lance was going to live.

CHAPTER 25

Harmony slipped from the ICU waiting room the next evening, moving past the throng of Lance's family, the Breeds
standing guard, and slipping carefully to the stairwell that
led to the first floor.

She had seen him as she stood at Lance's window, staring
up at her, his expression shadowed, and known that if she
didn't go down, then he would come up.

She knew exactly where to find Dane. He was lounging
on a bench in the small grassy park area next to the hospital,
a slim cigar clenched between his teeth, his expression re-
signed as she approached him.

She was unarmed. If she had to fight, she didn't think she
could find the energy.

"Where's Ryan?" She sat down on the bench beside him,
inhaling the tangy scent of the slim cigar.

"Calling Mother," Dane grunted. "I keep telling him this
crush he has on her is going to get him killed. Father will
make him wish he had never said the first flirtatious word."

Harmony inhaled slowly. She had listened to Dane chastise Ryan for years over his flirtatious relationship with Dane's mother.

"Are you a Breed, Dane?"

He lifted the cigar from his lips, blowing a stream of smoke as his eyes narrowed before turning his head to her.

"How long have you known me, Harm?" he questioned rather than answering, and he used the nickname he had given her so long ago.

"Long enough for me to know when you're avoiding a question." She sighed, pushing her fingers through her hair as she drew closer around her the jacket one of Lance's cousins had given her earlier. "You have no canines, no scent. I didn't even suspect."

"If I were a Breed, I would be careful not to let you suspect." His smile was a shade mocking, a shade saddened.

"Why?"

He sighed heavily. "Sometimes, the answers are more complicated than the questions. Suffice it to say, I was always your friend instead. And so I will always be."

His voice was firm, assuring her that he had no intention of answering the question.

"Why have you helped me then?" she asked instead. "You could have had that information at any time. You likely already knew where it was. Why the game?"

He leaned forward, flicking an ash from the cigar as he braced his elbows on his knees before answering.

"You needed a reason to live. I just helped you along." He finally shrugged. "Now that you have what you've always needed, Harmony, I'll take the information and make certain it can never be used to hurt anyone else."

She tilted her head and regarded him silently.

"But why? And answer me this time, damn you." She was tired of games, tired of answers voiced in questions and men attempting to manipulate her life. "Just tell me why."

"Because I love you, Harm."

That shut her up. She stared back at him in disbelief, her eyes widening at his heavy expression.

"Look at you." He shook his head with weary amusement. "You never knew. But . . ." He shrugged again. "I never meant for you to know. If it were meant to be, it would have been. You needed a reason to live, I couldn't be your reason, so I helped you with the one you chose at the time. It's that simple."

She swallowed tightly, uncertain what to say to him, how to feel about this man who had been such a large part of her life.

"How did you keep track of me?"

His lips quirked at her avoidance of his declaration.

"Shall I show you?" His hand lifted, moving beneath her hair until his fingers settled high beneath her hairline and pressed against a small, previously unfelt bump beneath the flesh.

She blinked at him, her hand flying back as she felt the area herself. It was no larger than a pinhead, but definitely there.

"It's a GPS locator with an added sensitivity to monitor your vitals. Heart rate, pain sensation, whatever." He shrugged. "I always knew within moments when you were in trouble and where you were. And I always came for you."

"Why?" Confusion, disbelief and a sense of frustrated anger filled her. "Why would you do this, Dane?"

"Because you mattered, luv," he whispered, his accent thickening. "You mattered to me, as well as to those you don't even know. You're vital to us, not because of what you are, or what you thought was hidden, but because of the heart and the soul of the young warrior you were. You mattered to us."

"No . . ." She shook her head fiercely.

"You needed to believe yourself to be alone, so we let you think you were alone. You needed to know you were a weakness to no one and that no one weakened you, so I let you believe I was rescuing you in exchange for a job only you could do." His smile was mocking. "You always knew better, Harm. If you hadn't, you would have given Jonas what he wanted. You would have betrayed me."

"How did you know?" She touched the hidden device.

"No, I can't monitor your voice or your actions." His grin was a bit amused. "I have other sources, sweetheart, within Sanctuary. I knew what Jonas wanted. I was quite curious how far he would go. Though I always knew I could trust you."

She clenched her fingers in the jacket, staring back at him miserably.

"You knew all along." She shook her head at the revelation. "Why didn't you tell me?"

Wide shoulders shrugged again. "What was the point? You were confused enough. Mating, falling in love, facing the danger you brought to your man. I wanted you happy, Harmony." His smile was rueful. "I would have preferred it had you fallen in love with me. But your happiness was all that truly mattered."

She'd had friends. A man who cared for her; she couldn't accept the love part right now. He and Ryan had risked their lives more times than she could count on both hands, for her. And she had never realized, even worse, she had never wanted what they had to offer.

"I'm sorry." She met his gaze fully, regret filling her. "You deserved better, even for a friend."

"No, sweetheart, you deserved more." He shook his head at her statement. "You were like a wounded lioness, fighting to survive. I merely helped you where I could. I did no more."

"You're wrong," she whispered. "It was so much more."

She rose to her feet then, knowing she didn't have much longer. As soon as Jonas learned she had disappeared, he would be searching for Dane again.

"Jonas thinks you're the first Leo and he's determined to capture you," she told him then. "Be careful of him, Dane. Even in the labs, Jonas was frighteningly adept at getting what he wanted. He's only grown stronger and more determined."

Dane smiled at that. "I'm not the first Leo, Harm. But should I ever run across him, I'll be certain to pass the message along."

He straightened, staring down at her, his emerald eyes brilliant even in the darkness.

"You're a Breed," she whispered then. "I think I've always . . ."

He laid his finger across her lips. "Go in peace, little lioness. And should you need me . . ." His hand slid to the small tracker hidden beneath her hair. "I'll always be close."

She watched as he turned then and moved toward the vehicles parked at the edge of the grass.

"Give Jonas my regards," he called back as he disappeared into the shadows. "And tell him we will meet again."

It sounded like a warning.

Harmony rushed back to Lance's hospital room then, slipping past the nurse on watch and sliding into the room to hide in the shadows as she had the night before. If they caught her, they always ran her off. And she always returned.

The curtains were still partially closed across the wide windows that looked out onto the nurses' station, allowing her to slide into the chair next to the bed.

Harmony let her fingertips touch his, aware of the tubes and wires that led from his body to the machines next to the bed. She needed that contact. Needed to feel his warmth, to share her own.

She laid her head at the end of the mattress and sighed deeply. She couldn't believe he was alive. That he was breathing, that the surgeons were certain he would recover, with few complications. The miracle of it still managed to weaken her knees and bring tears to her eyes.

"Harmony . . ." The fragile thread of sound had her eyes jerking open as she lifted her head and stared up at him.

His eyes were slitted open, the dark blue color clear and lucid as he stared back at her.

"Lance. Oh God . . . Lance." She lifted her hand, touched his brow, his cheek, his lips. "Are you thirsty? In pain . . . ?"

"Shhh . . ." That thread of sound. A gentle croon that eased her as nothing else could have.

"You're going to be fine . . . The doctors . . ."

"Shhh," he whispered again.

She frowned down at him.

"I love you," he whispered, his voice a bit slurred and weak.

His hand moved then, his fingers lifting to reach out to her, to touch her abdomen. The warmth speared into her, spread through her.

"It's a son."

Her breath caught at his words.

"I love you, Lance Jacobs," she whispered then. "And the minute you're well, I'm going to kick your ass for what you did."

"Shhh . . . Kiss me, baby. Let me feel you. Let me know I lived . . ."

She leaned down and let her lips touch his. Brief though it was, a tentative caress, it was an affirmation of life.

"I love you . . . ," she whispered, her lips feathering over his, her gaze locked with his. "Always."

And he smiled. "Always."

✦ E P Í L O G U E ✦

Three Months Later
Washington, D.C.

Jonas twisted his hips, slamming them against his partner, feeling the hot, tight clasp of her pussy around his aching erection, the slick, liquid heat that surrounded him, and calculating her rise to orgasm.

Her hands slicked over his back, sharp little nails piercing his flesh as long blond hair wrapped around them like damp strands of silk.

Bracing his knees on the bed between her spread thighs, he pumped into her, eyes narrowed as he watched her pleasure-filled face and held back his own release. Ladies first. It wasn't so much a motto as part of his sexual training. The scientists had wondered if pleasure and sexual release would overcome the genetic encoding that prevented female Breed conception. It hadn't, but Jonas had excelled so quickly in bringing that pleasure that he had become the lab's resident stud.

He was used to seduce wives, daughters and buttoned-down professionals associated with the targets the Council sought. Women talked to their lovers, especially women experiencing the full flush of their first experience with a man who knew all the intricate paths to completion, such as Jonas did.

As he stroked inside the tempting little lawyer, finding all the delicate little nerve-ridden areas within her soft pussy, his hands caressed and petted. His lips stroked over sweat-dampened flesh, nipping, licking, kissing over sensitive skin.

His pleasure came from hers, as odd as that should have been. Here, the only pain was the agony of need, of hunger that began to fill the air with her rising moans. Her hands gripped his biceps now, her hips lifting against him, pushing his cock farther inside her as he felt the warning ripples of release stroke over his dick.

Her gasping cries were rising in crescendo as he felt the rippling waves of sensation begin to pulse in his balls. He could have come thirty minutes before. Instead, he had kept moving, sliding inside the rich, hot depths of her cunt as she shuddered beneath him.

She was insensate with pleasure. Her eyes were glazed with it, her body flushed with it and soaked with sweat. Her head twisted on the sheets a second before her breath caught, her body jerking helplessly beneath his as her pussy sucked at his cock before tightening further and letting go the sweet, fiery moisture of release.

Jonas gave in to his own pleasure then, one hand gripping her hip as he began to shaft her furiously, fucking into her with furious strokes until his release whipped through him.

He held inside her, his semen spurting into the tight channel as he gritted his teeth and pumped against her, determined to wring each ounce of pleasure from the experience.

It was rare for him to feel anything beyond the driving need to ensure Breed security. At least here, he could immerse himself in warmth, allow it to touch him, if only for a brief time.

As the final pulses of release rippled through his cock, he knew it wasn't enough though. The restlessness that haunted his working hours was beginning to drift into these hours of pleasure as well. A vague dissatisfaction he had never known before while copulating. And it was starting to piss him off.

Inhaling deeply as the final shudders of release vibrated through his muscles, Jonas eased back from Jess's hold on him, sliding from the silken depths of her pussy as he ran a hand over the spiky length of his hair. He needed a haircut.

He was aware of her eyes opening as he moved from the bed and headed for the bathroom to wash up. She would be a few more moments before she rose behind him.

"You know, one of these days, you're going to find a woman you can't get up and walk away from," she murmured long minutes later, as he padded back from the bathroom, refreshed by a quick shower.

He grunted at the observation as he began to dress. He had work to do, and playing lovers' games wasn't on his agenda. He had a spy to find, and he was now one step closer to trapping her.

Propping the pillows behind her back, Jess stared back at him from intelligent gray eyes, an amused smile on her kiss-swollen lips.

"We need to move on the case pending against the Breed found beaten to death last week," Jess commented as he pulled on his socks before picking up his slacks. "I want those supremacists under Breed Law rather than international law. I'm sure the Ruling Cabinet can find a way to make them regret the errors of their ways."

"I disagree." He speared her with a dark look. "Let the justice system have them and oversee the case against them. The press will have a field day with it. A Breed videotaped attempting *not* to hurt its captors, to merely escape, and be-ing beaten nearly to death for his efforts. It will engender sympathy and compassion as well as outrage. Kill them, and the Breeds will be seen as no better than those striking against them."

A frown flitted across her face. "We have a right to justice," she said stiffly. "The same group raped and murdered that young female Breed the month before and you know it. We can't let this continue."

"Once they're free, I'll take care of them." He pulled the silk shirt over his shoulders and buttoned it before tucking it into his pants. "Such people disappear all the time. For now, it's better to let the humans believe they are policing themselves."

It helped that one of Alonzo's lieutenants had been found dead at the scene of Harmony and Lance's attack. Pinning the blame for the sheriff's near murder on the supremacist group had gone a long way to fracturing much of their power.

A bit of careful maneuvering and Jonas had laid in the groundwork for the demise of the assassin known as Death as well. He had laid it right at the feet of the supremacist lieutenant Harmony had killed.

To Jonas, that was justice. Harmony was now safe in Broken Butte with her mate, and those who suspected her as Death could no longer speak to betray her.

"These games of yours are going to get someone killed," Jess finally said and sighed as he finished dressing.

His smile was tight, cold. "Most likely," he agreed. "Blood supremacists and those damned purist groups if I have my way about it. The world would be better off without them."

"And so they say about the Breeds." She shook her head as she rose from her bed. "I'll make certain the case goes to trial, but you have twelve jurors who may well let them off." It wasn't unknown. Convicting the supremacists was never easy.

"Making them disappear is easy enough." The fact that they would get off didn't bother him nearly as much as the fear that it wouldn't go to trial.

If they succeeded in beating the charges after the clear proof that they had committed the crime, then he would know which direction he needed to go in terms of raising awareness to the prejudice that threatened the Breeds. Anything could be worked, especially emotion.

Until then, he needed to refine his plan to draw out the first Leo. If the Breeds were lucky, he could squeeze out another year before the world learned of the mating heat. Hopefully, this would give him and the scientists working on the phenomena time to learn the secrets of the delayed aging.

Callan Lyons, the Pride leader, was over forty now; according to his tests and his physical appearance, he might have aged a year since his mating, though Jonas doubted it. Kane Tyler, the human mate to Sherra, Callan's adopted feline sister, hadn't aged either. Nor had the women. Speculation was already growing, and keeping them out of the public eye was next to impossible. The situation was becoming explosive, especially with the spy working within Sanctuary.

But there would always be spies. Betrayal was commonplace to Jonas. That didn't mean he had to let the spies live once he learned their identities.

"You're zoning out again, Jonas." Jess's crisp voice had him gazing back at her as he pushed his feet into his soft leather wing-tip shoes and sat down to tie them.

He preferred boots, but he'd learned that in this arena of warfare, appearance meant everything.

"I have work to do, Jess." Playtime was over. "Take care of your end and I'll take care of mine."

Her laughter was smooth, and surprisingly warm. It was rare that he could piss her off, though sometimes he did try.

"Watching you mate is going to be so much fun," she drawled as his gaze jerked up to her, his eyes narrowing.

"I'm not mated," he reminded her carefully.

"Not yet." The open amusement on her face was damned offensive. "But when you do, it's going to be so funny, Jonas. I hope I'm there to see it."

Figured. And who said the females were the gentle ones? They had no idea what they were talking about.

"I have work to do." He rose to his feet and headed to the bedroom door. "I'll see you at the office in the morning. Remember we have to fly to Sanctuary."

Damned Vanderale Industries was threatening to pull the plug on the deal for weapons and vehicles the Breeds needed. They were sending one of their representatives in to discuss their concerns with the Ruling Cabinet. Just what the hell he needed, another damned liability walking into Sanctuary.

The woman they were sending wasn't even a major force within the far-flung holdings Vanderale owned. She was a damned paper pusher. A buttoned-down little prude that made him shudder at the thought of the funds that were likely to be cut off. Not that Sanctuary couldn't survive without them, but hell, it would bite to lose their support within the international community.

He also needed to meet with Ely to see if any of the readings coming from the implant beneath Harmony's scalp meant anything. The cryptic message they had received three months ago with the frequency for the GPS locator she possessed had saved her and Lance's lives. Ely reported her suspicions a month later that the feedback from the implant appeared to hold more information than just her location.

As he ran through the list of tasks ahead of him in the coming week, prioritized and filed them, he moved from Jess's home. He was aware of the team of Breed bodyguards that met him outside and the limo waiting on him. His eyes scanned the area, his senses automatically picking up the sights and smells of the night, the absence of danger.

Which was rare enough.

As he settled back into the limo, he opened the briefcase waiting on him and pulled out the first file. It was time to get back to work. He was getting closer to their spy, and soon he would be closer to the first Leo. He wasn't giving up.

LORA LEIGH is known for her deliciously intense and satisfying erotic romance. Her characters come to her in her dreams, inspiring her with the possibilities of *What If* . . . Most days, Lora can be found in front of her computer weaving daydreams while sipping the ambrosia of the gods, also known as coffee. When not writing, thinking about writing, or plotting what to write, Lora, a Kentucky native, enjoys gardening, fishing, and hiking with her husband and children. You can find Lora at www.lora leigh.com.